This book
characters, places and incidents are the product of the author's imagination or are used fictitiously. Any resemblance to actual events, locales, or persons, living or dead, is coincidental.

© Robert J Henry 2013-2014

There are so many people I would like to dedicate this book to. The list being so long it would warrant it's own chapter. You all know who you are that helped with this book and offered your encouragement for me to complete it. To each and everyone of you, Thank You.

With that being said, I would be remiss if I did not thank just a few people individually. Of course there is my mom, for she gave me the gift of life, the love of books.

Thank you to my two very bright, wonderful, and funny children. You are the lights in my life Danielle and Owen.

*I can't change the direction of the wind, but I can adjust my sails to always reach my destination.*

*~Jimmy Dean*

# The Rose

## an Owen Henderson novel

By Robert J Henry

# Prologue

## Part One - The Council

He sat at the one end of the large antiqued conference table.  His chair, that was appropriately ornate and throne looking, was not overly comfortable.  That really didn't matter to him, he would only be sitting in it for a short time.  Long enough to complete the matters at hand, build a solid foundation for his future, and finally close this chapter.  He scanned the 12 men seated around the table, most looking uncomfortable with the current topic of discussion.  He let them stare back at him, watching each one look away from his gaze as it fell on them.  Good, he thought to himself, I intimidate them, very good indeed.

His voice resonated against the aged stone walls, "Gentlemen, Brothers, this has been a trying year.  No, this has been a trying 50 years, with this last year being all that any of us can take.  We will not be held hostage and forced to be at their mercy any longer.  As we all sit here, and I speak to you today, the digest is getting closer to being back in our hands once more.  It has been far too long, too long indeed.  This time next week, the major obstacles will have been eliminated, and we will all be able to put this in the past and move forward."

There were nods of agreement all around, some murmuring chatter, and quiet looks of relief.  He rose from his chair, resting both hands on the large solid table.  He sighed, looked at each one again.  He spoke once more, this time with more authority, with more menace, "I have accomplished what none of you have been able to.  I have not only solved our problem, I have eliminated the threat that has plagued us for the last 50 years," he boomed.  All the men stared at him as he paused.  He felt in control, he knew this was his moment.  He started again, in a lower voice, with deeper compassion, "With this gift that I will bring you, I hope," he paused for effect, "I hope that you will remember me when we are asked again to cast our ballots."

## Part Two – Second In Command

The older man, walking with a slight limp, was a few paces in front of the odd young man with the yellow windbreaker. Wondering why he had been summoned at this hour, what was so important that it could not wait until morning? He was getting too old for these late night meetings, he thought to himself. He turned to voice his protests to his minder. He never heard the shot that came from the silenced pistol. His last thoughts draining from him as quickly as the blood from his chest. He felt at peace and swore he could see the bullet as it left the gun.

The younger man, in the yellow windbreaker, took three paces forward until he was standing directly over the dying man. He aimed his pistol at the man's head and took the final shot that landed squarely in the centre of his forehead. He felt there was no need for it as the old man was already dead, but it was his orders and he was very good at following his orders. He studied the dead man for a long minute. The crimson pool around his head almost made him look like an angel, an old one, but an angel none the less. He reached into the breast pocket of his windbreaker and pulled out a single yellow rose. He placed it on the dead man's chest. He crossed himself, said a silent prayer, closed the dead man's eyes, and walked away.

He hadn't noticed the elderly woman standing in her kitchen window three floors above him and he was not overly concerned if anyone did see him. His work would be done in a few short days and he would move on to other things. Besides, the light in the parking lot was so sparse, no accurate description could be made of him. He made a few short turns, moving through the old narrow streets, to finally arrive at his rental car. Parked as he left it, there were no signs that it had been tampered with or broken into. Again, he was not concerned with these things, nothing from the car's interior could identify him, and nothing of value was in it, not even a fingerprint. He reached for his map, scanned it for a brief moment, pointed his car in the right direction, and set off for his next destination.

## Part Three - The Boss

He pulled into the cul-de-sac and parked at the large house that occupied the entire end of it. Checking his Glock, he attached the silencer, and then placed it in his shoulder holster. He grabbed the manila envelope from the passenger seat of his rental car and headed to the front door. He rang the bell and waited. Thirty seconds later, the rotund man with the bad toupee opened the door. His red silk smoking jacket looked too warm for this weather, he thought, but then he felt the cool air from the house hit him. The old man didn't say anything, he just scanned the man with the yellow windbreaker up and down, turned, and walked back into the house. The younger man crossed the threshold and quietly shut the door behind him. The old man turned his head slightly and finally spoke, "I don't understand why it was so important that you come by tonight. It's late, and my daughter is here. I don't like to do business like this when my family is around."

The young man in the yellow windbreaker didn't say anything as he followed the old man down the hall, their foot falls echoing off the marble flooring. As the old man took the first step into the sunken living room, the young man pulled his gun, aimed it at the back of the old man's head, and pulled the trigger. A small pfft erupted from the gun and the old man's forehead detached from his head, followed by blood and gore. The young man reached forward and grabbed the collar of the old man's silk smoking jacket and let him slowly sag to his knees. Dead at the instant the bullet hit his head, the old man was now in a kneeling position. The young man placed the gun at the base of the old man's neck and pulled the trigger a second time. This, of course, was unnecessary, but again, he was doing as he was ordered. He kneeled, reached into his inside pocket, and pulled out a yellow rose. He placed it on the dead man's body, said a silent prayer, crossed himself, and stood.

The young man scanned the room for several seconds. Instantly he saw what he was looking for, and walked to it. He picked it up and felt the great heft of it. He was sure he could feel an energy coming from it. He knew immediately that it was what he came for. Opening the thick leather bound cover as instructed, he read the inscription that was scribed with broad strokes on the front cover.

# Quæ scripta sunt in servitute hic notandum deo sempiternum erit, et Apostolicae Sedis tutela

He pulled from his pocket a large cloth bag and placed the ornately carved leather bound book into the bag. He looked around the room one last time and headed out the door for his car. As he climbed in, he felt a surge of adrenaline run through his body. Never before had he seen such an item. Never before had he held something so sacred. He allowed himself a rare small smile as he held the carefully wrapped book to his chest. His mission was almost complete. He started his car and drove off with the sun just peaking over the lake to the east of him.

## Chapter One

Tyson Richards knew that if his phone was ringing at 2:00 am, it was not good news. No one called at 2:00 am with good news, even the telemarketers didn't disturb people at that time of day. He got the phone on the third ring. "Richards," he croaked into the receiver as it reached his mouth. He made a few grunts, said "30 minutes," and hung up the phone. He wasn't necessarily a light sleeper, however this job often had him up at the oddest of hours. He sprang from bed and was dressed and out the door as if he had not been sleeping at all. The drive to the crime scene took him less than 20 minutes at this hour and he was pleased to see he was at the scene exactly 30 minutes from when he hung up the phone.

As a 20 year veteran of law enforcement, he was no stranger to a crime scene, or death for that matter. Being head of the newly formed OPP Organized Crime Unit, or OPP OCU, he was even more familiar with execution style killings than he wanted to be. The OPP had always investigated organized crime as it had provincial jurisdiction, but with the increase in biker gangs, the ever present mafia, as well as various other gangs popping up, the Ontario Provincial Police felt the need for a more specialized department.  Richards, who recently had been instrumental in breaking up a major drug syndicate, was not the number one pick for the job.  He was the number two, and that suited him fine.  He really didn't want the job.  His partner, who was the true brain of the duo, was the number one pick.  The last case, the loss of his wife and the kidnap of his daughter all stemming from the same major drug case, had left its toll on his partner.  He was now on medical leave, with no one knowing if he would ever return to the job.

Richards sat in his car for a minute longer, taking in the big picture, as his partner often would say, "Buddy, no need to rush to see the dead, they are going nowhere!  Take in the big picture, see the forest, then go and investigate all the trees."  Richards, shaking the thought of his partner from his mind, walked over to a uniformed officer who was taking some notes.  They greeted each other and Richards asked for the details.

Officer Thompson told him a 911 call came in at 12:50 am.  An elderly woman, one Mrs. Willowtree, said she noticed two men walking through the parking lot, she turned to get a tea cup and when she looked back, one man was on the ground and the other man was walking away.  She felt it didn't seem right, so she called 911.  City Police responded at 1:15 am.  As soon as they arrived, they identified the dead guy as Vincent DeLatrota.  They contacted us and have since just kept the parking lot entrance blocked.

Richards scanned the parking lot and saw the old small apartment building on the opposite side of the lot.  He noticed what appeared to be an elderly woman standing in the only lit window in the building.  He asked Thompson if that was Mrs. Willowtree.  Thompson nodded and said it was.  He added that he had spoken to her briefly and that a detective would be up to speak with her at length shortly.  Richards thanked him, turned on his heel, and headed for the building.  Thompson called after him, "She's a bit of an odd duck," he said, "on the ball, but just a bit off," he added with a grin.  "Thanks," Richards said again and headed off to the building.

It was an older four storey walk-up, just one of many on this old block on the edge of Hamilton's downtown area.  Richards' mounted the stairs, taking them two at a time.  He reached the third floor just as a door opened onto the small landing.  He eyed the old woman and asked "Are you Mrs. Willowtree?"  "Oh, just call me Ethel, Officer," she paused, waiting for him to fill in the blank.

"Ok, Ethel," Richards said, "I'm Detective Richards, Tyson Richards, from the OPP. You can just call me Tyson," he added. "Well don't just stand in the hall," Ethel said, motioning Richards into her small apartment. Richards took a quick look around the apartment. Standard widows dwellings, he thought to himself. Family pictures on an old buffet style cabinet, wedding pictures of what looked to be a young Ethel and her husband on the wall. No crosses or Jesus or Holy Mary statuettes sitting on any tables. At least she doesn't appear to be a religious fanatic, he thought. They are always harder to deal with.

"Would you like a cup of tea or coffee, Tyson?" the old woman asked him as he followed her into a compact yet efficient kitchen. "Coffee if it's no trouble, Ethel," he responded, as he peered out the single kitchen window taking in the crime scene from this vantage point. He turned to face her and asked if he could sit. "Oh, please do," she responded. He pulled out a chair from the 1970's style kitchen set and sat. Ethel brought him a mug of steaming coffee and set a carton of 1% and bowl of sugar down in front of him. As he poured some milk into his coffee, he asked her to describe what she saw.

"Well, it was 12:45 am, and I had just come into the kitchen to make a pot of tea. I don't sleep much these days. My late husband always said that as we get older we need less sleep because the big sleep was fast approaching. I guess my big sleep must be really close because I only sleep two or three hours a night," she followed this with a hearty laugh that made her look 10 years younger. "He had a lot of silly sayings like that, my late husband, Clive, that was his name. Oh, I'm sorry Tyson, you want the facts, just the facts ma'am!" she said, laughing again. "Isn't that what they used to say on that TV show?" Tyson smiled at the old woman. Yes, bright, but a bit odd, just like the patrolman had said, he thought to himself.

The old woman continued on, "As I was saying, I came into the kitchen to make a pot of tea. I know it was 12:45 am because a news brief had just come on the TV and that funny looking man from Channel 10 started by saying it was 12:45 am. When I walked into the kitchen I saw two men walking across the lot down below. If you stand in the door way, you will see that it is the perfect angle to see down to where the light post is." Richards stood and walked to the doorway, nodding with agreement as he sat back down. She continued on, "I turned to the stove and put the kettle on for my tea.  I always fill the kettle with water after I use it, you see.  That was another of Clive's little things, 'An empty kettle is as useful as a bull with tits,' he used to say, 'can't get nothing from it'!" she followed this with another of her hearty laughs.  Richards smiled at this and gave her a small nod to continue on.

"Tyson," she said, "you're not writing any of this down."  Richards told her that he had a good memory.  She looked at him skeptically.  So Richards pulled his small note book and pen from his pocket.  He asked her to continue.  "Well," she said, "after I put the kettle on the stove, I walked back to the window just to take a look see.  This is not the greatest of neighborhoods and we do get our fair share of hooligans around here because of the so called 'club' over there," she said, pointing out her window across the parking lot in the general direction of the Canadian-Italian Social Club.  Richards interrupted her, "Why do you call it a 'so called club', Ethel?"  "Oh, come now Tyson," she snorted, "us old folks who have lived here for 20 years or more, know that it's nothing more than a mob hang out.  Oh sure," she continued, "they call it a social club, but we all remember what went on over there years ago."

Richards was too young to remember the beginnings of the social club, however, from his work on the OPP OCU, he was very familiar with the history of the club and its notorious past. Fronting as a social club, with apartments on the upper floors for immigrant Italian's looking for a new life and new start in Canada, it has been under surveillance off and on for the better part of 25 years. No less than 17 murders have been committed in and around the building. However, over the last 10 years or so, it has for the most part, been relatively quiet with only the odd badly beaten body dumped out the front doors.

"Go on, Ethel," he prompted. "Ok, well, I looked out the window and the younger of the two men was bent down over the one laying on the ground. My eyes aren't as good as they used to be, so I can't give you any more details, he was just bent over him. Then he stood up and walked away. I kept watching for the other one to get up, but he didn't. That's when I called 911." "And you didn't see anything else?" Richards asked. "Nope," Ethel replied. "Can you give me a description of the guy that walked away?" Richards asked. "Nope," Ethel said again. The pair sat in silence for a long moment. Then Richards said, "Well thank you for your information Ethel, and thanks for the coffee." He started to stand and leave when Ethel said, "Aren't you going to ask me what he was wearing?" Looking quizzically at her, he said, "What who was wearing?" "The one that walked away," Ethel said incredulously. Richards raised his eyebrow, "Ok Ethel, can you tell me what the man who walked away was wearing?" Richards said. "Well, not everything he was wearing," Ethel replied, but I did notice that he had on a bright jacket. Hard to tell the colour exactly," she continued, "but I would reckon it was yellow or orange. Hard to say with the funny light they have in that light post there."

Richards jotted yellow/orange jacket down in his note book. He stared at his sparse notes for a few seconds. He turned and looked out the window to see that the ME had arrived on the scene. He stood, took one last sip from his coffee, damn he thought, this is good coffee, then he looked at Ethel, "Thank you for all the information you have given me." He produced a card from his pocket, handed it to her and said, "If you remember anything else, please give me a call. You have been a great help, and your coffee was fantastic," he added. She stood with him, took the offered card, scanned if briefly and looked him directly in the eyes, "Well I hope I have been a help to you, Detective Tyson Richards," she said. They both smiled at each other. "You have been a great help, Mrs. Ethel Willowtree," he said with a smile. With that, he went out the door and back down the three flights to the crime scene.

Richards made his way over to the ME, Janet Heartland. She was a squat woman, late 40's, with bottle blond hair, pink rimmed eyeglasses, and four or five studs in each of her ears. Some of the guys in the department said she had both her nipples pierced as well. To each his own, Richards thought. When he approached Janet, she looked at him with a perfect smile. Well, she did have that going for her, he thought, the most beautiful smile. "Janet, what can you tell me?" Richards asked. "Not much at this point," she rambled, "to me it looks like a chest shot, then a head shot. If it was the other way around, there would be less blood loss from the chest wound as the brain shot would have stopped the heart. Either way, both shots were completely fatal shots. Not sure why the shooter would have wasted the bullet for the second shot. Found both shell casings and they look to be 9 millimetre, but the casings don't have a manufacturer's stamp on them that we can see. Time of death would be between 12:00 am and 1:00 am. I don't think we can be any more exact than that. Plus with the 911 call it pretty much confirms TOD." She paused for a brief second then continued on, "One other odd thing.  We found a yellow rose beside the body, but it had lots of blood on it.  It was laying on a dry patch of ground, so we are thinking that someone, maybe your shooter, put it on the dead man's chest. Maybe a gust of wind blew it off, or the guys first on the scene knocked it off checking for pulse and vitals.  That pretty much sums it up," she finished.

Richards made a small notation in his notebook, underlining yellow on both his jacket and rose notations.  He looked up at her, she was still smiling at him.  He smiled back.  "I don't think I have any other questions for you, Janet, your summation seems to coincide with the 911 and eyewitness accounts and timings," he said.  "So we can bag and tag the guy and get him downtown?"  Heartland asked.  "Sure," Richards responded.  "Where are you going to take him, Hamilton, or the OPP chop room in Burlington?"  The OPP chop room was the nickname given to the small but highly equipped morgue and forensics lab that Janet Heartland ran in the bowels of the Burlington OPP OCU headquarters building.  Heartland said, "I don't think there is really any reason to stink up my office with this guy.  Pretty cut and dry case.  Two shots, both fatal, cops arrived within minutes. Sound good to you to send him to Hamilton?" she asked. "Sounds good to me," Richards said, adding, "but all the other stuff goes back to your office right?" "Of course," she said, with the tone of 'duh yea' in her voice. Richards chuckled at her and walked over to where they were bagging the body.

Richards stood looking at the men working to bag the body. Scanning the parking lot, he looked up to see Mrs. Ethel Willowtree still in her kitchen window. He gave her a small wave, she returned it. His thoughts were going over all the information he had. Pretty straight forward hit, he thought, walk DeLatrota out to the lot and put a bullet in him, but how did he get the guy to come out in the lot, and why on his own? DeLatrota would never venture out with no protective detail around him. He always traveled with at the very least, two other guys. Why would they let him go out on his own? Unless he told them to wait, which would indicate that he knew his killer, and possibly was expecting to go with him. So was it a prearranged meeting, he asked himself. Who could get DeLatrota to go to a meeting without his protection, he wondered. "Janet," he yelled over to the ME, "did he have a cell phone on him and was he carrying a gun?"

Heartland conferred with one of her younger crew members for a second, then she looked over at Richards and said, "No on both counts. He had a roll of Tums, $425 cash in mixed bills, a wallet with standard credit cards, DL, union membership card, and a few family pictures. All the cards and DL were in the name of one Vincent Salvador Joseph DeLatrota," she finished.  "Ok, thanks," Richards responded. Going back to his thoughts, he became more and more convinced that old Vinny was expecting his killer but didn't know it was going to be his final meeting.  So who would put a hit on Vinny, and who had the power and control over him to go out in the middle of the night with no bodyguards and no gun?  Only one person had that control over him, The Boss, Louis DeDominicus, "Good old Louie," Richards mumbled to himself.

As Richards walked back to his car, the sun was just peaking in the east. He thought it looked like it was going to be a nice day.  A warm breeze was picking up with the rise of the sun.  He climbed into his car and was making his way back to the office to start his paper work.  He wondered if he could get phone records for the past couple of days to see if Louis had called Vinny.  Even if he could get them, what would it prove?  Vinny and Louie talked all the time, he assured himself, and Louie would not have pulled the trigger himself. He would have an iron clad alibi, probably at dinner with the mayor, or some other important person. No, he thought, phone records would lead him to a dead end or hundreds of loose ends. This murder was going to end up in the unsolved. "Not a great loss," he chuckled to himself.

As he was reaching the top of the Burlington Skyway, a large bridge that spanned over the inner Hamilton harbour, his Blackberry rang. He had it set to the old telephone ring. Snatching it from his belt, he thumbed the answer button and brought to his ear, "Richards," he said. He listened for a few seconds, his jaw dropping, "Hold on," he said, "let me pull over." He tossed his Blackberry on the seat and flicked on his police lights that were a thin band tucked up high in the front and rear windows of his car. Cutting across two lanes of traffic, he pulled to the shoulder just at the base of the bridge. He reached for his phone, noticing his hand trembling just a bit, the adrenaline had kicked in. "Ok, go ahead," he said.

## Chapter Two

It took Richards almost an hour and a half to get turned around and make his way to St. Catharines.  As he arrived at the opening of the cul-de-sac, he was not surprised to see the half dozen or so news trucks, or the same number of police vehicles, blocking and filling the small street.  He left his car at the barricade and walked over to the patrolman who had the unfortunate duty of keeping the gawkers and onlookers out of the street. Showing his badge, he was immediately let past. Trying to keep away from the camera crews, he made his way to the front door of the huge house that took up the entire end of the tiny street.  Again, his way was blocked by a patrolman.  He produced his badge and was let in.  The scene inside was chaotic, with crime scene forensic people, all with booties and gloved hands, going over every space with dusting powder, tweezers, and magnifying glasses.  He was stopped by a burly guy who immediately reminded him of Columbo, complete with the rumpled over coat and stub of a cigar hanging out the left side of his mouth.

Richards pulled out his badge for the third time to show it to Columbo, "No need to badge me, Detective Richards," the Columbo look alike said, "everyone knows who you are." Richards nodded and asked what his name was. "Detective Steve Glass," he responded, adding "I'm glad you guys are here. I don't want anything to do with this case. Old Louie is somewhat of a prominent figure in this town. Donated tons of money to the local hospital, parks and kids sports. I know that don't make him no saint and all, but most people around here think he is. Most of these folks don't believe the rumors and talk that he's some big crime boss." Richards looked at the man for a moment, then asked, "What do you think of Old Louie Detective?" "What I think don't matter much now that he's dead, does it Detective?" the Columbo wannabe scoffed. "Ok," Richards said, can you fill me in on what we have here?" "First you have to put on some booties, or the techies will flip," said Glass.

Richards put on the booties offered to him and reached into his coat pocket to don a pair of latex gloves. He followed Glass down the marbled hallway, heading towards a sunken living room. Standing at the opening to the room, Glass turned to Richards and said, "What we can figure so far, is the shooter was standing here, pointing to the bottom of the two stairs going down into the room. Mr. DeDominicus was kneeling facing into the room and the shooter popped him once in the back of the head and once at the base of the skull. A bit of overkill if you ask me," Glass shrugged. "The one shot blew half his fucking head across the room, the other one I guess ripped through the base of the skull, taking out most of his throat. Looking at the in and out of the base of the skull shot is how we figured Old Louie must have been kneeling. They appear to be on a downward angle." Richards was impressed with Glass's reasoning and detective skills.

"That's all we really have for you, Richards," Glass said. Richards scanned the overly large living room. He figured it must have measured 20 by 40 feet. Set at the far end was an oversized and very old looking desk. Polished to a high gloss, it sat facing into the room. In front of it was a low backed black leathered sofa. Directly in front of the two detectives lay the body of Louis DeDominicus, laying face down. In front of him sat three more sofas situated in a U shape facing into a large stone fireplace. Hanging above the fireplace was a painting of what looked to be an original Picasso. The room looked like something you would see in the movies. Everything had its place. There were lots of other overstuffed chairs scattered around, probably enough room to comfortably seat 20 guests, Richards thought.

He turned to Glass, "Who found the body?" he asked him.  "It was the maid," Glass replied, "she got to work at 6:00 am, just as she has done for the last 20 years," he added.  "So no one was here when he was shot?" Richards asked.  "Yea, his daughter was here," Glass told him, "but she didn't hear a thing.  Said she was asleep in her room by 11:00 pm last night and didn't hear anything until the maid started screaming and running down the hall."  Richards looked back down the hall in the other direction from the living room.  It spanned just as far on the other side of the front door and looked to open into a dining room.  Three doors came off the long hallway on the opposite side of the front door.  "Which one of those is her bedroom?" Richards asked, pointing to the doors in the hall.  "None of them," Glass said, "one of them is a powder room, one is an office, and the other is a large walk-in closet.  You have to go through the dining room, then through the kitchen, which is off the dining room, and the bedrooms are all in the back," Glass told him.

"So you think she wouldn't have heard two gun shots from back there?" Richards asked Glass.  "Well the house is big," Glass said, "but even with a house this big, one gunshot would be heard, two you would for sure hear." "So you're thinking silencer then?" Richards asked. "Yup, that's what we figure. We asked a couple of the neighbours if they heard anything last night, 'not a peep', they all told us." "Ok," Richards said, "where's the daughter and the maid now?" "The maid is at the hospital, she fainted shortly after running down the hall. We have an officer posted there with her. The daughter is back in her room with a friend who came over. A girl who lives across the street or something. She's been back there crying since we arrived," Glass said. "Can you add anything else?" Richards said. As Glass was about to respond, the familiar voice of Janet Heartland could be heard at the front door and she didn't sound too happy.

"Like fuck I can't go in there," Richards heard Heartland saying to the patrolman at the front door, "this is my fucking crime scene and I will go anyplace I need to go. Do you understand me Officer," there was a pause as Richards assumed she was reading his name tag, then Heartland barked, "Officer Kennedy." Richards and Glass exchanged looks and both made their way to the front door as Janet Heartland was muscling her way past Officer Kennedy. Slightly out of breath, carrying cases, and followed by her ever present entourage of junior forensic specialists, Heartland looked at Richards and said, "So Richards, we have to stop meeting like this," her smile flashing on him. She nodded her head towards Detective Glass and said, "What's with Columbo here?" Richards couldn't help but smile at that comment. Glass didn't look too impressed and gruffly responded to her question. "I'm Detective Glass, St. Catharines PD, and who the fuck are you?" he said, looking at Janet Heartland. She sneered at him and said, "If you don't get your flunkies out of my crime scene, I'm going to be your worst nightmare," she responded. With that, she elbowed her way past the men and stopped at the top of the stairs of the sunken living room.

"Ok," she said loudly, "everyone stop what you are doing. Put down everything in your hands and get the fuck out of here. This is now an OPP crime scene and you are all relieved. Leave any and all evidence you have collected where you found it, if it is already bagged ensure your marker tags are clearly marked on the evidence bags. My crew will sign off your evidence as you exit the building. Come on people," she bellowed, "we don't have all fucking day, let's move it." Glass looked at Richards and said, "Quite the piece of work she is." "Yea, she does have a way with people," Richards said, "but she is the best of the best at what she does," he added.  "That's what I have heard," Glass said.  "So are we relieved too, Detective Richards?" Glass asked him.  "I can take it from here, Detective Glass," Richards said.  "Thanks for your insight and for securing the scene.  Can you leave your patrolmen at the front door and street until my guys get here?"  "Sure," responded Glass, as he turned and made his way to the front door.  As Glass reached the door, he turned, "One more thing, Richards," Glass said, as he turned.  Yup Columbo, Richards thought.  "What is it Detective?"  "That yellow rose on the table," Glass said pointing, "it was laying on the body when I got here.  Not sure if it's part of the scene, or if the maid dropped it when she came in.  We have not had the opportunity to talk to her yet.  One of the tech's just set it on the table when they rolled the body to examine it.  They took pictures before moving him.  "Thanks," Richards said, as Glass turned and walked out the door.

Richards scanned the living room and decided that it was best to stay out of Heartland's way while she and her crew did their thing.  He walked back down the hall, heading towards the dining room and the rest of the house.  He entered the dining room and noticed it was almost as large as the living room.  The table, made of some exotic hardwood, was polished to a high shine. There were 20 chairs around the large rectangle. The one end sat in a curved bay with 10' high windows overlooking the manicured front yard and the street beyond that. Turning to his left, he walked towards a swinging door that took him into a restaurant style kitchen with some sort of stone counters and a stainless double door, industrial sized fridge and freezer tucked to one side. The eight burner, stainless stove was gas, with what looked like a bbq grill at one end of it. Large white double sinks, big enough to bathe two small children in each, were in the centre of the main counter. A window centered over the sinks looked off to a side yard and into part of the neighbour's yard, which was still a good 100 feet off into the distance. Off the back wall of the kitchen, were French doors that emptied out onto a deck. Richards could see a pool back there and small flower gardens spotted here and there.

To his left again, Richards spotted another hall that led across the back of the house. One side of this hall was lined with more of the 10' high windows. By the looks of it, Richards thought to himself, this hall must run across the back of the house. The doors leading off to the left, he assumed, were the bedrooms.

Five, he counted, all spaced at a minimum of 20' apart.  At the far end of the hall, he noticed a large wooden door.  Walking down the hall to the far door, he passed the second door on his left and heard murmurs behind it, and what sounded like a girl sobbing.  He paused a second listening, then rapped gently on the door.  A short heartbeat later, a twentyish girl opened the door, peering at him with reddened eyes and running eye makeup, her nose red from blowing and wiping, a tear still standing high on her cheek.  He held up his badge and ID, "Miss DeDominicus?" he asked.

The young girl shook her head, "No, I'm Keira, Jessie's friend from school," she said shyly.  "I'm Detective Richards," he said, "I need to speak to Miss DeDominicus."  "Jessica, Jessie," she whispered, "the policeman is here to talk to you," she said over her shoulder, still keeping the door open only a few inches.  Richards heard the muffled voice from inside the room reply, "Tell him to go away.  I don't know anything and I don't want to talk to anyone," she said between sobs.  The young girl, Keira, tilted her head, shrugged in an apologetic way, and started to close the door.  Before it got more than an inch, Richards had his hand firmly planted on the door.  He looked at Keira with an empathetic smile, "Sorry Keira," he said, "I have to talk to her now."

Richards pushed the door open further as Keira moved away.

Jessica DeDominicus was laying in a bed that was fit for a princess, complete with a lace canopy and a couple dozen oversized pillows. She was a pretty girl, with a thin athletic body, natural blonde hair, and stunning blue eyes. The room was painted in orange and purple, with hockey posters and the latest boy bands covering much of the walls. It was a large room, with the oversized bed, a small settee along one wall, and a nicely refinished dressing table. The one wall housed a full length walk in closet. On the far wall, was a row of windows that looked over a private garden, complete with a waterfall. Richards thought about that a moment, orienting himself to his position in the house. He quickly figured it out, there was a private secluded garden in the centre of the house. This gave all the bedrooms natural light without having the need for the windows to face the outside of the house.

Jessica groaned and rolled over so she was facing away from Richards. "Jessica," he said in a calm voice, "I know you are going through a lot right now, and I am very sorry for the loss of your father. I know this must be very trying and very scary for you right now." As much as he despised the dead man in the other room, this was a young girl who had just lost her father, he thought.  He needed to approach this with as much tenderness and sympathy as he could.  Richards continued, "I just need to ask you a few questions and then I will leave you to be alone with Keira.  Do you need me to call anyone?" Richards asked.  "Have your brothers been contacted yet?"  Richards was familiar with the DeDominicus family, or at least he was familiar with the male members of the family.  He knew DeDominicus had a daughter but she was young and had never been on the radar.  The one son Mark, who was older, was not part of the mob family.  He was from a former marriage and had moved with his mother to the States at a very young age.  The other son, Justin, was a thug and couldn't be much more than two years older than Jessica.

Keira spoke up and said, "I spoke to Mark a few minutes ago.  He and his wife are flying in from Connecticut and should be here later this afternoon.  Nobody knows where Justin is." Jessica mumbled something.  Richards asked her if she could repeat what she said.  "Justin is in the Dominican with his girlfriend," Jessica repeated between sobs.  A quick passport check should verify that, Richards thought. "Jessica," Richards said, "I need you to sit up and look at me so I can ask you a few questions." She moaned again, Keira rubbed her back a few strokes and said come on Jessie, just get it over with. Jessica moaned again and rolled over to face Richards. She finally sat up, curling her legs under her, and holding one of the purple overstuffed pillows in her arms. She really was a beautiful girl. By the looks of it, she had no makeup on, or hers was not of the type that ran from too many tears. She snuffled once, wiped her nose on the back of her hand, and with a sigh said "Ok, what do you want to ask me?"

Richards pulled the chair from the dressing table up to the edge of the bed. He sat down and opened up his note book and said, "The other officer told me that you were here all night." "Yes," she said, "I was going to go out but I felt kinda yucky so I just stayed in and hung out with Daddy." "Were the two of you alone all night?" Richards asked. "Well, Camilla was here until 9:30 pm," she said. "Who is Camilla?" Richards asked. "Oh, she's our housekeeper," Jessica said. "Does she normally go home at that time?" Richards asked. "No," responded Jessica, "she normally leaves around 6:00 pm, but she stayed a bit longer to help show me how to make risotto. She has been giving me cooking lessons." Richards smiled a small smile and nodded,

"Doesn't your father have any men who stay here with you, like protection or body guards?" he asked.  "Gawd no," Jessica snorted, "his two secretaries, as he calls them, always leave by 5:00 pm every day.  Daddy said he built this house to keep us safe and there is no need to have anyone but family here at night."  "So is it just you and your father here now that your mother has passed away?" Richards asked.  "Yeah," Jessica sighed, with a look of sadness and sorrow crossing her face.  "Well sometimes Justin stays with us," she added.  Richards knew all this.  He also knew that the girl's mother, DeDominicus' second wife, died in an auto accident three years prior.

"So you weren't feeling well and you went to bed early.  What time was that?" Richards inquired.  "I think it was around 11:00 pm," she said.  "Daddy wanted us to watch a movie but my stomach was feeling all shitty."  "No one else was here when you went to bed?" he asked.  "NO," she snapped, "I told you that.  It was just me and Daddy."  "Ok," Richards said, raising his hands in surrender, "is there anything else you can tell me about the evening, anything that you can remember, anything at all that might give us any clue or insight into who may have come here to kill your father?"  "No," the girl sighed again, "it was just an ordinary night.  Camilla showed me how to make the risotto, then she left. Daddy took a call around 10:00 pm and then I went to bed."  Richards quickly picked up on the new information Jessica had provided.  "Do you know who the call was from?" Richards asked.  "No," Jessica paused a second, "but it did seem to irritate Daddy.  He sounded a bit angry with whoever it was.  He almost slammed the phone down, but then he just came and sat with me for a bit, then after awhile, I went to bed."

Richards stood, looked around the room once more, and slid his chair back under the dressing table.  He looked at the two girls sitting on the bed, Keira still rubbing Jessica's back, Jessica snuffling and staring into her pillow.  "Jessica," Richards said, "I am very sorry that you lost your father.  We will be finished up shortly.  Before we leave," he paused, "I am going to need you to come into the living room and take a look around to see if anything is missing or out of place."  She started to sob again, big tears running down her face, "I can't go in there, I can't see my father that way.  I can't do it," she said.  "Jessica, it's ok," Richards said, "I will make sure that your father's body is gone and that anything that may be disturbing to you will be covered up or cleaned up.  I promise.  I don't want to upset you further."  He reached over and stroked her hair once, he really did feel for the poor girl.  She looked up at him, "You promise it won't be all gross like it was?" she asked.  "Of course," Richards responded, "it will be all cleaned up."  "Ok, I will try," she whispered.

Richards closed the door gently as he left the room.  He stood in the hallway a moment looking out the large windows into the back yard.  He was fairly certain that it was some sort of gang or mafia related hit that killed DeDominicus, so bringing the girl into the living room was really not necessary, however, he thought there could be more to it.  Maybe a jealous boyfriend took Daddy out, or it had something to do with the girl.  He couldn't take the chance and make assumptions.  He needed to see her reaction, see if she did notice something.  There had to be a reason for the hit, had to be a motive.  Maybe her being in the room might help pull it together.  He turned towards the large wooden door and moved down the hall.

## Chapter Three

As Richards was reaching the door, his Blackberry erupted with its classic telephone ringer. He put it to his ear and said, "Richards." He got a response and then said, "So what can you tell me BJ?" He had to pull the phone from his ear as a barrage of expletives, curse words, and some Spanish, came blasting back at him. He smiled to himself, "Ok, calm down," he said, "I'm sorry Brian, what news do you have for me?" The person on the other end was Brian Jones, one of the detectives on his squad. Most of the time, the nick name that many in the squad called him from time to time, was taken in fun. It didn't appear to be that way this time. On the other end of the phone, Jones said, "Sorry Boss. The baby was up all night teething and I didn't get much sleep. I must be grumpy." "No worries," Richards replied, "just tell me what you have so far."

Jones continued on with his summary, "Well, we canvassed most of the neighborhood around the Social Club. Nobody saw or heard a thing. The old guy who owns the convenience store a couple blocks away said it was a slow night. He did see a guy walking away from that end of the street, but he had no description. Said he had a few teenagers in the store and just caught a glimpse of someone walking by. That's all we've got," he finished. Richards paused a minute then said, "Ok, sounds like dead ends out that way. Why don't you grab Butters and Ingers and come down this way. See what you guys can dig up around here." He got a reply and hung up the phone.

He reached for the handle on the door, just as it was opened. Startled, figuring this was the master bedroom and knowing there should be no one in it, he took a quick step back. Janet Heartland stood staring at him on the other side of the threshold. "There you are, Richards," she said, "did I scare you?" she giggled. "No," Richards replied, "I thought this would be the master bedroom. I didn't know it led back into the living room." "Oh," Heartland said, "the master bedroom is on the other side of the living room. That door over there," she said, pointing across the room to the other side of the big desk. Richards walked into the living room with Heartland and asked what she had for him this time. Heartland began in her professional mode, "Pretty much the same as the hit in Hamilton. Two shots, both fatal. Two shell casings, again with no identifying marks on them. This guy really does a job on his vics and he is not really too worried about what he leaves behind. We haven't found any stray fibres or any prints that don't belong to the vic," she finished.

"Does the desk look like it was gone through?" Richards asked. "Nope," she replied, "not as far as we can see. It looks all neat and orderly, everything seems to be in order." "I want to bring the girl in to see if she notices anything out of order," Richards said, "so can we cover up the mess and get the body out of here?" "The body is gone," Heartland said, "I didn't think you needed to see it anymore." She turned to bark an order to one of her techs to cover up the gore that was DeDominicus' forehead and brain matter. She looked at Richards, "Ok, anytime you want to bring her in," she said. "Thanks," Richards said. As he turned to go back down the hall to get Jessica DeDominicus and bring her in, he discovered she was standing a few paces back, Keira holding her up with a tender arm around her shoulders. Richards looked at the two girls, "Are you up to this now, Jessica?" he asked her. Jessica nodded, a tear slipping from her eye. The two girls started moving slowly towards the entrance of the living room.

Richards let the two girls pass by him. As gently as he could muster, he said, "Ok Jessica, I just need you to take a look around the room, see if anything is missing, anything out of place, or if something doesn't seem right."  The two girls made their way into the room.  Jessica was slowly looking around, her bottom lip quivering just a bit.  Keira, although visibly shaken, was being strong for her friend.  After a few quiet moments, Jessica turned to Richards and said, "I don't see anything wrong.  From what I can see, everything looks normal.  Daddy didn't have anything special in here.  All his work stuff he kept in the desk and I wouldn't know what was what."  "So the room looks normal?" Richards looked at the two girls again.  "Ok," he said, "thanks for doing this for us.  We will be out of here in a few more minutes.  I'm going to have a police officer stay out front until your brother arrives."  He pulled out a card from his pocket and handed it to her.  "If you think of anything that can help, please give me a call," he said to her.  Again she nodded, sniffled once, and was turning to leave the room when she swung back, "Wait," she said.  "What is it?" Richards asked.  "Something's missing," she told him, recognition washing over her face.  For the first time, she stood on her own, looking at the desk.  Intelligence could be seen in her expression now that the immediate emotions of the ordeal had been removed.  She scanned the room again, then stood staring at her father's desk.  A long moment passed, and she walked over and brushed a hand across the far corner of the desk.  She looked at Richards and said, "Here! Daddy had a big old book that used to sit here."

"What kind of book?" Richards asked her. "I'm not sure what it was," she replied. "It was this big old thick thing. It was Daddy's most prized possession, he used to say. He had it for as long as I can remember. Once, when I was young, I opened it up and was flipping through the pages. All the writing was old and in some old language, Latin I think. Well, Daddy came in when I was doing this. He didn't get mad at me, but he gently closed the book on me. I remember he sat me down and told me that it was very old, very valuable, and that I was never, ever, to touch it again. He said one day he would explain it to me, he said something about it being my future, my security. I never understood what he was talking about and never paid much attention to it again," she finished.

"Can you describe it in more detail?" Richards asked. "Did it have a title on the outside, or any markings?" he continued. Jessica shook her head, "No, not that I can remember," she said. "It was about this thick," she said, holding her two hands apart about 5" or 6", "and maybe this big again," holding her hands apart to show dimensions of about 10" by 14", "other than that, I can only tell you it was old." Heartland cut in at that moment, and said, as she was measuring a space on the corner of the desk, "From the trace dust accumulations you can see here," she said pointing at the corner of the desk, "it looks to be 11.5" by 14.4" in size."  Richards walked over to where Heartland was, she said, "Bend down and bit, you can see faint dust when the light hits the desk.  It covers the desk except in this area."  Richards bent down, nodded his head in agreement.  Standing, Richards said, "Ok, thank you for your help Jessica."  "Does it help at all?" she asked the detective.  "I'm not sure," replied Richards, "we have no idea what the book was and it's really hard to say if it was worth killing over."  At that, Jessica's features changed back to the emotions she had earlier.  "I'm sorry, Jessica," Richards said.

As Jessica and Keira were leaving the room, she once again turned and said to Richards, "I know Daddy would often bring up the book in conversation when he had some men over.  They would say something and laugh and Daddy would pat the book and say 'my precious, my precious', just like that creepy guy in the Lord of the Rings."  With that, the two girls left the room and went down the hall.  Richards looked over to Heartland, "What's your take on it?" he asked her.  "Beats me, Detective," she replied, "that's your area of expertise, not mine." "Right," Richards said, slowly nodding his head.

"Are you just about finished up here, Janet?" Richards asked her. "Probably only another 30 to 45 minutes," she responded, "oh, and our uniformed guys have shown up. They relieved the locals. One is at the end of the street, the other at the front door," Heartland told him. "Thanks," Richards said, I'm going to head back to the office and start the report." He added, "Jones, Butters and Ingers are on their way here. Can you give them a briefing when they arrive?" "Sure," she said over her shoulder.

When Richards made it out the front door, he was greeted by a throng of reporters and camera men. One reporter shouted at him, "Detective Richards, why is the OPP Organized Crime unit here? Are the reports that this was a mafia hit true? Was Louis DeDominicus the crime boss he has been made out to be?" Another yelled, "How was he killed?" And another added, "Are all his business dealings just a front for the mob?" Richards held up his hands to silence the shouting and quell the crowd. Microphones were shoved in his face, still cameras began flashing, cameramen aimed their sights on him. "Ladies and Gentlemen," Richards said, "at this time, we have no comments. When, and if, we have any information that we would like to share with the public, we will issue a formal press release."  More shouts erupted.  Richards combated them with, "I said we have no comments to make at this time."  He elbowed his way past the crowd with more questions still being thrown his way.

He made his way to his car and was leaning against it to check for messages and emails on his Blackberry, when a pretty reporter approached him.  He looked up and said, "Look, I already said we have no comments to make at this time."  The pretty reporter, whose name he could not remember, dropped the microphone to her side and told her cameraman to go back to the van.  "Detective Richards," she said, Patricia Lambton from Channel 7.  Can I just get an off the record from you?"  Richards looked up from his Blackberry and sighed.  He looked into her hazel eyes, which were more green than hazel, "Look Ms. Lambton," Richards began, "I really can't give you any information at this time."  Patricia Lambton said to him, "Can you just give me a few facts?  I won't quote you.  I will use you as an unofficial source close to the scene."  Richards scanned around to see who was watching, who may be in ear shot.  He had to give her credit for her persistence, and it was hard to resist that smile and those eyes of hers. Richards sighed again. "Ok, unofficially," he began, "Louis DeDominicus was shot twice last night sometime after 11:00 pm and before 6:00 am. There were no witnesses, and the maid found his body at 6:00 am this morning when she came to work. Other than that, we don't know much more." Ms. Lambton said to him, "Was his daughter or son home at the time of the shooting?" Richards raised his eyebrow, she knew her facts he thought. "His daughter was at home at the time," Richards said, "but she was sleeping in her room and did not hear anything until the maid's screaming woke her at 6:00 am when she found the body. It was the daughter who called 911 and she has not been able to add anything to the investigation. I'm sorry, I really can't give you any more information than that. It is all we have right now. When we get more, I will issue a release." She looked at him, flashed her warm smile, and said, "Thank you, Detective Richards." With that, they parted ways and Richards climbed into his car.

## Chapter Four

Richards returned to his office to find a stack of phone messages and other paperwork that needed his attention. The top phone message though made him smile. It was to return a call to Alisha Henry. His mind drifted off to when she was just a little girl, now a grown woman attending university in Australia. Alisha Henry was not her real name, it had been changed from Danielle Henderson shortly after she was rescued from her kidnappers. Danielle Henderson was the daughter of his partner, and long time friend, Owen Henderson. During Richards' and Henderson's last case, Danielle and her mother were taken from their home by members of the Cortez Cartel to intimidate, control, and force Henderson to not testify in the case in which he was the lead investigator. One member of the Cartel, in a fit of rage, shot and killed Danielle's mother when she would not cooperate in making a video recording for proof of life.

Richards and Henderson stumbled into the case when they were tracking shipments of coke that were coming across the border in Niagara Falls. A trucker, who they thought was a small time distributer, was arrested when they found 60 kilos of coke in the fuel tank of his transport truck. During questioning, he broke down and gave them more information than they could have hoped for. The shipment he was carrying was a sample for some Canadian buyers operating out of Montreal. The larger shipments, if the product was satisfactory, were going to begin in the weeks that followed his arrest. The quantities of coke that were going to be crossing the border were in the tons and not kilos. Originating in Mexico, and being shipped through the United States for a final destination of Montreal, the coke was being hidden in carefully configured trailers that would be hauling fresh vegetables. With all the loads being pre-cleared by customs, the chance of detection of the drugs was minimal.

With traffic routes and shipment timetables, Richards and Henderson were able to quickly put together a multi-national task force of Mexican Police, DEA and OPP Officers. Their plan was to track the first load from its origin in Mexico to its final destination. After the first load, they would then be able to fit all the players together and in a coordinated effort make the biggest busts that the drug world had seen. Over 100 people, including Jesus Cortez, were arrested in these sweeping raids that took place on the same day across the 3 countries. It was later during the trials that the death threats against Henderson, and then ultimately the kidnap of his wife and daughter, happened.  This is what pushed Henderson over the edge.  It was these events that put him on sick leave.  Still dealing with the loss of his wife, and a daughter that he felt no longer looked at him the same, Henderson had become a recluse.

Richards picked up his desk phone and punched in the numbers to return Danielle's, aka Alisha's, telephone call.  It took several seconds for the number to finally go through.  Richards sat in his chair staring at a picture of Danielle that he had on his desk.  "Uncle Ty, is that you?" Richards heard through the telephone.  She always called him Uncle Ty, even though they were not related.  "Danielle," he said.  "How are you doing?  How is the weather down under?"  Danielle responded in a verbal flood of information.  Weather is hot she was telling him, with a number of bush fires that were filling the skies with smoke and the smell of burnt wood.  She continued to tell him that school was really good, the dorm accommodations were better than she had hoped for.  She told him that school was hard but she was managing ok at keeping her grades up.  He was sure she was not struggling too hard as she was a very bright girl.  The tone in Danielle's voice changed some.  It took on the ring of concern and he was pretty sure he knew what was coming next.

Danielle said, "Have you spoken to Dad recently?" Richards paused for a second and said, "I called him last weekend. He wasn't in a chatty mood." Richards remembered the conversation that was mostly one sided on his part. Danielle interrupted his thoughts and said, "I spoke with him last night and he doesn't sound good. Can you please stop in and make sure he is ok. I feel he needs to get out of that house. He needs to let go of the past and move on. It has been almost 10 months since Mom was murdered and I don't think he has spoken to anyone. Well anyone other than you or I," she continued. Richards thought for a moment then he said, "I will stop in to see him tonight on my way home from work if I can get out of here at a decent time." "That would be great," she said. "He always calls after you have visited him and he always seems like it lifts his spirits some. I wish you could talk him into going back to work. I think that would be good for him. Living the way he does is a waste of a great man." Richards smiled when she said this. He knew their relationship was strained and he also knew that Danielle loved her father very much, just as Owen Henderson loved his daughter. "Give him my love when you see him," Danielle said.

"I will," replied Richards. With that, they said their goodbyes with promises to talk again in a few weeks.

Tyson Richards did manage to get away from the office at a decent time. The current double murders that he was investigating produced no added information that day. Up since 2 am, he felt he owed it to himself to get away from the office and start fresh the next day. He drove across town and headed out the familiar country road on the edge of the city that would take him to the Henderson residence. Set back a couple of hundred feet from the road was the old farm house. Owen and his wife had purchased it just before Danielle was born and spent several years remodeling and repairing the once run down house. Now the front yard was starting to look neglected, the grass full of weeds, something Owen would never have let happen when his wife was alive. Richards parked his car near the house and sat for a moment to take in the country air and familiar sounds. He got out of his car and walked to the front door. He could hear the news playing on the television from the open window.

## Chapter Five

Sitting in a reclining chair, square in front of the flat panel television, Owen Henderson was sound asleep, or more likely passed out. A half empty bottle of Grey Goose vodka sat next to the telephone on a table that was near his side. He wasn't sure if it was the insistent banging, or the endless ringing of the phone, or the pretty news woman on the TV that woke him. He sat a moment, a bit disoriented. Probably still a little drunk from his afternoon binge, something he had taken to lately to ease the pain of his recent past. The woman on the TV was that pretty girl with the hazel eyes that he always liked. Patricia he thought her name was. He often wondered if people called her Patricia, or Pat, maybe Patty, or he wondered, did she go by Trisha or Trish. With the banging still in the background and the phone still ringing, his head cleared a little more. Then what the girl on the TV was saying really caught his attention. "An unnamed source close to the investigation told this reporter just today that Louis DeDominicus was shot and killed in his home late last night," the reporter said. She continued on, "There is speculation that the murder of Vincent DeLatrota, also last night, may be linked somehow."

Now Owen Henderson was fully awake and he reached for the phone to stop the gawd damn ringing.  "Yea," he said into the hand set.  "Open your fucking front door," he heard through the receiver.  "What?" replied Henderson.  "Owen, it's me Ty.  I'm at your front door.  Open up you idiot," came across the phone.  Henderson's head was clearer now as he fully gained his senses.  He stood, walked over to his door, and opened it to find his long time friend and partner standing there with a sour look on his face.  "Hey Ty," Henderson said to the other man.  "Geez buddy!  You sure look like shit.  When was the last time you shaved or washed your fucking hair?" Richards said to the bigger man.  "Oh yeah," Henderson replied, running a hand through his mop of dirty blonde hair and then itching at the three days of growth on his face, "it's been a bad week.  This was the week that Danielle's mom and I bought this house," he continued on, "I guess things kind of got to me," he said as he walked back into the living room.  "Sure looks like it," Richards said.

The two men sat down in matching oxblood leather recliners and listened to the final bit of the news cast about the double murders.  Henderson looked at his partner and asked, "So is it true?  Both DeDominicus and DeLatrota were killed?"  "Yup," replied

Richards. "Wow! Incredible!" Henderson remarked. "Do you have any theories yet, any eye witnesses?" "Not yet," said Richards, "just happened early this morning and we have not really gone over any of the evidence yet. But it does look like an execution on both of them. All I can tell you is that there will be chaos in that band of misfits," he continued on, "if the DeDominicus crime family is without the number one and number two, it leaves the family ripe for take over from a huge number of people. There literally could be a blood bath in the streets as they fight this out." Richards pause for a second, he looked at his partner, "I, no, the department can really use you on this one Owen. We need what you have in that brain of yours." He continued to look at his partner. He looked older somehow, withdrawn. He thought he even may see some grey in the three days growth on Henderson's chin.

Henderson picked up the remote for the television and flicked it off. Shuffling the remote from hand to hand for a second, he set it back on the table beside him. He looked at his partner, "I don't know Ty," he said. "It's really tough, I feel lost most days, and the others I'm just drunk. I feel like I let everyone down, that I fucked up. Danielle doesn't sound the same when she talks to me, and I don't blame her.  My actions, or my fucking inactions, changed her life, changed my baby girl's life forever," he finished.  His eyes becoming watery, he reached his hand into the ice bucket that was on the table between them, scooped a few cubes and dumped them in his tumbler.  The rattle of the ice in the crystal glass was the only sound that could be heard.  He reached for the bottle of Grey Goose.  As he wrapped his hand around the neck of the bottle, Tyson Richards reached out and wrapped his hand around his partners.  Henderson looked at him.  Richards, his eyes moist now as well, said, "Look Owen, you're drowning your life, your sorrows, and the memories of your wife and daughter, in this bottle.  You need to stop this self pity party now.  We all miss Tracy, she was an awesome girl, the best. Everyone saw the love you had," he paused, "still have for her.  And we all respect that love, but she is gone.  Your daughter, your life, and your career are not.  Stop washing away the pain with this bottle.  Deal with it and move on."

Richards removed his hand.  He stood and looked down at his partner.  Henderson let his hand slip from the bottle.  "Owen," Richards said, "I need you on this case.  I need your help.  Please think about it," he finished.  He turned to the door, grabbed the handle, and

turned back again to face Henderson.
"Danielle is worried about you," Richards said, "she is all alone out there while you waste yourself on the vodka. If you can't come back to work to help me, do something to help yourself, help your daughter." He turned and walked out the door, not even closing it as he left. Henderson sat for a minute until he heard Richards' car start. He stood and walked to the big window that overlooked the once beautiful front yard. He watched his lifelong friend drive away without looking back.

## Chapter Six

Owen Henderson stood staring out the front window for several minutes. He wasn't really looking at anything, yet looking at everything at the same time. He reached for the cordless phone where it lay on the cluttered table with his remote, his bottle of vodka and the ice bucket. He dialed the number of his daughter and waited for the overseas call to be connected. As he listened to the now familiar beeps, crackles and clicks of the connection being made, his mind drifted to a day 10 months ago. He was sitting in his office at the OPP Burlington detachment, the then home of the quasi organized crime division. He had just had a meeting with the Crown Prosecutor who would be handling the case of Jesus Cortez. His phone rang and he answered it with his standard greeting, "Detective Henderson". What the caller on the other end of the line said froze his blood. "We have your wife and daughter Detective," the voice said in broken English with a strong Spanish accent, detective coming out like DEETICTIVE, "If you want to see them alive again," the voice went on, "you will go on permanent vacation before the trial starts." The caller then hung up.

Henderson was pulled from this nightmarish reverie by the familiar voice of his beautiful daughter, "Daddy, are you there?" Danielle said. He cleared his throat and with as much joy as he could put in his voice said, "Hey Baby Doll! How ya doin'?" He paused, his hand gripping the phone so tightly that it turned his knuckles white. "I just wanted to let you know that Ty was here," he continued, struggling to keep his voice in control and not break down over the phone with his daughter. He waited for a response from his daughter. After a long moment of silence, his voice cracking just a bit, he said, "Danny, you there?" She sighed, "Daddy," after a small pause, she continued again, "Daddy, I love you," she said. That was all he could take. He broke, his sobs came in rasps, his body wracking. "Oh Baby," he said, "I'm so sorry. I'm so, so sorry." He repeated again, "I'm sorry, I'm sorry," his voice trailing off as the sobs overtook him.

"Daddy," Danielle began, her voice trembling, "it wasn't your fault. They were bad men, doing bad things. You didn't do anything wrong." She took a long breath and continued on, "I have never blamed you for what happened to Mom, never blamed you for what happened to me. I was pissed that you walked away. You closed up after what happened. You abandoned me Daddy. You left me alone. Sure you were in the house with me, but you never talked, you never said you loved me. You never said you missed Mom. You just shut down." Henderson didn't say a word, he just listened as his daughter continued on, "I only wanted my dad, the only person I had left in the world. I just wanted you to hold me, to tell me that everything was going to be ok. But you didn't do anything, you hugged me once at the funeral and barely spoke a word to me after. I want my dad back, I want my hero back. I know you miss Mom, I do too, but you're all I have Daddy. Please come back."

His sobs were coming almost uncontrollably now as he listened to his daughter, his grip so tight on the phone he heard it crack under the pressure. She had finished and was letting him get control of his emotions. He wiped at his face, his big hand clearing his eyes. He stood a moment gathering his thoughts, listening to his daughter breathe. He looked out the window, it was now fully dark outside, his only vista being shadows and dark grey blobs of bushes and shrubs. He cleared his throat, "Danielle," he said, "I am sorry I abandoned you. I'm sorry for all the bad things that happened to you and I'm sorry that your mom was killed," his voice becoming just a bit stronger. "This has been an exceptionally hard week," he continued. She interrupted him, "I know Dad. It's the anniversary of when you and Mom bought the house, but those should be good memories for you, not bad ones." He sighed, "Yes, they should be. But some days it just hurts and I can't get past the hurt." The two were both silent for a long moment. "Daddy," she said in a more cheerful voice, "I have a surprise!" Henderson smiled, probably the first time in months. "Well, don't keep me hanging," he said. "I met a boy," she said with too much happiness and glee in her voice. "Oh gawd," he groaned in mock despair. "Oh stop Dad," she said, "he is a great guy. He's from Canada." "Well that's one thing he has going for him," Henderson said with genuine humour in his voice, "well tell me about him," he continued. With both their spirits perked up, she rambled on about her new boyfriend. This pleased Henderson, not that she had a boyfriend, but that she was getting back her life, starting to enjoy it again. They continued their talk for another 20 minutes, mostly one sided from Danielle. With sweet goodbyes and I love yous, they said their goodbye.

## Chapter Seven

Owen Henderson flicked on his stereo, the familiar sax of Clarence Clemons from Springsteen's E-Street band wafted from the speakers.  It was a favourite song of his and Tracy's.  He paused to listen for a second.  He picked up his bottle of Grey Goose, the ice bucket, and his crystal tumbler.  He walked into the kitchen, setting everything on the counter.  He looked out the window over his kitchen sink, the moon full and bright hung low in the eastern sky, reflecting brightly off the small lake at the back of his property.  Again his thoughts drifted back to the day almost 22 years ago that his then new bride, Tracy, and he came to look at the property.  They both laughed as they pulled into the driveway of the rundown farm house.  Sure it was in their price range the real estate agent told them.  Only needs a little TLC he had said.  Owen and Tracy debated on whether to even get out of the car when they drove on to the property.  The weeds out front were waist high, the front porch was sagging, and there were only three shutters hanging on the wall for the six or seven windows on the front of the house.  He remembered looking at Tracy, she had that glint in her hazel green eyes, "Oh what the fuck," she said, "we're here, might as well take a look!"

They got out of the car, did the customary hand shake of the real estate agent, and began their tour. Walking in the front door, there was a short hall, a worn wooden staircase was set to one side just past a door that led into a living room. A doorway on the opposite side of the hall led off to a formal dining area that had tall windows looking into the side yard, and a door at the back leading into the kitchen. At the far end of the hall was the entrance to the kitchen at the back of the house. It had everything they were looking for; high ceilings, wood flooring throughout, and a couple of working wood fireplaces. The eat-in kitchen was made for a family of 10 with space to spare. Upstairs had four bedrooms and two bathrooms. Owen and Tracy instinctively agreed, both pointing out the one room that would be the office/sewing room. It really was exactly what they were looking for except for one thing, it was really run down, had not been lived in for 20 years, and all the paint, wallpaper, and wood floors were in need of laborious hours of work and stripping. Neither of them were afraid of hard work, but this project, they thought, was just too big for the pair of them to tackle.

The agent told them about the two out buildings, one a barn, the other, a workshop type storage shed. He told them to take their time, look the property over.  He handed them a fact sheet and said he had to go make some calls in his car and would leave them alone, but he was here at their disposal.  The pair, hand in hand as they always were, wandered through the house, talking of colours, of the hours and months of work it would take, both agreeing that it would be a great house, but too much work for them at this stage in their young lives.  They walked out the back door that was off the kitchen and were greeted with weeds even higher than the ones in the front yard.  Standing looking around, it was Tracy who first spotted it.  "What's that over there?" she said, pointing to the far back of the yard.  "I'm not sure," replied Owen, "looks like a deck of some sort."  He, even being 6'3", had a hard time looking over the weeds and brush that had grown up over what they thought to be a back deck.  "But why put a deck 100 feet off the back of your house?" Tracy asked him.  "Beats me," he shrugged, maybe it's an old building that fell down."

He let go of her hand for the first time since they arrived and started to whack away at the bushes and overgrown weeds making a path back to what they spotted.  Tracy, standing only 5'2", followed in his wake, barking mock orders to hurry up!  They were both laughing.  Henderson stopped and she almost ran into the back of him. "Holy shit!" he gasped. "What is it?" Tracy asked. "Babe, you have to see this," he replied. He banged down some more weeds and stepped to the side to let her take a look. She stood at the end of the object that they had both spotted, with weeds growing up through the dock and high on either side, the lake in front of them had been totally obscured from their view. "Oh my gawd," Tracy said, "it's absolutely beautiful." At the end of the dock stood a pristine lake, maybe one square kilometre in size, in the centre sat a tiny island with two blue pines spouting up from it. The pair, with eyes beaming, looked at each other, again that glint in Tracy's eyes. All she said to him was yes. Henderson nodded his head and said "Yes."

At that moment, the pair knew that they had found their house. The amount of work was a small sacrifice for the small piece of paradise that they had on the property. They quickly made their way back to the agent who was still sitting in his car on the phone. They stood patiently waiting for him to get off the phone. He hung up his call, got out from his car, and looked at the beaming couple. "What?" he said inquisitively, "Did you find a pot of gold at the end of your rainbow?" Owen, barely able to contain himself, said, "How much property comes with the house? How far back does it go?" The agent referred to his paperwork. "Well," he said, "the back of the property goes to the next road over which," he paused for a second, "is about two kilometres back. Wow, there is a lot of property with this old house." A smiling Tracy, with her hazel green eyes glinting and the dimples in her cheeks growing larger, said, "We will take it."

Taking Owen's hand, she said, "We want the house. We want to put in an offer now and we are not leaving until we have a final answer." The agent smiled at the pair. "Ok," he said hesitantly, "let's get in the car and see what we can do." Two and a half hours later, their final offer had been accepted in principal by the selling parties. Now it was just up to the bank, but they both knew that the finances would not be a problem. The couple parted company with the agent and wandered back to their lake. Standing on the end of the dock, the sun just starting to set, Owen looked over at Tracy, "We did it Babe," he said, "we bought our house." "No," she corrected him, "we bought our home."

They took possession of the house at the beginning of October and spent most of the fall clearing the yard, cutting down the overgrown brush, and making their lake and house visible. Over that first winter, they tackled what they could in the house. To their joint surprise, it was in far better shape than they had both thought. Finishing first a bedroom, the pair then tackled one of the bathrooms, followed by the kitchen, and finally the living room, finishing this phase just in time for spring to arrive. When their first spring came, they spent most of their time working the yard, taking down more brush, and opening up the view from the house out to their lake. Owen spent countless hours rebuilding the dock that spanned almost 20 feet out into the clear cool water. Once that was complete, he began other work; replacing the missing shutters, rebuilding the aged and sagging front porch, and working on cleaning up the junk that had been collected over the years around the two out buildings. It was during his junk cleanup that he stumbled upon the old row boat. It was an old Medway Skiff made of cedar strips, about 10 feet long with a wide shallow body and flat bottom. Numerous coats of paint had been added to it, but the hull looked sound.

Without Tracy's knowledge, he dragged the old skiff into the back of the barn and worked on it tirelessly when she was at work or occupied with other things, like her gardens or sewing. It took him most of his spare time throughout the summer to strip the layers of paint from it, sanding and scraping it by hand, and applying numerous coats of varathane.   He was finally ready to present his find to Tracy in late September.  It was a beautiful Saturday to have a birthday, her 25$^{th}$, and he could barely contain his excitement when he woke that day.  Waking before Tracy, he went down to the barn and dragged the newly re-finished skiff down to the dock.  With new rigging and ropes, he tied it to a cleat he had installed the night before.  He raced back into the house, poured some champagne and orange juice into two glasses, grabbed a bowl of fruit, and went back up to his sleeping bride.  He was sitting on the bed staring at her when she opened her eyes.  Their mimosa's and fruit sitting on the bedside table at her side.

"Good morning Princess," he said to her as she smiled at him.  "Go away," she said, giving him a small shove.  "You're a creeper you know," she said smiling, "sitting there staring at me while I sleep," a bigger smile crossing her face.  "Ya, I know," he sighed, "just a creeper looking at a beautiful Princess," he said.  He bent down and kissed her, her lips soft and warm against his.  He let his hand slowly run up her thigh lifting the old dress shirt that she would often wear to bed, exposing her naked hip.  Slapping at his hand, she smiled at him, "Enough," she said, "I need to pee before you start your pawing at me." Again she beamed her smile at him, padding off to their bathroom, swinging her butt from side to side just to get his attention.

She returned from the bathroom and crawled into their bed. Handing her a glass he said, "Happy Birthday Babe!" She took the glass from him, smiled back, they clinked their glasses and both sipped the smooth fizzy drink. "Ok," he said too loudly, startling her. "Geez, can't you warn a girl when you're going to shout like that? I almost spilled my mimosa." "I really want to give you your birthday present," he said to her." "Ok," she smiled, holding out her hand. "Oh no, you need to come see it," Henderson said to his wife, taking her hand and practically dragging her from the bed. Barely able to contain himself, he led Tracy down the stairs and into the kitchen. She looked around and said, "So, where is it?" "Close your eyes," he told her. She complied, then lifted one eyelid slightly. He smiled at her, "You're bad," he said, "surprises need to stay secret until you get them." Wrapping a towel around her head to cover her eyes, he said, "There, that should do it."

He led her out the back door. She walked gingerly along the stone pathway the two had built over the summer.  "Slow down," she said to him.  "No, you hurry up!" he retorted.  They were both smiling.  He led her on to the dock and positioned her so she was facing directly at the skiff bobbing on the water.  "Ok," he said, "take off the towel, take a look."  She reached back and untied the loose knot of the towel.  Blinking her eyes a couple times to adjust to the bright morning light, she stared in astonishment at the small finely crafted boat bobbing on the water.  "Oh my gawd," she said in hushed amazement, "I love it Owen."  She reached over and wrapped her arms around his neck, planting a warm wet kiss on his lips.  They hugged for a long moment, pressing their bodies together, Owen feeling her warm naked body under the oversized shirt.   She eventually pulled from him to study her gift more closely.  "It's beautiful, where did you ever get…" she said, stopping in mid sentence, "you named her the 'Naked Grape', that is perfect."  Naked Grape was their favourite brand of wine.

"When can you take me out in it?" she asked him.  "As soon as you get dressed," he told her.  She giggled and went running off into the house.  Five minutes later, she came back out, still barefoot, carrying a wine bottle and two glasses, and the bowl of fruit that Owen had put together for her breakfast. "A little early for wine isn't it?" She looked at him with a mock stern face, "It's my birthday, I will do what I want, plus we have to christen her." Again she darted back to the house. Henderson placed the wine, glasses, and fruit in the bottom of the boat. He put the oars in the boat and when he stood back up, Tracy was coming back across the yard, this time her arms were full of every pillow she could find in the house. Dragging behind her was their favourite quilt that she had made over the winter months. Plopping it all in the boat, she asked him to help her in. "Well are you not going to get dressed?" he asked her. She smiled again, "I'm as dressed as I'm going to be silly," she said. Taking her hand, he guided her into the boat. She sat on the front bench and laid the pillows out. On top she spread the quilt. Now nestled into her new nest, she unbuttoned a couple of the top buttons on the shirt she was wearing. Winking and smiling at him, she asked, "Are you ready Capitan?" while offering a very badly executed salute.

Owen paddled them out to the middle of their tiny lake, letting the boat drift while they sipped the wine. They were both now snuggled into the nest that Tracy had built with the pillows and quilt. They talked of their future, their plans, and held each other close. It wasn't too long before Owen had slowly undone all the buttons on Tracy's shirt, opening it up, he smiled as he looked down at her naked body.  She was truly a beautiful girl, never wearing make-up except for her favourite vanilla flavoured chapstick.  She had freckles that speckled the tops of her firm breasts, he traced his finger over these and around her nipple.  He looked her in the eyes, "I love you Tracy Henderson," he said, "to the moon and back."  "I love you too Owen Henderson," she smiled warmly at him.  He squeezed some of the juice from a piece of fruit onto her naked breasts.  "Hey, that's cold!" she said with a smile.  He bent over her, kissing and lapping up the juices off her breasts.

He did this a second time, again kissing the sweet liquid from her breasts.  He cupped her perfect breast in his hand slowly licking the fruit juice from her nipple.  Taking it into his mouth, he felt it get harder.  Tracy let out a soft moan and pulled his head closer to her breast as she arched her back to him.   "Make love to me," she whispered in his ear.  He set their glasses to the side, again cupping her breast gently, he kissed her with the same passion as if it was their first time.  Looking into her eyes, that had now turned the colour of green glass just as it hits its melting point in a fire, he ran his hand down the soft supple skin of her side, gently caressing her naked hip. He ran his hand up the inside of her soft thigh, he paused on this spot fondling her gently, he felt she was very ready and wanting of him.

They made love several times through that late September morning and again in the early afternoon. Both spent, they lay side by side, hand in hand, Tracy's one leg flopped over Owen's, letting their naked bodies soak up the warm sun. They lay like that for some time, searching for pictures and objects in the clouds, saying sweet words to one another. It was that warm late September day that Danielle was conceived, out on the water in their boat.

They made love often out in Tracy's little boat over the years, sometimes through the day, and often at night under the stars. It was their favourite place, eager to race to their love nest on the water when there was a warm gentle rain to make love in. On a particularly mild Christmas Eve, they even snuck the boat into the water. No ice had been present that year and the lake looked like a sheet of glass when they slipped the boat into it. They made love most of the night under the quilt in the cool night air, waking in the early morning hours to a light dusting of snow covering them and the sun just about to peak above the horizon.  Giggling and shivering in the cold, they raced in the back door to find seven year old Danielle rubbing her eyes and asking if Santa was outside.  They both smiled at her naivety.

Henderson looked up to the moon that had moved little while his mind had drifted off to happier times.  They were not only extremely compatible at making love, they were compatible at most things in their life, true best friends and equal partners.  Their love was the true kind of love, the kind where you know the other always had your back, the kind that only came once in your life.  It was the type of love you could see in the other's eyes or feel through the tender gentle touches as they would pass each other in the hall or kitchen.  "I love you Tracy Henderson," he said to the moon.  "I love you to the moon and back," he whispered.  He reached for his Grey Goose, hands trembling slightly, undid the lid, dumped the bottle in the sink, and left its clear contents to slosh down the drain.

## Chapter Eight

Owen Henderson found himself standing in front of a pair of opulent front doors with finely crafted crosses carved in them, the doors to Cathedral Basilica of Christ the King, the largest catholic church in Hamilton. It was the same church he, Tyson and Wyatt had attended while going to catholic school. The same church he and Tracy had married in and the same church where her funeral was held. With seating for over 1000 people, it held the old world charm and grace of times gone by. A steeple close to 100 feet rose to the sky, intricate stained windows depicting hundreds of different scenes and pictures of Mary, Jesus and the twelve disciples. His hand trembled as he reached for the door, get control of yourself he thought. Pulling his hand back he was second guessing his decision. He woke with purpose that morning. Almost feeling if a small burden had been lifted from him through the night. He slept well, sound, no nightmares this time to leave him in a cold sweat and unable to go back to sleep.

He had showered, shaved and put on his standard uniform, or what he classified as his uniform. Casual tan pants, off white dress shirt, a tweed jacket and his trusted Nike running shoes. Although not as professional looking as his superiors wanted him to dress, they overlooked minor things like that.  Saying you cannot judge a book by its cover.  They over looked a few things when it came to Owen Henderson.  He was an exceptional detective.  He was always good at being not just one step but three steps ahead of the criminals and cases he was working on.  They often joked that it was good he was on their side, if not, they would never catch him.  He looked good in his choice for this day.  He could always pull of the casual business look, well, except for the shoes.  Not like his partner, who would always be in a perfectly pressed suite, starched shirt and silk tie.

He knew he needed to start someplace; this was the best way to do it he thought.  The last place he had been able to look on to his wife's face.  Start here, move forward.  He steadied himself, running a hand through his mop of dirty blonde hair, he drew in a deep breath, reached for the large wooden handle on the door and walked in.

At this hour, just past 8:30 in the morning, he was surprised to see as many people in the church as there were.  A few workmen fiddling with lights off to one side, a group of old women in a pew about 5 back from the altar.  Another crew of cleaners were going over the pews on the far side.  Walking in Henderson was always shocked by the magnitude of the inside of this church.  Pews were four wide, with a narrow aisle between the left set of double pews and the right set.  The centre aisle was larger, maybe 15 or 20 feet wide. Walking in you go down 3 stairs to the main floor of the church, this too gave the interior the appearance of a huge cavernous space. The ceiling was no closer than 50 feet, with the stained windows raising two stories, the acoustics incredible.  You could stand at the pulpit and speak in a normal voice and be heard in every corner of the main chamber.  To the left and right of him were an identical grand sets of stairs that led to more seating, the balcony overhung the spot where Henderson was standing and stretched another 20 feet forward seating for another 250 worshipers.  Gazing around he spotted the person he came to see.

Father Wyatt was in the right wing of the main stage area talking with what Henderson assumed were some maintenance men. Henderson stood looking at him, still amazed that Wyatt had taken the path of God and became a priest. Most thought Wyatt would try for Hugh Heffner's job.  Wyatt was Tyson Richards' older brother.  The trio, Owen, Tyson and Wyatt, were for years inseparable.  Where you found one, you found the other two. However Wyatt always fancied himself as more of the ladies man. Or at least that is the appearance he tried to put forward. That and the consummate partier, usually the first to puke his guts out, or wander off in a drunken adventure he thought apt for the situation. Before their senior year Wyatt started to drift away from the trio. He got more into partying of the heavy kind. Running away from home a few times to hang with a different, not so nice, crowd. Senior year came and most of the kids in their grade were talking of University, Wyatt was talking of grow ops and girls.

It wasn't until February of their senior year that something happened. No one really knows what , he never spoke of it, but Wyatt became withdrawn. He settled down some, but there was more too it. If invited to a party he may show, but would sip one drink for a few hours then leave with the excuse of parents or curfews. Less and less was seen of him. At graduation, many were actually surprised that first he showed and that second, he did qualify to graduate. The last summer before everyone went off to University very little was seen of him. He was either at work or at home with his parents. One end of the summer party he did show with Owen and Tyson. Everyone was talking of what school they were going to, who their roommates would be and all the things young people talk of at summers' end parties.

Someone asked Wyatt what he was going to do, what university he was going to. That caused a bit of a hush as most figured he could not get in with poor grades or he didn't have the ambition. He was the partier for most of the four years they spent in high school. At first he didn't say anything. Both Tyson and Owen looked at each other as well, wondering what he would say. Very proudly, very confidently, Wyatt looked at the questioner and he said, I have been accepted into the University of Minnesota's Theological Program, I'm going to become a priest, Wyatt said with a straight and very proud face. At that moment you could hear a pin drop. And to see the jaws that dropped in unison was something Henderson had never seen. Someone spoke up and made some derogatory comment, others just laughed and made comment of sure when hell freezes over. Wyatt never argued with any of them, never made a wise crack and the look of pride never left his face. One week later he left on a plane for Minnesota. No one saw him for 5 years.

Now he stood at the far end of the church, his pleasant smile always present on his face. His hair was shorter now, thinning some.  His face was aged appropriately, the same as the rest of the groups faces had.  He wore faded jeans, his ratty U of M sweatshirt, and underneath his black shirt with the white banded collar.  Wyatt looked away from the people he was with when he noticed the bright light from the front doors.  Not expecting anyone he was both curious and surprised to see his long time friend standing at the entrance to the church, gazing over the pews and few people scattered here and there.  Excusing himself from the people he began to make his way over to Owen.  Raising his hand with a small wave, hey Owen, he said in a voice just above talking level.  Henderson turned his attention back to Father Wyatt, he grinned broadly and started to make his way in man's direction.

The two men embraced warmly where they met almost in the centre of the church.  Hey buddy, Wyatt said to the bigger man, having to look up to meet his eyes.  Hey Father, Henderson said with a sardonic grin.  Come on, Wyatt sighed, I'm still Wyatt, you can drop the father crap.  The two men laughed together and moved to take a seat part way in of the pew rows that was closest to the centre aisle.  Wyatt looked at the bigger man for a long moment then said, so, how are you doing.  You look good, well as good as you will ever look, he added with a chuckle. Henderson with his head hung low, hands fidgeting in his lap, he let out a long breath. Wyatt could see his friend was fighting to control his emotions, he could see the jaw muscles clenching as Henderson struggled to gain control of himself. Finally Henderson said, better I think, It's been tough, I have good days, then bad, then worse. Seems like the worse or bad ones have been outweighing my good days though. He finished with another long exhalation.

Neither man said a word for a few minutes. Father Wyatt, having spent a number of years after leaving the seminary studying Human Psychology, and true he was also now a doctor, he knew to give his friend time to collect his thoughts, control his emotions. He knew that Henderson would eventually let out his words. When Father Wyatt could see that Henderson had become more relaxed he said to him, I know this has been tough on you. You, Tracy and Danielle were the perfect family. Everyone saw it and everyone knew it. We saw the way you cared for your girls and we saw the love and affection you have for your wife. With Tracy being gone, it has not broken your family, it has only changed it. She is still with you, and she always will be. Tapping Henderson on the chest in the vicinity of his heart, she is always here, he said. With a little more strength now, Henderson looked at his friend and confidant, she was my best friend, I feel lost without her, he said.  Letting his head drop down again.  He looked back up at Father Wyatt, his eyes moist he said, but I know I have to let go, I know I have to move forward, I have to be here for Danielle.  I'm working on it, he finished.

## Chapter Nine

The pair of men sat in silence for a few more minutes, it was Father Wyatt that spoke next. I think coming here is a good first step, I know it was the last place you were able to see her. I also think it's a good thing that you are going back to work. You are going to work right, that's why you are dressed that way, and in a lower voice said, any why you brought a fucking gun into my church, he finished. He may be a man of God but Father Wyatt Richards had not lost any of his street talk or charm. Probably why he was so popular with the kids in his therapy sessions as well. Both men smiled at Father Wyatt's last comment. Yes, Henderson replied. I just came here to see you and then I'm heading to the office and see if they will let me help with the murder cases going on, he finished. Ya, Ty was telling me about those last night, Wyatt said. We went for a beer after he left your place. I actually had a feeling that you may show up here, although I didn't expect to see you today. Pretty busy place you have here today, Henderson said, trying to get the subject on to other things.

Father Wyatt said, well I'm sure you are aware that. His voice trailed off in Henderson's head, it wasn't that he was ignoring Wyatt or uninterested in what he was saying.  It was that funky prickle on the back of his neck, the one he got when something was out of place, or not right for the current situation.  This $6^{th}$ sense, as his work colleagues called it, has always helped him, and more times than he would care to count saved he and his partner's lives.  He didn't know what triggered it at this moment, his eyes looking at the all people he had seen when he entered, nothing had changed there.  What was it he thought, what caught his eye.  He heard Father Wyatt say something about the Pope, and then his eyes narrowed on the man that had just past them, walking up the centre aisle.  He was all wrong, but why he asked himself.  He is moving to slow came the immediate response from his brain, and the clothes, they are all wrong.  Dark blue pants, military style, too many pockets, the jackboots, the man's gaze scanning the church from side to side.  The dark blue jacket, again too many pockets, looks like army surplus, all wrong he said to himself again.  Hair cropped short, dark hair, middle eastern or Mediterranean features, darker skin.  His synapses were firing on all engines.  This is not right he kept thinking.

He caught another snippet of what Father Wyatt was so animatedly talking about, huge crowds he thought Wyatt had said.  It was then that Henderson saw the tell tale bulge under the strange man's right arm.  Shit, shit, Henderson thought.  Not good.  This guy has a gun.  Only police officers can carry guns in Canada, even military cannot carry a gun off base.  And this guy was no cop, he was paramilitary, he was all wrong.  Henderson put a hand on his friends knee, sorry something's not right, he said cutting Wyatt off in mid sentence.  Henderson's brain did not register Wyatt's protests as he rose, his hand reaching to his side to unclip the safety on his weapon.  With grace, speed and stealth, something a man his size should not possess he had sprung from his seat and was one pace behind the strange man.  With one hand on his weapon, ready to draw if needed, he reached out his right arm to spin the man and confront him.  In a blur of blue the foreigner silently spun on Henderson, catching him completely off guard.

The foreigner's left hand and arm scooped under Henderson's right arm, he then reached around Henderson's neck, locking Henderson's arm high in the air.  The foreigner then kicked the back of Henderson's knee, this forced the big man to the ground with his right arm wrenched up and useless.  The foreigner was now behind Henderson applying so much pressure to his arm it would have snapped a smaller mans.  With Henderson facing the wrong direction, the other man behind him, his gun was useless.  He felt the hard cold of steal press against the base of his skull, this is it Henderson thought, the last place he saw his best friend will be the place he gets to join her.  But it wasn't his time and the survival instincts kicked in.  With all the strength that he could muster in his awkward positioning he ploughed his free left elbow back and up and made surprisingly solid contact with the man's crotch.  The gorilla grip on his right arm immediately released, he heard the clatter of the gun as it hit the floor.  The man behind him gurgled like a drowning man and slumped behind Henderson both hands clutching his crotch as he lay in the fetal position.

Henderson spun on the other man drawing his gun as he did, just as he placed a knee on the man's legs to pin him to the ground his senses widened to his entire surroundings.  He heard shouts and screams from the other people that had been in the church, he heard Father Wyatt with a commanding voice you would not expect from a priest yell, wait, wait, everyone just take a chill.  As Henderson looked up four more men dressed exactly like the man Henderson was pinning to the ground surrounded him, guns drawn, pointing them to the ground, but in his general direction.

Father Wyatt pushed his way through the group of men. Stop, he yelled, he's a cop, facing the men with the guns he repeated, he's a cop, only this time it was in perfect Italian. Just stop now. Father Wyatt looked at Henderson and said with his voice a little bit more under control, get off him Owen, it's ok. Let the man breath. His adrenaline still running fast through his body it took a second to register what Wyatt had said. Again Wyatt said, Owen get off him as he reached his hand under Henderson's arm to help raise him off the fallen man. Standing Henderson hesitantly holstered his gun, the other four men followed suite with as much trepidation as Henderson. What the fuck is going on Wyatt, Henderson said through gritted teeth. Wyatt again faced the other men and in Italian said something to them. He looked at Henderson, Owen, it's ok, he said. These guys are with the Swiss Guard, he said. Henderson's brain not really registering what his friend said looked at him quizzically. The Swiss Guard, Wyatt repeated, you know the police that protect the "Holly See" you know, Vatican City and the Pope. That is what I was telling you back there when you went all commando and zoned out on me.

Come on Owen, Wyatt said grabbing his friend by the elbow to usher him away from the foreign police officers.  Henderson gently pulled away from him, he bent down beside the fallen man, placing his big hands under the man's arms he helped him to his feet.  With honest sincerity he looked the man in the eye, I am very sorry, he said, I thought you were someone up to no good.  He repeated I'm sorry.  The other man still bent slightly cupping his groin reached out a trembling hand, he looked up to Henderson as the two men shook hands, it is, pausing, how do you say it, OK, I may have done the same to you if  you where in my country, the man said in broken English, his voice just a little shaky.  Henderson let the man's hand go and followed Father Wyatt back to the pew they had occupied.  He heard the 5 Italian police speaking, the one groaning some, a few chuckles and he thought he caught the words "No Bambino".

Well you certainly haven't lost any of the fight in you, Father Wyatt said, shaking his head and grinning at Henderson.  So what's going on, Henderson asked?  Laughing Father Wyatt said, that's what I was telling you.  Man, you really have been out of touch for the last 10 months.  You know there was a new Pope elected right, he asked?  Yea, I think I heard that on the news, Henderson replied.  Pope (Place Name here), is a more moderate and understanding Pope, Father Wyatt said.  He is way more in touch with reality than any Pope in the last 200 years. He read and liked the paper I wrote a few years back on the social impact of intolerance and non-recognition by the Church on gay and lesbian marriages. So during his current world tour he has picked this church for one of his stops. He is coming here, Father Wyatt finished with a beaming smile. Coming here, to this church, to see you, Henderson asked? Well not just to see me, but it has been mentioned that he would like to meet me in private, Father Wyatt said. Wow, very impressive, Henderson said, reaching his hand out to shake his friends. Father Wyatt beaming with pride now said, Yes, I was very surprised that he read it. But like I said he is very tolerant and more in touch with his flock than any of his predecessors. And that is what I was telling you, he continued with a raised eye brow.

Father Wyatt explained to him that this special unit of the Swiss Guard are much the same as the Secret Service or the RCMP. They have diplomatic immunity in every country. They are the advance team that go to each of the stops on the Popes current agenda. They look for security concerns, scope out the travel paths for the motorcade and generally provide all the security the Pope will need at all his stops. They never rely on local police, which can be a huge expense for a community if the Pope decides on a visit. He continued to explain that the men are highly skilled in many forms of self defence, anti-terrorist tactics, hostage negotiations and anything else you can think of. The men are fiercely disciplined and highly educated. So they are here checking security concerns on the church, Henderson asked his friend? Yes, and if you had just listened to me for another 10 seconds I was about to tell you that the guy walking up the aisle was a police officer and that you should not be alarmed, Father Wyatt said laughing at the bigger man. Well, I guess no harm no foul, well I guess I did harm him a bit, said Henderson. I hope he can still have kids, Henderson chuckled. Doubtful, Father Wyatt said, they take vows of celibacy.

So do you feel better now that you have that out of your system, the priest asked his friend? Well, I feel better that I came here, it was good to get out of the house, and really go to see you, Henderson replied. Me you and Ty need to go out, grab a couple beers and shoot the shit. It's been way too long, maybe we can get in touch with Tommy have him tag along as well, Father Wyatt said to Henderson as both men stood. That would be good, Henderson replied, I would like that, like that very much. As Henderson reached for the other man's hand to shake it, Wyatt looked at him with compassionate eyes, I am truly sorry for your loss Owen, I'm always here if you need to talk. The two men embarrassed, broke from the clutch and shook hands one last time. Hey, how is Danielle doing, Father Wyatt asked. Beaming Henderson looked at him and said, I think she is doing ok. She sounded really good on the phone last night. She has a boy in her life she said. God Help us, Wyatt said both men rolling their eyes and ginning.

## Chapter Ten

For the second time in the past two hours, Owen Henderson found himself standing in front of a set of doors, anxiety welling up in him, wondering if he was doing the right thing. Taking a deep breath, he steeled himself as he walked in the front doors of the new OPP Organized Crime Unit offices. The building, actually a mansion that was confiscated under the "Seizure of Goods Obtained Through the Proceeds from Crimes" laws that had been passed a few years back, was a home that Jesus Cortez had purchased to stay in during his trial. He never got to use it because the kidnapping of Henderson's wife and daughter impelled the judge to remand Cortez in jail throughout the trial. The building had been extensively renovated. The main floor offered an entrance foyer for a receptionist and two assistants, as well as a kitchen, large conference room, and a tactical room. The upper floor was reworked to provide a second smaller conference room and 10 offices for the unit, along with a few over the top bathrooms. The basement of the building was the chop shop, Janet Heartland's domain.

When he made it through the front doors, Mrs. Sandhill was already standing to greet him. Spying him coming through the glass front doors, she was around her desk with a speed befitting a woman much younger than she.  An older woman, with grandmotherly features not unlike Mrs. Doubtfire from that Robin Williams' movie, she embraced him with a firm motherly hug.  "Owen," she said, pulling back, gripping him by his big shoulders and looking him in the eyes, she continued, "how are you doing my child?"  She embraced him again, he almost melted in the sweet motherly hug.  Pulling back to look at him again, "You have lost some weight," she said, "but you still look healthy.  You know," she continued on, "I stopped by your house once to check on you.  You never answered your door so I walked around back.  I saw you standing out on your dock.  I left, feeling I didn't want to interrupt your private time."  "Thank you for coming by, you should have come out to the dock," Henderson said, "it's just a spot I go that centres me."  She hugged him one last time, "We all loved Tracy, you know," she said.  "Yes, she was a great girl," Henderson replied.  Swatting the big man on the ass she said, "Now get upstairs, there is lots going on around here and I'm sure you will be well received."  He smiled at the stern old woman and mounted the stairs.

When he reached the top landing and rounded the corner, Brian Jones had just stepped out from his office. Jones stopped, and started a slow methodical clap, which brought the rest of the squad who were in the building rushing from their offices. Soon there was a full standing ovation in that hall to greet Owen Henderson on his return to work. Tyson Richards was in his office at the end of the hall when he heard the ruckus. He opened his office door to see Henderson receiving handshakes and hugs of both condolence and welcome from his co-workers. "Alright everyone," Richards barked, "we have lots of work to get to and I'm sure Detective Henderson has had all the attention he wants for today." No one actually paid attention to Richards' bellows, not that they did not respect his authority, but they knew his bellows came half heartedly. Richards elbowed his way through the small group and stuck out his hand to Henderson, "Welcome back Detective Henderson," Richards said. The men shook hands and the crowd went back to what they were doing.

"Come on in," Richards motioned towards the office at the end of the hall. Henderson closed the door as he entered the office and both men took a seat. Richards, looking a bit uncomfortable, sat behind the desk while Henderson took up the guest chair. "Look Owen," Richards began, "I didn't think you would be back in so soon when I talked to you last night. I haven't had time to clear my stuff from your office, I'm really sorry about that." "What the fuck are you talking about Ty?" Henderson said. "Well with you back, I figured you would assume the task of Unit Commander," replied Richards. Henderson looked over his shoulder and pointed at the glass on the door, "Can you not read Ty? That says Unit Commander, Organized Crime Unit, Detective Tyson Richards," Henderson said, "it doesn't say Acting Commander." "No," Richards rebuked, "you know this has always been your job, I was just keeping your seat warm. You know you deserve this." "No, Tyson," Henderson said, "you deserve this. Remember, I was the one who walked away when they offered me the job. It's your unit, you're the commander. I'm here to help in any way I can. Besides, you have done a great job over the last 10 months, everyone respects you."

The two men sat staring at each other, neither wanting to budge on their respective stands on the issue. Henderson spoke first, "Look, I don't know how stable I am. This unit needs someone stable without all the emotional baggage that I currently tote around with me. Just give me an office and tell me what you want me to do," he finished. Again there was silence as the two men contemplated each other.  This time it was Richards who spoke, "Ok, fine.  We will do it your way," he said, "but I feel the higher ups will want a different arrangement."  "Well I will tell them the same thing then," Henderson said.  "So," he continued on, "are we going to bicker all day or do you have a place I can park my ass and maybe be of assistance to your team?" Smiling as both men stood, Richards said, "Sure Owen, we have an office next to mine. It's kind of where we have stored your stuff. Honestly, I didn't think you would be back this week so everything from your old office is still packed in boxes."  "That's fine, I can unpack my stuff," Henderson said, "it will give me a few minutes to settle my nerves and take a breath."

Opening his office door, Richards pointed to a door that was down the hall a few feet. "That's yours there," he said.  "Welcome back Owen," Richards said giving his partner a pat on the back as he walked the short distance around the hall.  "Oh and Detective Henderson," Richards said with a huge grin on his face, "I'm not sure I approve of your choice of attire, we try to be a bit more professional around here!"  Henderson faced his friend and now boss, so as to keep the conversation between just the two of them, he smiled and mouthed the words, "Fuck You, Asshole," throwing up his middle finger at Richards. Both men smiled and walked into their offices.

Henderson leaned against his closed office door, "Ok, I can do this," he said to himself, "everyone has done the condolences, my hand is not shaking as much. Get through the first day, the rest will follow." Isn't that what Wyatt told him, or something like that? He eyed the boxes sitting on his new desk. It was these kinds of things that scared him, the unknown, opening a box and not knowing what ghost would pop out and send his mind reeling back, put his emotions to the test. He knew he had to get it done. He placed all but one box on the floor and sat down at the desk.

The first box that he tackled was mostly files and notebooks that he quickly stored in the desk. The last item he pulled out brought the biggest smile to his face in more than 10 months. As he sat admiring the silly little object, there was a knock on his office door. "It's open," Henderson said. Tyson Richards poked his head in the door and said, "What's with the stupid smile?" Henderson laughed, holding up a tin can covered in multi-coloured macaroni noodles. "Remember this?" Henderson asked. Laughing, Richards said, "Yah, I think I do. I remember you freaked out when someone picked one of the noodles off and popped it in their mouth.  It was BJ wasn't it?"  Both men were laughing now.  "Ya," Henderson said, "it was the first school Father's Day gift that Danielle made for me."  Still smiling, he said, "What's up?"  Richards, pointing behind him said, "We are going to have an evidence and update meeting on the murders, down the hall in the conference room."  "Great," said Henderson, "give me two minutes."  "Last door on the left down the hall," Richards said, closing the door as he left.  Owen Henderson rolled the can around in his hand a moment.  He placed it on the left corner of his desk and reached into the top desk drawer, pulling out a handful of pens and letting them slide from his hand into the can.

## Chapter Eleven

Henderson walked into the small conference room to see Tyson sitting at the head of the rectangular table. Seated to his right was Janet Heartland, and to her right was Brian Jones. "Hey Janet," Henderson said. "Well, look who has finally returned to grace us with his presence," Heartland said with a sardonic grin. "Great to see you too Janet," Henderson replied, smiling at her. "Hey BJ, how is the new baby?" Henderson said to Brian. Seeing his face turn a slight shade of pink, Henderson added, "Sorry Brian, how's the baby?" "She's good, up all night right now though," Brian replied, shifting in his seat and looking every bit the proud new father. To Richards' left, was Steve Ingles. He and Henderson nodded at each other and exchanged brief pleasantries. Henderson sat down next to Ingles.

"Ok," Richards said, looking at Ingles he continued on, "where are Butters, Thompson and Sunland?" Ingles replied, "Butters is following up with a witness in St. Kitts. Got a call from him early this morning, he should be here soon. Thompson and Sunland are off today, they are doing nights this week remember?" "Right," Richards said nodding his head. Looking at Henderson, Richards said, "This is the team we have on this case for now; Brian Jones, Steve Ingles, Harry Butters, Sue Thompson, Cyrsta Sunland, and now you, Owen. Oh, and don't forget Janet here," he said, nodding curtly in her direction. "Sounds like a decent team," Henderson said, "everyone else is on other cases, I presume?" he added. "Yes," Richards said, "but if things start to pick up and we need more manpower, we can always pull someone else in." "Perfect," responded Henderson. Richards looked over to Janet Heartland and said, "Do you want to start with the forensics and pathology Janet?"

Heartland went through a detailed explanation of both murders as far as body condition, points of entry, and cause of death. She was then explaining that there was very little other physical evidence other than a few as of yet unidentified shell casings and two yellow roses. Henderson cut in and asked, "So the shell casings had no distinguishable markings on them?" "None that you can see with the naked eye," she said, "I haven't had time to put them under a scope yet, we just got back here from the second scene about 3 hours ago," she added. "Will you get to them today?" Henderson asked. "Oh sure, I don't need any fucking sleep like the rest of you, I just run on coffee and cigarettes," she said in a voice laced with sarcasm. Holding up his hands in mock surrender, Henderson said, "Geez Janet, I was just asking! You don't need to bite my head off." Richards cut in, and in a stern voice said, "That's fine Janet. Get to them as soon as you can. Tomorrow will be fine." Heartland looked over at Richards, sighing, "Do you guys need me for anything else? I think I have given you all I've got." She was about to stand up when Henderson asked, "You said something about yellow roses Janet?" Again, sighing heavily, she sank back into her chair. "Right, the roses," Heartland said. "At each of the crime scenes, we found a single yellow rose laying on or near the body. We can only assume that the killer or killers placed them there, but there is nothing remarkable about them and there is no way to tell where they came from other than canvassing every florist in the city. Are we done then?" she asked, eyeing the group. No one dared say a word. She stood and left the room.

As Janet Heartland was leaving the room, the men around the table all rolled their eyes and exchanged smiling glances. Richards was just about to start speaking again when Harry Butters came rushing into the room, flapping his note book in front of him. Harry Butters was the youngest member of the squad, having only made detective a year ago. He had about him the classic look of the boy next door, clean cut, clean shaven, always smelling not of cologne but Ivory soap, dark brown hair cut in a funky new "Metro-Sexual" style with lots of styling gel to keep the just messed up look holding strong all day.  He always dressed conservatively in off the shelf blue or grey suits with white shirts and tasteful ties.  Sitting down in the chair that Heartland had just vacated, he glanced over at Henderson.  "Oh hey, Mr. Henderson.  Welcome back," he said.  "Come on Harry, I'm not that much older than you.  Can you cut the Mr. and just call me Owen, or Henderson?" Henderson said with a small grin, shaking his head, "and thank you," he then added.  Looking down, Butters said, "Sorry Owen.  Welcome back."  Storming ahead, he said, "I've got something," holding out his note book as if to say "look, proof, I wrote it down!"

"Well what do you have?" Richards asked.  Without a pause Butters said, "Well yesterday, when we were all in St. Kitts, one of the neighbours was not home, or wouldn't answer the door.  Either way, I left my card in his door with a note to call me as soon as he returned.  Well he called me at 7:00 am this morning.  I was barely out of the shower, woke both my mom and the dog."  With a chuckle, he added, "I guess you don't need all those details."

Taking a breath, he said, "Anyways, the guy calls me, said he saw a car, so I raced down there to get his statement," he finished. "And?" Richards said. "Oh, yea," Butters said, flipping his note book open and peeling the pages back until he found the one he was looking for, "the guy's name is Robert J. Henry," he looked at the men, "don't forget the J, he gets a little pissy about that!" Drawing in another breath, he carried on, "This Robert J. Henry was at home the night of the murder. He said he is a crime novelist and does his best work at night. So when I knocked on his door, he was home, but sleeping. He didn't know anything happened until he went out to get his newspaper last night." "Why didn't he call last night?" Henderson asked. "I asked him that," Butters said, "and he told me that he didn't see my card until this morning when he was going to go get a coffee from Tim Horton's. It must have fallen by the wayside when he got the paper."

"Makes sense," Richards said with a slight shrug of his shoulders. The men all nodded in agreement and Butters continued, "He said he was writing up in his writing room as he called it. It looks down onto the street. He lives across, and up the road two houses, from DeDominicus' place. It took me a few minutes before he would let me go into the room to take a look out the window. He said it was his sanctuary and no one was allowed in there, it messed up his stories and vibe for his writings." "Has the guy published anything?" Ingles interjected. With a chuckle, Butters said, "Nothing in print. I did a quick search on the internet and couldn't find any authors by the name of Robert J. Henry. There was one of those stupid sex fantasies that people write and submit to Playboy that had his name on it. I don't know if it's the same guy, or if that makes him an author! The guy is a real geek," he added with a grin. "Once I threatened him with getting a warrant to search his house, he became more cooperative, and sure enough, when you sit at his desk, you can see right down the road to DeDominicus' place. He said it was about 2:30 am and he saw a car pull up in front of the house. He told me that was odd because in all the years he has lived there, he has never seen a car arrive anytime after 11:00 pm."

"Did he get a make, model or colour on the car?" Richards asked. "He said it was a four door Toyota Camry, 2012 or 2013 model. He owns one so he said he was sure. He can't be one hundred percent on the colour, because it was under one of those sodium lights that cast an orangeish glow, but he said it was either light blue or grey, and that's not all, he said it had a Discount car rental sticker on the back of it." The energy and excitement in the room rose tenfold with that small piece of information. Swallowing and taking in a breath, Butters reached for one of the full water bottles in the centre of the table. Looking at Richards ever so politely, he said, "May I?" "Sure, sure, have one," Richards said, wanting the man to continue. He looked at the men seated across from him, "Wait," he said, opening his water and taking a long pull, "it gets better." The excitement in the room was now palpable. You could almost feel it bouncing off each of the men. "He gave me a pretty decent description of the guy," he finished with the proud look of a man who just landed a three hundred pound tuna after a six hour fight.

"How good?" Henderson asked. "Really good," replied Butters, "he saw the guy from the back, going into the house. Said he was between five foot ten inches and six feet, short dark hair, slender body type. When the guy went up onto the front stairs, the outside light came on and he saw that he was wearing a yellow jacket. Maybe a windbreaker style, definitely not a winter jacket he said, it looked too light," he added. Butters forged ahead, "About 10 minutes later, the guy came back out and he saw him from the front in full light. He has darker skin, not black, but he thought maybe middle eastern, or eastern Indian. He said it looked the colour of a Tim Horton's coffee with single cream. Said the guy was carrying a bag of some sort. He thought it looked dark blue or purple and it was about a foot square. The guy held it close to his chest as he walked back to the car. He also added that the guy has a perfect smile and dark eyes." All the men were listening with great intensity. Sitting on the edge of their chairs, they looked as if they would pounce on Butters at any moment. "And finally," Butters said, pausing to add as much weight to the last piece of information as if he was reading the Best Actor winner for the academy awards, "the guy only has three fingers on his right hand. Pinky finger was missing."

The room was dead silent, only the air whooshing in from the air duct made any sound. Ingles spoke first, "How sure is this guy about the pinky finger?" he asked. "Very sure," Butters responded, "he said that when he was walking towards the car, he noticed his hand looked funny, but thought to himself that the guy could have it bent in or folded in. When the guy got to the car, he placed his full hand on the roof of the car and you could see as plain as day that he had no pinky." "Did he get a licence plate?" Henderson asked. "No," Butters said, "he told me the car was parked directly in his line of sight, didn't see the back in clear view, just the Discount rental sticker that was on the top left of the trunk lid." "Does he think he could pick the guy out in a line up or picture set?" this was Richards who asked the question. "Sir, I asked him and he said he is not sure, but would try if we needed him to," Butters said. "He said that the guy was 200-300 feet away so he couldn't give accurate feature descriptions, only what he gave me," Butters added. "Well guys, it fits the time line, that's for sure," Richards said, "and the yellow jacket is what the old woman in Hamilton said she saw as well." "I'd say he's our shooter for sure," Henderson added in. "Good work Detective," Richards said, nodding towards Butters, who was now beaming. "Thank you, Sir," Butters said.

"Ok, so how do you want to work this guys?" Richards said. Instinctively, Jones, Butters and Ingles all looked to Henderson. He had always been the leader. Henderson looked to Richards and the men, visibly embarrassed by their mistake, turned and looked at Richards as well. Feeling the uncomfortable awkwardness in the room, Butters broke the silence by saying, "I will start with Discount car rental agents." This got the ball rolling.

Richards then said, "Brian, I want you to lend him a hand.  Steve, you start calling hotels and motels to see if anyone fitting the description has checked in, start in Hamilton and work your way out from there.  I will get Mrs. Sandhill to call in Thompson and Sunland early, one of them can lend a hand on car rentals and the other can help with the motels."  "Henderson," Richards said, "can you write up Butters' description and get a BOLO out, then I want you with me to go back to both crime scenes so you can familiarize yourself."  "Yup, no problem Boss," Henderson said, a small smile on his lips.  "Alright guys, we have our work cut out for us, time is ticking," Richards said.  As the men were all standing, three quick raps were heard on the door and Mrs. Sandhill poked her head in, "The Chief is in your office and he wants to see you two," she said, pointing at Richards and then Henderson.  She left as quickly as she entered, not waiting for a response.

## Chapter Twelve

Richards and Henderson entered Richards' office to see the Chief sitting in Richards' chair. Working on his blackberry with his sausage like fingers, he was grumbling and throwing out a number of curse words. He looked up at the two men as they entered. "Hey boys," he said, "just let me finish this email. Fuck they make the buttons small!" Looking at Richards he said, "Can you give me and Owen just a minute alone?" "Sure," replied Richards, turning and shutting the door as he left. Chief Joe Smith, although he had an innocuous name, was far from it. He wasn't an overly big man, standing 5' 9" with a bit of a gut from good eating and good drinking. He had pale blue eyes, the lids slightly hooded. His nose looked to be from Greek ancestry, but Joe Smith was Scottish through and through. You could even get him to put on a classic Scottish brogue when he was in one of his many jocular moods. Always dressed conservatively, with tasteful ties and highly shined black leather shoes, he held an air of cool confidence, not arrogance. He had an excellent command of the spoken word and could hold a room in rapt awe, or have them bent over in howls of laughter.

He finished his email and dumped the blackberry on the desk.  Noticing that Owen Henderson was still standing, he rose and walked over to the bigger, younger man and embraced him in a fatherly bear hug.  "How are you doing buddy?" Smith said.  They separated and then shook hands.  "I'm good," Henderson said, "well I'm doing better.  Getting out of the house and coming here has been good.  I wasn't sure about it when I left the house this morning, but now I think it was time."  Smith looked him over, "Good," he said, "I'm glad you're back to the land of the living.  I know this has been a tough time, but maybe now is the time to start to move on.  However," he continued, "if you feel you need more time, your benefits don't run out for another two months, and after that we can look at other things."  "No, really, I think it's time that I got my life back together and this is the best place to start," Henderson said.  "There are no ghosts here to haunt me and it keeps my mind active and working."  Smiling at Henderson, Smith said, "Good, I'm glad to hear that and I'm glad that you're back.  Sit down."  Smith and Henderson had known each other for almost 20 years.  When Henderson first started with the OPP as a young patrolman, Smith was a Sergeant and was assigned as Henderson's training officer.  They quickly forged a strong bond.  Often people would comment that they were just like father and son, and to Henderson, Joe was the father he wished he'd had, always caring, always interested in your life. The two men would never admit it, and never be caught dead saying it, but they did have love for each other like a father and son would have. Smith sat down and bellowed loudly enough to be heard in every crevice of the building, "Richards, get your ass in here!"

Richards was back in the room in less than a minute and found the two men talking about the weather. Taking a seat beside Henderson, Richards sat patiently until the two men finished. Smith looked at Richards, "Ok," he said, "so what do we have? Bring me up to speed and don't leave out any details." Although Chief Joe Smith was the Chief of Police for the Burlington Detachment of the OPP, he still had administrative and oversight authority on the OCU. He let Richards run the division on his own, with minimal oversight, but weekly updates on cases were mandatory. Richards cleared his throat, looking first to Henderson and then to Smith, he said, "As I told you on the phone, I think Detective Henderson should assume command." He hadn't even finished the last word of his sentence when Henderson turned on him, his face taking on the colour of a stop sign and his jaw clenched so tightly you could see the muscles working.  "I told you Ty," he spat, almost with rage, "I am not taking your fucking position.  You are the Commander."   Richards, raising his hand in quick protest, said "Dude, mellow out!"  Chief Smith just sat looking at the two men with a small smile creasing his face.  Richards, lowering his hand and patting Henderson on the knee in a patronizing way said, "As I was saying, I think Detective Henderson should assume command of the current investigation, be lead investigator, with me as his number two and backup.  I have other cases to oversee and tons of administrative work to attend to."  Henderson, now feeling foolish and embarrassed, sat with his head hung low and his hands folded in his lap like a scorned little boy.  He looked up at the two men, "Sorry," he said, "I thought Ty was going down a different path."

Smith, still smiling, said, "You two act like a fucking pair of lovers with all your bickering and carrying on, but I think that is an excellent idea.  Owen has more information on the two," he paused, "victims," he continued, "stuck in his head than anyone.  I agree he can focus all of his attention on the case and organize the other detectives.  You do have lots of other things on the go Tyson," he said, clearing his throat and raising his eyebrow as he finished,

"including the monthly budget report."
"Right," Richards said, "almost got that done. You will have it on your desk by Friday."
"Good," said Smith, "now why don't the two of you bring me up to speed on the cases and tell me what the next steps are. I have had the press hounding me and the fucking Mayor of St. Catharines calling me every 10 minutes wanting to know what we are doing about the murder of one of their city's most prominent citizens." For the next 45 minutes, the two younger men filled the Chief in with as much as they had so far, with Richards doing most of the talking and Henderson absorbing the facts he had missed in the earlier meetings.

"So what's next?" Smith asked. "After our meeting here, I want to take Owen to the two crime scenes so he can see everything for himself. That will use up most of the day, unless the car rental or hotel rental inquires bring up any leads," Richards replied. The three men sat in silence for a few minutes. Smith, with his hands clasped in a steeple pose, sat nodding. He then looked at the other two men, "I think you should stop in and talk to the author guy yourselves," Smith said. "I'm sure Butters did a bang up job, but I would feel more comfortable if the two of you got a feel for the guy as well. He could be our killer and have led the young detective on a wild goose chase," he finished.  All the men smiled, "It is possible, and a second set of eyes on what this guy saw from his writing room might help as well," Henderson said.  Richards and Smith both looked at Henderson.  "What?" Henderson said.  "Nothing really," Smith said, "you just sounded like your old self.  Good to have you back," Smith finished.

With that, Smith relinquished his chair.  Pointing to it, he looked at Richards with a broad smile.  "There you go Commander, you can have your chair back," he said with a sardonic grin, "made it nice and warm for you."  Smith made his way down the hall, stopping to poke his head in each office and speak to the other detectives.  Fifteen minutes later, you could still hear him downstairs laughing and joking with Mrs. Sandhill.   As Chief Joe Smith was leaving, Henderson looked at his long time friend and partner and said, "Look, I'm sorry.  I thought you and the Chief were ambushing me and trying to get me to take command of the unit.  I guess that was pretty presumptuous of me.  I'm sorry," he finished.  "Don't be," Richards said, "when I spoke to the Chief on the phone, I actually told him that I was going to do that and I wanted his support.  He, like you, shut me down.  He said things stay as they are."  "Good," said Henderson, "I think you are doing a great job and I am really not ready for more than I have now. Are we done with this then?" he added. "Yup," replied Richards, "you ready to head to Hamilton and St. Kitts?" "Whenever you are," Henderson replied.

Richards and Henderson drove in silence for the first 20 minutes of their trip, both getting over the awkwardness of friends who had grown apart over time and neither knowing exactly what subjects to avoid or talk about. It was after they had been to the first crime scene in Hamilton and were back on the road that the ice finally melted. They began discussing different facts about the case, the scene, and the one witness in Hamilton, and before long, their conversation moved to other topics. By the time they reached the second crime scene, the two were deep in animated discussions about sports, movies, and Henderson's daughter's new boyfriend. It was as if the last 10 months had slowly vanished.

Garnering no new information at the second crime scene, the pair did quick follow up interviews with Jessica DeDominicus, her housekeeper, and the author, Robert J. Henry. Again, all the facts from the previous interviews had remained the same, with them learning little. Jessica's older half brother and his wife had arrived and occupied one of the spare bedrooms in the house.  While Richards was busy with some emails on his blackberry, Henderson had a brief chat with the half brother.  He too could add little to the investigation and commented that he thought this would have happened to his estranged father long ago.  Obviously, there was no love lost in that distant relationship.  The two men made far better time on the afternoon's tasks, and had made it back to the office with daylight to spare.  They sat in the parking lot of their office building for a short time discussing plans for the next day.  Within five minutes, the two parted and headed off in separate directions, Richards heading downtown to his apartment, Henderson heading out to the country to his empty farm house.

Henderson walked into his house and immediately the loneliness and loss hit him, as it usually did at this time of the day.  He hated that Tracy was not here to share in his day, or for him to share in hers.  It had been a ritual of theirs for years, to come home, have a glass of wine or a drink, and share their days as they worked in the kitchen preparing their dinner.  It was the small things he knew he missed the most about his best friend, lover, and as they would often say to each other,  partner in crime.  He searched in the cupboard and found the bottle he was looking for, a bottle of Sailor Jerry's Spiced Rhum. It had dust on it. A favourite drink of the pair was Jerry's and Dr. Pepper. After mixing himself the familiar drink, he walked out to the dock. On the end, sat the two Adirondack chairs, his painted a sky blue, Tracy's painted a sunshine yellow. His was on the left and hers on the right, this way their free hand could always hold the others. He sat looking off over the tiny lake, not thinking of any one thing, yet thinking of everything at once. He reached his right hand over towards Tracy's chair as he often had done in the past. For a small moment, he thought he could feel her small warm hand in his. A single tear slid down his cheek. Not wiping it away, he just sat and sipped his drink.

## Chapter Thirteen

The man in the yellow windbreaker paced back and forth in his tiny gardenview room, walking from the front door to the sliding glass doors overlooking the gardens, back to the front window, and back to the sliders.  He mumbled to himself, "What a pathetic excuse for a garden."  Then repeatedly mumbled, "Why? Why?  This makes no sense."  Running his hand through his hair, he stopped and looked at himself in the mirror, staring blankly into the eyes that stared back at him.  "This makes no sense," he said to himself.  "I have the book.  What need is there for the next assignment?  Pathetic gardens.  The book was the main goal," he continued muttering.  Again he would pace from front to back, pausing to look out the sliding doors, then back to the front of the room to look out the one window. Sighing with anxiety, he had a hard time coming to grips with the final part of the plan.

The other two were bad men, he thought to himself.  Their bloody murders will give no one grief, they were thieves, liars, cheats, and in a league with the Devil himself.  But the last man was good right?  He was pure of heart. What purpose could his death serve?  He was a man of God, a holy man who devoted his life to good.  What purpose could this serve?  He had never rebuked any of his assignments, always carrying them out with precision and speed. He had to check if he understood the message correctly, if he understood the target. He paced again, waiting for the phone to ring, needing that confirmation that this was what he was to do. He sighed again, starting his mumblings, "Pathetic." Yes, he thought, if the message and target are confirmed, he would do as he was told. He too was a servant and would do as instructed. It was his duty, but first he must get the confirmation.

Six hours later, at 3:00 am eastern standard time, the phone in the tiny gardenview room rang once. He snatched it from its cradle before the second ring had started. "Yes," he said into the receiver. The calming, familiar voice of the old man came over the long distance connection to him, "What troubles you my Son? Why do you question the orders you have?" he heard the old man say. "No Father, I am not questioning you, please you must understand that. I just want to make sure I understand correctly. I don't want to make any mistakes," the man in the yellow windbreaker said. "Marcus," the old man soothed, "I'm sure you won't make any mistakes. You know the target, yes?" "Yes Father, I know the target. I know his schedule, but is he not a man of God? All my other targets have been bad people Father," Marcus finished.  With more authority and indignation in his voice, the old man said, "Marcus, you do not know of what you speak.  People with more knowledge than you have made this decision.  Now you must carry out your assignment."  "Yes Father," Marcus said with a morose tone to his voice, "it will be done."  The line went dead.

## Chapter Fourteen

It was 7:30 am and Owen Henderson sighed as he was reaching down to pick up one of the boxes that sat on his office floor, knowing, but not liking, that he had to get this task done. As he was straightening out, Janet Heartland stuck her head in his door and said, "Boo!" Looking up, he said, "Hey Janet, what's up?" "I ran the shell casings under the microscope to take a closer look at the three dots on them," she said. "They are actually not dots at all," she continued on, "they are three circles with interconnecting lines, like a triangle." Walking over to Henderson's desk, she set a number of 8x10 glossy photos in front of him. Looking up at her, he said, "Triangle eh?" "Well take a look for yourself," she said, tapping the photos. Picking up one of the highly magnified photos of the shell casing, he studied it for a long moment. Again, looking at Heartland, he said, "What do you make of it? A Triad gang symbol, maybe Chinese made? Do they match any registered munitions companies?" he asked. "None that I have," she responded, "I went through the entire catalogue. I just sent requests off to the FBI and CSIS to see if they have a match." "Excellent work," Henderson said. "Well I'm more than just tits and dimples," Heartland retorted. Seeing the blood drain from Henderson's face, watching it take on a sullen ashy look, she said, "Oh my gawd, what's wrong?  Are you having a heart attack or something?"  Henderson quickly recovered, "No, no,  I'm sorry," he stammered, "it's just, well, that's something that Tracy used to say.  Just caught me off guard."  Placing a tender hand on his shoulder, Heartland looked at him and said, "Owen, I really am sorry about your loss."  "Thank you," he replied.

As she left the room, Henderson thought to himself, man I have to get a grip on things, and where the fuck does she come off having a heart after all these years, he chuckled to himself.  Henderson picked the pictures back up and scanned them more closely a second time.  Still smiling to himself, he set them down and was about to start again on one of the boxes on his floor when he heard a familiar voice say, "Hey Big Bro!"  Looking up, he saw Cyrsta Sunland standing in his door, her ever present and beautifully radiant smile brightened by her chocolate skin.  Smiling even more broadly, he replied, "Hey Little Sista!  How ya doing?"  Cyrsta and Owen had known each other for many years, she being younger than him, they had always called each other brother and sister.  Cyrsta was a long time friend of Tracy's and one of the few people he had confided in and seen over the past 10 months. She was born in Guyana and emigrated with her mother when she was a young child. She had radiant long black hair that she often wore in a braid that stretched down to the base of her spine. Her flawless skin was the colour of melted chocolate, she carried herself with confidence and had the most wicked sense of humour, maybe something acquired from being raised in an abusive, poverty stricken home. Standing barely 5', you never wanted to tangle with her as it was said she had killed a man with her little finger when he had pulled a gun on her.

"It was good to see you smiling," she said to him. "What brought that on?" "Did you know that Janet Heartland actually does have a heart and maybe even a soul?" he said laughing. "Really, you could have fooled me," she replied. "I thought she had ice water running through her veins," she added, with them both now laughing. "So are you just stopping in for a social visit?" Henderson asked. "No actually, it's work related," Sunland said. "Well Detective, take a seat and talk to me," Henderson said pointing to an empty chair. As she sat, he said, "I thought you were on nights?" "They called me in early to help make calls to car rental places and that's why I'm here," she said. "I just got a hit on our rental car, I think." "Well that's damn good news," Henderson said, "whereabouts?" Sunland looked down at the sheet of paper she had in her hand, "A 2012 Toyota Camry, grey in colour, was rented from the Ottawa airport Discount car rental agency six days ago," Sunland said. "The renter was wearing a yellow windbreaker, had darker skin, and signed and produced a valid Ontario drivers licence in the name of Mark Able," she finished. "What about the missing finger? Did the clerk say anything about the missing finger?" asked Henderson. "No. The clerk," Sunland paused, referring to her papers, "Miss Michelle Carry, said it was really busy and she had a couple of people doing rentals at the same time."

"Hmmm," came out of Henderson's mouth as his smiling face slowly turned to one of concentration. "What about a video?" he asked her. "They do have video, but they think it's on a five day loop and that would mean that transactions six days ago would be overwritten by now," Sunland replied. "They are going to go through it this morning to see if they have anything left from that day." "Tell me your thoughts, Cyrsta?" Henderson asked. "Well, if he rented at the airport, my guess would be that he had just come in off a flight, and that means he may have been, or is staying at a hotel or motel in Ottawa," she said. "That's the way I'm leaning as well, but we know he was here too," Henderson said. "How long was the rental agreement for?" Henderson asked abruptly. Again Sunland checked her notes, "The agreement was for two weeks," she said, "so if he doesn't get spooked between now and then, we may be able to nab him when he brings the car back." "Yea," Henderson sighed, "but if I had just popped two of this country's biggest mob bosses, I don't know if I would be too worried about taking a rental car back. Ok, tell the others to stop with rental agencies, I have a feeling this is our guy. Everything except the missing finger matches. Get the car licence to Canada Customs to make sure he didn't skip the country in Niagara or any of the bridges for that matter, and have everyone focus on hotels and motels at this point." "What about Ottawa airport security tapes?" Sunland asked. "They are on a loop as well," Henderson said. "We tried that on another case a few years back and they overwrite every 48 hours unless they pull a tape because of something suspicious. Not quite like the movies, I'm afraid, where we can go back months and months," he added, "but just in case, have someone call Ottawa and see if they have any tape for six days ago by chance, and while you're at it, check inbound flights on the day the car was rented to see if we get a match on

Mark, what's his name?" "Able," Sunland said. "Right, Mark Able," Henderson repeated. As Sunland was getting up from her chair, Henderson said to her, "You should go home and get some sleep." "Soon," she replied, "and you should do that more often, it looks good on you." "Do what?" he asked. "Smile," she said, turning and leaving his office.

Grabbing a pad of paper, Henderson began jotting down notes in point form. Starting with missing finger, he added yellow jacket, roses, three circles with interconnecting lines. He continued on like this for few minutes, organizing his thoughts, reading the list, then adding another thought that would come to him. When he had finished, he looked at the note blankly, letting his mind drift, trying to picture the man they were currently tracking. He picked up his phone and dialed Cyrsta Sunland's extension, "Sunland," came back the response after three short rings. "Hey Cyrsta, did you run the guy's licence?" he asked. "Yes we did. It's a fake. There is no such person as Mark Able with the licence number he gave Discount," she said. "Well that blows," Henderson responded. "He paid by credit card though, didn't he?" Henderson asked. "Yes," Cyrsta said, "it was a pre-paid visa with a value of a $1000. Card was registered to Mark Able with the same address as on the licence," she added. "Where is the address?" Henderson asked. "It was a Toronto address. Already been checked out and it's a building that they haven't even started to build yet," Sunland said. "So that leaves us with all dead ends then," Henderson said. "Yea, pretty much, but maybe we will get a hit on a hotel," Sunland said. "Ok, talk soon," Henderson said hanging up the phone. Going back to his notes, he scratched off all the questions that he had written down, all dead ends.

Tyson Richards walked by Henderson's open door. Just as the men were about to great each other, Henderson's desk phone rang. He picked it up, "Henderson," he said. Richards leaned against the door frame waiting for Henderson to finish his call. Henderson's expression immediately changed after he had listened to the call for only 10 seconds, the smile on his face widening with each passing moment. Henderson finally spoke into the phone, "And this is a positive ID? Perfect," he said, "thanks and good work." Finishing the call, he wrote a few notes on his pad and looked up at Richards. "We have a positive match on a three fingered man with darker skin checking into the Pool Garden Motel on the 417 just outside Ottawa. Night clerk said the guy showed up a day ago and has been in his room since.  Car is parked in front of the building now, and the Ottawa detachment has been told to send an unmarked over to keep an eye on the room," Henderson finished.  Looking at his watch and doing a quick calculation of the drive time, Henderson said, "If I, or we if you have time to come along, leave now, we can be there by six."  Richards smiled and said, "If we leave now, we can catch the eleven o'clock commuter out of the island airport and be there in an hour."  "We have the budget for that?" Henderson asked.  "Yes we do," replied Richards.  "I will have Mrs. Sandhill arrange to get an unmarked taken to the Ottawa airport."  "Do we have time to slip by my place?" Henderson asked.  "I want to grab a few things."  "Sure, but let's go now," Richards said.

## Chapter Fifteen

With lights flashing the entire time, it took Richards and Henderson only 75 minutes to make it from the OCU to Henderson's house and out to the Toronto Island Airport.  They still had 10 minutes to spare prior to boarding when they arrived.  Since it was a domestic flight, they had less security to deal with and only Henderson's bag as carry-on luggage.  When asked to put the duffle through the x-ray machine, Henderson produced his OPP badge and asked that the officer check it by hand so as not to set off alarms.  Richards, likewise, opened his jacket to reveal his side arm and held out his badge for inspection.  Out of courtesy for law enforcement, the pair were quickly and quietly walked around the standing metal detector and escorted to a security office to wait for the flight to be called for boarding.  Both anxious to get moving to follow their first solid lead on the killer, they said little as the minutes ticked by.

Their flight landed at exactly 11:53 am and the pair were allowed to be the first to de-plane.  They were greeted at the bottom of the portable stairs by a pair of uniformed OPP officers out of the Ottawa detachment.  The older of the two asked, "Are you Detectives Richards and Henderson?"  "Present and accounted for Officer!" Richards said with a smile.  "If you two want to follow us, we have a car waiting over here and have been told to assist you in any way we can," the older patrolman said.  "Do you know if the rental car is still at the motel?" Henderson asked as the four men walked along.  "No, we dispatched a car as soon as we got the call from you guys, and as of 20 minutes ago, the car was no place to be found."  "Shit," Henderson said.  "Ok, follow us over but stay well back," he continued, "we will go into the lot and I want you two to keep driving by.  Find a spot that you can watch the entrance to the motel without being seen," Henderson finished.  The younger of the two officers led them over to a squat building.  In front, sat a non-descript older brown Crown Victoria and a stealth marked Mustang 5 litre.  You had to look at the car in the right direction to see the police markings on it.  From a distance, the car looked like any black Mustang.  Henderson placed his bag on the roof of the old Crown Vic and opened the back door.  He took off his sport coat and then removed his shirt.  The other three men just looked at him.  He opened the bag and pulled out a clean white t-shirt with an OPP crest on the front breast.  He then pulled a black Kevlar vest out and put that over his tee.  Over this, he put on a navy blue OPP windbreaker with bold yellow POLICE printed on the back.  Turning, he looked at the three men staring at him, "What?" he questioned.  "I have a daughter.  I can't take chances."  Richards piped in with a laugh, "If you knew how to shoot, you wouldn't have to worry!"

It took just over 15 minutes for the two cars to make it to the motel.  As Richards and Henderson pulled in, the Mustang drove on by and blended in down the road.  The motel consisted of two buildings, both L shaped, with one of the L's being inverted.  From the road, it looked like a long row of doors across the parking lot with a break in the centre where a 30 foot wide walkway ran up between the two buildings.  Not visible from the street, the walkway had doors on either side for the rooms on this leg of the L.  The large parking lot spanned the entire front of the two buildings facing the road.  On the far end of the right hand building was an attached two story structure, which offered an office and tiny lounge on the bottom floor, and an owner's or manager's quarters on the second floor.  Scanning the parking lot, Henderson noticed that Mark Able's rental car had not yet returned.  They parked their Crown Vic around the side of the office and went in.  They were greeted by a portly little fellow, with a ring of grey hair surrounding his head, giving him the appearance of Friar Tuck.  "Good afternoon Gentlemen," the man said with a curt nod as they walked in.  "Good afternoon," Henderson said.  "I'm Detective Henderson and this is Detective Richards," he announced, both men showing their badges.  "I believe someone from our offices has talked to you today?"

Clearing his throat, the Friar Tuck lookalike said, "Oh yes, right, they said some detectives would be by.  So is he a really bad guy?  Do I need to be concerned for my guests?" he asked.  "Right now he is just a person of interest, someone we would like to speak with," Henderson said.  "Do you know when he left in his car?"  "No, sorry Detective.  I just had a bus load check in and I was so busy.  It's just me here, you know," he said.  "Do you think you could give us his room number and a key so we can go take a look in his room?" Henderson asked.  "Ah, don't you need a warrant or something to do that, Officer?" the little man said.  "Not for a motel if the owner or manager gives us permission," Henderson said with noticeable irritability in his voice.  Looking a bit alarmed, the little man turned to face a board covered with keys.  He scanned it for a second and then plucked a key that was on the left side under a big 'GV'.  "Here you go, Officer," he said, "gardenview room 10.  Straight down the front of the building, turn at the walkway and it will be the 10$^{th}$ door on your left." Taking the offered key, Richards said, "Thank you," and the two men exited the office.

Once they were back out in the parking lot, they both scanned the parked cars to make sure their suspect had not returned. Not seeing his car, they made their way to the room. Standing off to either side of the door, Henderson on the left, Richards on the right, Henderson slipped the key into the lock and paused a second. Richards then knocked on the door with a trite double knock. In a very good, high pitched female voice, with a slight Spanish accent, Richards said, "Room service." Henderson looked at the man with a raised eyebrow and a small smile. Richards just shrugged at him. After waiting for 15 seconds or so, Henderson slowly and quietly turned the key, then just as slowly, he turned the knob. Swinging the door open a foot, both men held back, then in turn, they both did a quick look around the door. When it appeared that no one was in the room, Henderson said, "Well let's take and look and see what Mark Able has left for us." Entering, they noticed the bed appeared to not have been slept in, or was recently made. The drapes to the sliding glass door overlooking the gardens were open half way. At first, they thought their man had left, but then Henderson spotted a small duffle bag on the far side of the bed.

"He's still staying here," Henderson said, holding up the bag. "Yea, there is a shaving kit in the bathroom here," Richards said, as he walked into the compact bathroom. Having found nothing useful in the bathroom, Richards returned to the main area. "Anything interesting?" Richards said over Henderson's shoulder as he went through the bag. "Nope, nothing other than clothes and a bible." Dropping the bag on the bed, the pair went through the dresser and small fridge, still finding nothing to give them clues. Richards bent down and was checking under the bed when he hollered back over his shoulder, "Bingo!" Henderson went over to the bed as Richards was getting up off the floor, "What is it?" "This," Richards said, holding up a heavy dark blue bag. They walked over to the dresser that stood at waist height and placed the cloth bag on it, studying it for a second. The bag looked to be of a heavy velvet, deep blue, almost black in colour. The braided gold cord used to close the bag was in brilliant contrast to the bag's darkness. Flipping the item over, they saw it was intricately stitched with a crest neither could identify.

Both donning rubber gloves, Richards opened the bag and slid out the ancient book. The cover was made of heavy leather and was intricately carved with a scrolling swirl around the edge. In the centre, was a deeply carved cross showing detail as if the cross were made of wood. It had a bush or vine with a flower wrapping around the cross. Time had aged most of the cover so it appeared to be a dark, almost burnt brown colour, however, in a few spots, colours could be seen, as if the leather had been dyed but had faded over the years. "Looks like we found our man," Henderson said. "Or at least the book that was taken," Richards replied. "Do you think it's worth so much you would kill two members of the mob over it?" Richards asked. "It has to be pretty valuable to risk your life like that," replied Henderson. Not knowing what they were looking at, Henderson carefully opened the front cover. There was a waft of musty, mouldy fragrance that emanated from the book when they opened it, reminding Henderson of an old bookshop or antique store. On the inside page was written something in a fluid script, "Can you read that?" Henderson asked Richards. "Not on your life, English is my first and second language!" Richards chuckled. Flipping in a few pages, the pair were studying the scrolled writing in awe, having no idea what they were looking at or what the words said.  Henderson pointed to a spot about 40 pages in, "Is that a thumb print in blood?" he asked Richards.  "Hmmm, could be, must be a fucking old thumb though," Richards said.  "Why?" asked Henderson.  "Look here," he said pointing halfway down the page, "doesn't that look like a date to you?"  Henderson said, "I guess, it's hard to tell.  It's all so faded."

The book was thinner than had been described by Jessica DeDominicus, closer to four inches in thickness with thick covers measuring almost half an inch each.  The pages were of a thick ancient paper, maybe cotton, or other fibrous material, some pages even having loose fibres protruding.  In appearance, it was more like an old ledger book, the kind you would find in any store before the advent of cash registers and computers.  The writings on the pages they had studied were of varied styles and ink colours, mostly black, or deep indigo, others in red, some faded so badly they appeared pink.  Flipping the book over and opening it from the back, they both noticed that the last inch or so of pages were blank, as if waiting to be filled in by the old accountant who had used the book.  As Henderson was carefully turning the pages of the near crumbling paper to find the final entry in the book, he and Richards noticed a blur go by the partially opened curtains of the front window. Both men immediately drew their side arms and went to the window, momentarily forgetting about the old book.

Peering out of the window, they saw nothing in their field of view. Moving to the door, they each took opposite sides, Richards leaning on the door frame closest to the parking lot, Henderson on the opposite one. Richards did a quick peek around the door, he saw nothing and nodded at his partner to now do the same. Henderson followed suit and took a longer look out the door. Not certain if it was a guest or hotel staff, the two men eased out the door, guns ready, but both pointing to the ground. Richards was first out the door, facing towards the road, with Henderson a pace behind him and facing in the opposite direction. Seeing no danger towards the rear of the property, Henderson turned in his partner's direction. As he reeled around, a flash of yellow sprang from a bush at the end of the walkway, Henderson's weapon was coming up to the ready. Richards as well was attempting to draw a bead on their target. Mark Able, moving with the speed and training of a highly skilled military combatant, dropped to one knee as he came from behind the bush. His gun was at the ready and aimed before either of his would be attackers could target him.

Two small pffts erupted from his gun and he was on his feet and running before his target felt the pain.

The two bullets pounded into the center of Tyson Richards' chest as if he was wearing a bull's eye. The impact pushed him back into his partner, causing him to lose his balance as he was about to fire off a shot. Clutching his chest, Richards fell into his partner's arms and was slumping to the ground. Henderson saw his target had vanished as he struggled to slowly lower the wounded Richards to the ground. Every emotion was now racing through Henderson's head. The awful feelings of dread, anger, fear and sorrow, his breath now coming in gulping gasps as he tried to gain control of the situation. Yelling, Henderson said, "Buddy it's ok, it's ok. I'll get help, hang in there, just fucking hang in there Ty." Richards' head was lulled back, his eyes closed, his mouth was working in a pained grimace gasping to suck in oxygen. Henderson reached for Richards' neck and felt a strong but very fast pulse. Henderson's training kicked in and he swatted Richards' clutched hand from his chest and tore open his shirt to assess the wounds and apply pressure. "Fuck," was the first word from Henderson's mouth, and then a great sigh expelled from him as he slumped lower to the ground with

Richards in his lap.  Henderson was now staring down at two shiny brass mushrooms contrasted against the black Kevlar Richards had under his shirt.  A smile crossed Henderson's face and he said "Buddy, Tyson," giving him a gentle shake.  Richards gasped in a breath, exhaled, then took another ragged breath as his lungs began to work again.  Henderson heard his friend say something in a struggled voice, "What?" Henderson asked.  With a longer, bigger pull of air, Richards opened his eyes and between gritted teeth said, "This was a fucking $150 shirt!"

Henderson, laughing and shaking his head said, "You're good, you're ok right?"  "Yea," in a gasp, "just the fucking wind knocked out of me," replied Richards, "and a broken rib, I think."  "Come on, can you get up?  You ok?" Henderson said.  "Yea, I'm good," said Richards.  Struggling to help Richards up, Henderson said, "Come on, he went to the left.  I'll go first this time."  Henderson was at the corner of the building in three long strides, cautiously peering in the direction he saw Mark Able go.  Looking over his shoulder, he saw Richards rubbing his chest and taking up the distance between them.  Taking one more look around the corner, Henderson went around.  Keeping his back to the wall, he slowly made his way toward the office.

Richards was soon on his heel.  They reached a door part way down this section of the motel where a maid's cart sat out front.  Both men could see the door was slightly ajar.  Pressing his back against the wall, Henderson did a quick peek in the slit of the door.  Richards, crouching low, snuck around the maid's cart for cover and came up on the other side of the door.  In his high pitched female voice, Richards said, "Esmeralda, are you in there?"  Henderson was shaking his head in awe of the quick recovery and the return of his partner's sense of humour.  He then held up three fingers.  Richards nodded and they mouthed the countdown together.  When they hit three, the two men burst through the door, Henderson going high, Richards low, as they moved in with guns aimed forward.

Their man was not in the room.  What they saw was a pair of women's sneakers attached to chubby legs sticking out from the far side of the bed.  The two men rushed to see the maid, laying on her side, with a huge purplish bruise and small cut on her temple.  Richards bent and felt for a pulse.  He nodded a yes to Henderson and the two men rose to move toward the partially open sliding glass doors.  Peering out, they saw a large pool surrounded by cement and lounge chairs.  There were no guests in any of the chairs and no Mark Able to be seen. "Shit," Richards said. They again moved cautiously out the door and began a slow sweep of the area looking for open doors or probable hiding places. Splitting up, Henderson crept down the building at the left of the pool, while Richards went to the right. As both men were almost at opposite ends of the pool, they heard the loud rev of a car's engine and the squeal of tires. Racing back through the open sliding door, they made it back to the front door and out into the parking lot just in time to hear a police siren start up off to their right. It took several seconds before they finally saw the black Mustang work its way past the front of the motel, weaving and honking in the heavily congested traffic.

The pair looked at each other, holstering their weapons, Henderson said with a heavy sigh, "We don't know the area, we won't be much help." "Agreed," said Richards. Henderson then turned and went racing back towards Mark Able's room, over his shoulder he yelled, "The book." Slower, as the adrenaline was wearing off and the pain was setting in, Richards followed in his wake. When Richards made it to the room, Henderson looked at him shaking his head, "It's gone," he said. Both men shook their heads, pursing their lips, sighing. As they were leaving the room, Henderson's phone rang with the old phone bell.  Snatching it from his pocket, he said, "Henderson," with anger in his voice.  "Gee, don't sound so chipper there Henderson," said Janet Heartland's familiar voice.  Not being goaded by her, he responded, "What's up Janet?"  "Bad day, eh?" Heartland said.  Not waiting for a response, she continued on, "I got a match for your shell casings."  Henderson's heart did a triple beat in his chest, "And?" he said.

## Chapter Sixteen

"Well, you're not going to believe this," Heartland said, "but the bullets were manufactured by Remington."  "What?" Henderson queried.  "Why don't they have Remington stamped on them then?"  "Well, let me finish," Heartland said.  With a sigh, not wanting her shit right now, Henderson said, "Sorry, can you finish your story?"  "That's better," Heartland said, "it seems," Henderson cut her off, "Janet, wait a second, I want to put you on hands free so Richards can hear this too."  Placing the phone on the hood of the car, Henderson hit the hands free button.  "Ok Janet, Tyson is here with us.  Can you repeat that?" Henderson said.  With another long sigh, she said, "As I was saying, back during the 40's, well actually starting in 1938, all the munitions companies were eager to earn money from the big war machine that was happening over in Europe.  The Remington company, not knowing what way the impending war was going to go, started to make bullets for various countries, but, and that's a big but, they didn't want their name on them just in case things got really ugly and American troops were sent over.  You see, they didn't want their bullets to be blamed for killing American soldiers.  Once the war really got going, they stopped this practice because the US was purchasing more munitions than any of the munitions companies could produce.  However, one country has never stopped purchasing unmarked ammunition, or private brand ammunition if you want to call it that, from Remington."  "Who?" blurted Henderson, clearly losing his patience.

"The Holy See," said Heartland.  "What?" responded Henderson.  "Vatican City," Heartland said, almost adding 'you idiot'.  "I know what the Holy See is," Henderson responded, "I meant, 'what' as in that can't be.  They don't have an army."  "Not anymore," Heartland said, "but they still have the Swiss Guard.  All their side arms are 9 millimetre Glocks or Glock 19s to be exact, and they purchase the ammunition for them from Remington, under their private label.  The three circles with the interconnecting lines, or," she never got to finish as Richards cut her off with, "The Father, The Son, The Holy Ghost."  "Exactly," said Heartland.  "So Gentlemen, it would appear that your killer would be a member of the Swiss Guard, not a Chinese Triad member."  "This can't be right Janet," Henderson said, "is there any way that Remington could have made a mistake and shipped some to a gun retailer or some other place?"  "Nope," replied Heartland, "I just got off the phone with a rep from Remington.

They manufacture and ship under very strict and stringent guidelines as well as about a dozen or so quality checks, not to mention the government oversight and inspections.  They assured me that there is no way what so ever that these bullets came from any place other than Vatican City itself."  "Thanks Janet," Henderson said, "and thanks for looking into this so quickly.  Do you have anything else?"  "No, that is about all I have for you right now," Heartland said.  "Ok, thanks," said Henderson clicking off the phone.  Both men stood by their car looking at each other in total disbelief.

"This case just went from strange to stranger," Richards said.  "You're telling me," replied Henderson.  "I just can't believe that the Swiss Guard would be assassinating mob members over a book.  That just makes no sense at all.  There has to be another explanation for this.  Do you have your brother's number in your phone?" Henderson asked.   "Yea, why?" asked Richards.  "Give him a call and put it on speaker.  Let's see what he can tell us about his friends who he has doing security at his church."  Dialing the number and putting it on speaker, Richards set the phone on the roof of the car.  Four rings later,  a compassionate sounding, familiar voice came over the tiny speaker, "Father Wyatt Richards".  Laughing,

Tyson Richards said, "Gee Wyatt, it sounds like you're answering the suicide line!"  "Ha, Ha! Very funny Ty," Father Wyatt said, "just so you know, that is my professional voice.  I really never know who could be calling me, it could well be a troubled young teen contemplating suicide."  "I guess," Tyson Richards said.  "Hey listen, I'm here with Owen, I have you on speaker."  "I kind of figured that out, unless you have what sounds like a highway running through your mouth," Father Wyatt responded.

Henderson cut in, "Can you two stop with the crap and sarcasm for a second?  Wyatt, are your friends from the Swiss Guard still there?"  "You need to breath deep and find your Zen Owen," Father Wyatt said over the phone, "you're sounding too stressed."  "Well, being shot at and chasing killers can do that to a man," Henderson said.  "Oh, Mother Mary!  You guys have been in a gun fight?" Father Wyatt said.  "I really don't like the sounds of that. Nobody was hurt, or worse," Father Wyatt paused a second, "killed?"  With a little chuckle, Henderson said, "Well now that you mention it, your baby brother was shot twice."  Henderson looked over at his partner, who had dropped his head and was shaking it back and forth.  He looked up at Henderson and mouthed, "You should not have told him." After a very long pause, Father Wyatt said,

"Dear God, please tell me you are kidding, that he is ok?"  "Relax Wyatt," Tyson Richards said, "it's no big deal.  I'm not hurt, not even a scratch.  Remember it was me who called you."  "Thank you Lord," Father Wyatt said, "I don't want to hear anymore about it.  I worry enough about you two, I don't need to hear about this stuff.  Why did you guys call again? Just to give me a heart attack, or raise my blood pressure?"  "Sorry Wyatt, didn't mean to frighten you," Henderson said.  In a calmer and more relaxed voice, he began again, "The guys that I, um, ran into the other day, the Swiss Guard, are they still hanging around your place?"

"No," replied Father Wyatt, "they left this morning."  "Where did they go?" asked Richards.  "They moved on to Ottawa, the Pontiff is doing Friday Night Mass there with the Prime Minister and other dignitaries, so they have gone to do their security stuff there."  "This Friday night, like in tomorrow night?" Henderson asked.  "Yes, tomorrow night," Father Wyatt said.  "The Pontiff lands tomorrow morning, does some meet and greats and visits a hospital, followed by a private meeting with the PM, and then the Mass."  Henderson and the younger Richards were staring at each other slack jawed.  Over the tiny speaker they heard, "Are you guys still there?" Then, in a muffled voice, "Fucking cell phones." This brought their attention back to the phone. "Yes, we are still here Wyatt," Richards said. "When did the Swiss Guard leave Hamilton?" Henderson asked. "About 11:00 am this morning," Father Wyatt said. "How are they traveling? Henderson asked. "By a couple of vans," was the reply. "Hey, what's with all these questions? What's going on, you two?" Father Wyatt asked. "Can't really say right now, just trying to put some puzzle pieces together," Henderson said. "Do you by chance have a phone number for the guy I met?" asked Henderson. "Not on me," Father Wyatt said, "but I have it in my office. "I can text it to you in 15 or 20 minutes." "That would be great," Henderson said. "We have to run. We will give you a call later, ok?" "Ok guys, please stay safe," Father Wyatt said.

"One other thing Wyatt," Henderson said before hanging up, "do you know of any religious books or journals that have gone missing that the Swiss Guard would be looking for?" "Oh yea sure," Father Wyatt said, sarcasm dripping from his voice, "it was in last month's newsletter from the Vatican, under the lost and found section. 'Old book taken, please return to the Pope if found, small reward offered'!" Henderson said, "What?" "Come on guys," Father Wyatt said, "there are hundreds of lost, missing and misplaced religious and historical documents that people all over the world are looking for. You honestly think the Vatican advertises that stuff, or that I would even give a shit?" he finished with a chuckle. "And," he continued on, "the Swiss Guard would have nothing to do with that. They are for the protection and security of the Pontiff and Vatican city. There is a whole other department of old geezers who look after the library and historical documents. If you're talking about the book that Tyson told me was taken from DeDominicus' place, I would not think that is any religious book, not in that man's possession. Sure he went to church and said he was Catholic, but his heart was pure evil. I think you two are grasping at straws and trying to connect dots," he finished. "Yea, connecting dots," Henderson said, more to himself than the Richards' brothers. "Ok Wyatt, and thanks for the sarcasm," Henderson said. "Hey anytime, maybe next time you will not scare the shit out of me by telling me my little brother was shot," Father Wyatt finished. "Chow," Henderson said and ended the call.

## Chapter Seventeen

As both men checked their phones for any missed messages or emails, the black stealth marked OPP cruiser rushed into the parking lot and pulled up alongside them.  The passenger window closest to them lowered.  Henderson and Richards bent down to see the two police officers who met them at the airport.  The older officer, who was driving, leaned over and said, "Really sorry about that guys.  He must have slipped in as one of the transport trucks was going by.  We totally dropped the ball on that one."  "Please tell me you found him?" Henderson said.  "We found the car, he ditched it about two kilometres down the road at the mall.  We were lucky we even spotted it.  We have both City and OPP searching the mall and surrounding area," the older cop stated.  "We called in the K-9 unit as well," the younger one added, "but it's doubtful the dogs will be able to track a scent at the mall."  "Well it's worth a shot," Richards said.  "No witnesses saw him get out of the car?" Henderson asked.  "No, sorry.  We asked some people who were near the car when we found it and they saw nothing," the older cop said.  "So what now?" Henderson asked.  "Well, like I said, we have the City and OPP looking for him with the description we used to find him at the motel.  He is now on foot, so we are moving out from the mall in our search grid." "You guys will keep us posted?" Henderson asked. "Yes, absolutely Detective," the younger cop said. Henderson, looking over at Richards, said, "What do you think, do we stay around or head back?" "I say we stay for the night and see if anything turns up," Richards said. "Is there a better hotel to stay at than this one?" Richards asked the two uniformed cops. "Yea, sure, if you go up the road that way," said the younger cop pointing north, "you will find all the big chain hotels, up there about five kilometres, once you get closer to the city centre." "Thanks guys. We will let you know where we check in," Henderson said. "Right," said the older cop, "and if anything turns up, we will contact you ASAP. Really sorry about not seeing the guy come into the lot." "Don't worry about it," said Henderson, "shit happens. Can you call your division and get some people to go over his room for prints?" "Sure thing Detective," the younger officer said, "we will tow the car in as well and see if he left any in there."

As the two OPP officers where leaving the lot, Richards' phone chimed, indicating a new text message. "I got the number for the Swiss Guard dude you tried to neuter!" Richards said with a smile. "You want to call him now?" "No, not yet," Henderson said, "I need to think.

This case is getting bizarre and I want to know what I'm going to ask him before I talk to him. We can go down the road and get a room and call him after that."  "Ok, you're the lead detective," Richards said.  "You drive," he added, "my chest hurts something fierce."  "You got it Boss," Henderson said.  Just as the two men climbed into the car, Richards' phone chimed again.  "Another text message from Wyatt," Richards said.  "What about?" Henderson asked.  "He says if you want to find out about religious books or texts that have gone missing, or are being searched for, you should contact this guy, Professor Daniel Brown at Oxford University," Richards said.  "Give me a fucking break," Henderson said.  "Your brother never gives up.  That's the guy who wrote the Da Vinci Code, isn't it?"  "Well, yes, but no!  Same name, different guy," Richards said.  "His text reads, 'give this guy a call.  I have been to a couple of his lectures on religious history.  He knows everything about it, and no, it's not the same guy who wrote those books,'  and he sent a number that looks like it's for overseas," Richards finished.  "What time would it be overseas?" Henderson asked.  "Um, well it's 2:00 pm here, so it's about 6:00 pm there, I think," Richards said.  "Ok," Henderson said, "let's go get a room and make some calls."

## Chapter Eighteen

Marcus, aka Mark Able, saw the cop car with the stealth markings on it long before he got close to it.  He'd been circling the motel for over an hour since the first cop car showed up.  How did they track me down he thought to himself?  There had been no witnesses, he didn't leave any prints, and the bullet casings would lead them on a wild goose chase.  This was not good, he thought to himself, sighing and running his hand through his hair.  He was able to lose them in the chase and ditch the car.  Now what should he do until tomorrow night when the assignment would be concluded?  His brain was firing in all directions.  Should he contact the old man and tell him what had happened, he wondered, or should he just take to the ground and make his way to the target?  He had the book and he had his gun.  He only needed to wait 24 hours and then his work would be done.  No, do not call the old man, he decided, he would just lay low and make his way to the target, he told himself.  No one would be looking for him there.  He decided to make his preparations, prepare for the final target, and then go home.

Walking between the rows of cars in the rear of the parking lot, he spotted a battered old pickup with the keys still hanging in the ignition. Stupid people, he thought, probably some young kid without a care in the world, or an old man who would forget his hat was on his head if someone didn't tell him. Crouched low, he reached up and tried the door handle. "Stupid people," he mumbled to himself as the old door creaked open on its tired, rusted hinges. Staying low in the seat, he scanned around him, checking his mirrors to see if there was anyone close by, or if the cops had made it to this part of the lot. As he was about to turn the key, a police car turned into his aisle. He paused, slunk down a bit in his seat, and watched in his mirrors as the car cruised by. Peeking his head up just enough to see over the other cars, he watched as the police car moved down another three rows. Lazy, he thought, should be checking every row. He turned the key and the old truck purred to life. The body was old and neglected, but the engine sounded well maintained. Easing the truck into reverse, he eased out of the spot, not racing, but not going too slow, as he did not want to draw attention to himself. He made it to the end of the row, made a right turn, and headed directly for an exit. As he stopped at the exit, waiting for his chance to go, three more police cars pulled into the lot passing right by him. His heart raced and then he smiled, "They don't even know who or what they are looking for!" he laughed. Calmly and confidently, he took to the street and headed in the direction of his third and final target.

## Chapter Nineteen

Henderson and Richards had checked into a Holiday Inn Hotel and Suites, finding it cheaper to get a suite than two rooms.  Richards was sitting on the small couch, with Henderson facing him in an arm chair.  "So, what have you come up with, oh great wise one?" Richards asked Henderson.  "I think I'm going to approach this head on," Henderson said.  "The way I see it, the Swiss Guard has a bad apple.  Maybe they know it and are all involved, maybe not.  Either way, things point in that direction.  They were in Hamilton on or around the time of the first murder.  From there, it's a short drive down to St. Catharines.  Now we find that the Guard are on their way, or already here, and our shooter is also here.  As much as your brother has dispelled that the book has any religious significance, I tend to think it does.  The cross on the front, the age of the book, and to tie it all together, the shooter is using ammo that can only come from the Swiss Guard armouries."  "So you think they are all brothers in arms?" Richards asked.  "It does appear like that," Henderson replied.  "So we question the guy you took down at Wyatt's church, see what he can tell us, and follow the trail from there," Richards concluded.

"Do you want to call him now?" Richards asked, pulling out his phone and scrolling through his text messages. "Yea, let's see what this guy has to say," Henderson said. Finding the message, Richards said, "His name is Lieutenant Colonel Pedro Hauptmanns." He clicked on the number and set the phone on the table between them. After a few short rings, the phone was answered with an Italian greeting. "Lieutenant Colonel Hauptmanns?", Henderson said questionably. "Si, this is Lieutenant Colonel Pedro Hauptmanns, who am I speaking with?" came the reply over the phone in a strong Italian accent. "Lieutenant Colonel, this is Detective Owen Henderson from the OPP Organized Crime Unit. We met the other day at Cathedral Basilica of Christ the King, in Hamilton," Henderson said. "Ah yes, Detective. I am still feeling a little tenderness after our meeting," the Lieutenant Colonel said with a small chuckle. "Please Detective, call me Pedro. May I call you Owen?" "Yes, of course," said Henderson. "I am here with my partner, Detective Tyson Richards." "Yes. Yes, of course," Hauptmanns said, "his brother spoke of the two of you after we parted company the other day. What can I do for you, Owen?" Hauptmanns asked. "We are working on an investigation and some of the pieces seem to be pointing in a direction that may involve you, or the Swiss Guard,"

Henderson said. "I can assure you Owen that we have been involved in no criminal wrong doing since being in your country. Like you, we are police officers and work at upholding the law, not breaking it," Hauptmanns said. "Pedro," Henderson said, "we have found shell casings at two crime scenes that have been positively identified as Remington 9 millimetre, manufactured under the Vatican City private label." There was a long moment of silence, Hauptmanns then said, "This is impossible Owen. No one except the Pontifical Swiss Guard has access to our armouries, and none of my men would be involved in such a thing." "I think we should sit down and talk," Henderson said. "I understand you are on your way to Ottawa. When do you expect to arrive?" "We checked into our hotel just 15 minutes ago," Hauptmanns said, "we are at the Holiday Inn." "The one on Parliament Street?" Henderson asked. "Yes," responded Hauptmanns. "We are staying at the same hotel. When can we meet?" Henderson asked. "Soon, soon," Hauptmanns said, "let me make some quick calls, then we can meet. I think I saw a small bar when we checked in. 20 minutes and I will meet you there." "I thought you guys didn't drink?" Henderson said. "No, Owen, we take vows of celibacy, not vows of prohibition," Hauptmanns said. "20 minutes then," Henderson said, clicking off the phone.

Standing, Henderson grabbed his sport jacket, "Let's go downstairs now. We can keep an eye on the front door and see if anyone comes or goes," Henderson said. "He really didn't sound like he was going to bolt," Richards said. As the two men left their suite, Henderson said, "No, I don't think he is going to bolt either. He sounded somewhat shocked if you ask me, but if one of his men is our shooter, or there are a couple of bad apples in his group, maybe one of them may get cold feet." "I see your point, Buddy," Richards said as they stepped into the elevator. Arriving in the lobby, they could see three identical black SUVs sitting out front in the parking lot, and a few quests checking in. Looking around, they spotted the entrance to the lounge bar. They seated themselves and took a booth that looked out into the lobby area. Only five minutes had passed when a very fit looking Italian man, dressed in what looked to be blue military clothes, stepped out of the elevator. Henderson pointed and said, "That's our man." They both stood to great Lieutenant Colonel Pedro Hauptmanns as he approached. Extending his hand, Hauptmanns said, "Owen, it is very good to see you again, but I am not liking the accusations or situation that we are meeting under." "I agree," said Henderson, "we don't like this either." Pointing to Richards, he said, "This is my partner, Tyson Richards." Now taking Richards' hand,

Hauptmanns said, "Yes, I see the resemblance to your brother."

The three men sat in the booth, Henderson and Richards on one side, with Hauptmanns facing them. A waitress came by to take their order. Richards and Henderson both ordered a beer, while Hauptmanns ordered a single malt scotch. No one spoke until the drinks had been brought back. Holding up his glass, Richards said, "Cheers." Hauptmanns, raising his glass, said, "Salute." After each man had taken a drink, Henderson began speaking, "First off, I would like to say we are not specifically pointing a finger at the Swiss Guard, or you for that matter. However, we have a bunch of loose ends that do seem to point to your police department." "Are you at liberty to tell me some of these loose ends?" Hauptmanns asked. "Absolutely," Henderson said. "Two nights ago, two of Canada's biggest mob bosses were assassinated by who we think is the same man. Both men were killed with two shots, either of which would have been fatal on their own. We have vague descriptions of a person who was seen at both locations at the time of the shootings, but no solid identification. We managed to track him down to a motel here in Ottawa. Tyson and I were going through his room today when he showed up. Tyson took two bullets in the

chest, thank goodness for Kevlar."
Hauptmanns was listening intently, nodding his head, as he was absorbing the facts. "And," Henderson said, "as I said on the phone, at each crime scene, we found these," handing the Italian police officer one of the shell casings that he picked up from today's ordeal.

Hauptmanns carefully looked at the shiny brass object in his hand. Grasping it at the open end, he stared intently at the three small dots on the bottom of it. Nodding his head, he said, "Yes, this is a bullet from our stores." Handing the casing back to Henderson, he reached into his jacket and pulled out a Glock 19. Seeing the reaction from the two men sitting across from him, he quickly ejected the magazine cartridge and handed it to Henderson. "Please," Hauptmanns said, "take one of the bullets out so you have a positive match for your records. Richards and Henderson relaxed at this gesture. Henderson did as he was asked and handed the magazine back to Hauptmanns. He took the magazine and placed it in one coat pocket and the gun in the other, further setting the other two men at ease. "This is very troubling, Gentlemen," Hauptmanns said. "I do not believe your killer is one of my men, but the fact that he uses our private brand ammunition causes me great concern."  "How can you be sure he is not one of your men?" Henderson asked, "I have not even given you a description or the rest of the information."  "Even so, I am quite certain that it is not one of my men," Hauptmanns said.  "If I give you some identifying characteristics, will you be honest and tell us if it is one of your men?" Henderson asked.  "Most definitely Owen," Hauptmanns said, "we have nothing to hide and are here as guests of your country.  Please tell me what you can about this man?"

"I think I got a better look at him," Richards said, "I was looking right at him when he shot me."  Hauptmanns, looking at Richards, nodded with concern on his face.  Richards continued on, "He was about 5' 10" to 6', had short dark hair, black, not dark brown.  He had fairly thick dark eyebrows with barely a space between them.  I think the kids would call it a uni-brow.  His ears were close cropped to his head.  Skin colour was darker, but not black, a milky coffee colour.  Narrow chin and nose, broad shoulders but a slender man."  He paused to gauge a reaction from Hauptmanns. "Tyson," noted Hauptmanns, "that would be the description of exactly one half of my men.  The other half would be about the same build but with fair hair and fair skin, most with blue eyes."  "I have not finished," Richards said, "he has one very peculiar identifying mark."

Hauptmanns sat up a bit straighter and paid close attention. Richards said, "He is missing his little finger on his right hand." Holding up his right hand, he wiggled his little finger then tucked it into his palm with his other hand to show the other man. Hauptmanns looked first at Henderson and then over to Richards, he said, "You make a very good witness Tyson, your description will go a long way in finding this man, but again, I must tell you he is not one of my men. He is not of the Swiss Guard." He then looked at Henderson for a long minute, both men with their eyes locked. Henderson broke the silence and said, "How can you be so certain sitting here, that this is not one of your men? Maybe he's one you are not familiar with, a new member of the Guard, or one who has not yet brought attention to himself."

Hauptmanns took a sip from his drink. He set his glass on the table and stared at it as if in contemplation. When he looked up at the two men, he had a small smile on his face, not one of contempt, but more of coming to a realization. Looking from one man to the other, he said, "Gentlemen, I don't think you understand the Guardia Svizzera Pontificia. The Pontifical Swiss Guard, or the Swiss Guard, as you and most others know us and refer to us, has a very rich and colourful history. The

Guard has taken on many roles, and at one time in history, had been called the Defenders of the Church's Freedom. The first regiment of the Swiss Guard was created in 1427, and the first Pontifical Swiss Guard regiment was created in 1471. In the very early days, the Swiss Guard was just that, Swiss men who joined to fight for, or protect, whoever the Swiss had made a deal with to provide men. There have been many regiments that have protected various European Courts, Kings and Queens. Often, the only Swiss in the regiments were the officers, the others being French or other Europeans. They had a reputation of unwavering allegiance to the King, Queen or Court they were to protect, and yes, the Swiss Guard has fought many battles, some were won and some were lost. At one time in the 1600's, you could even say the Swiss Guard had numbers upwards of 120,000 fighting men. In the 1800's there were 1800 Swiss Guard that served in the revolution, but those numbers, and those men, are not, and have not been, what most people have come to know as the Swiss Guard."

"The Pontifical Swiss Guard was formed in 1471 by Pope Sixtus IV and its numbers have been only as big as 200 dedicated men. Over the years, the Swiss Guard was mainly a force to provide protection for the compound that you would know as the Holy See, or Vatican City.  There have been other forces who provided protection and security for the Pontiff, but in 1970, under Pope Paul VI, the Palantine Guard and Nobel Guard were disbanded.  At that time, the Swiss Guard became the only security force for the Vatican and the Pontiff.  Today, we have 135 members, including myself, the Colonel, and our Chaplan.  We are the defacto military for Vatican City, and the security force for the Pontiff.  I am there on May 6 of each year as new recruits come forward and ask to join the Guard.  I have been a member for the last 17 years.  So you see, Gentlemen, I know each and every member of the Swiss Guard personally, and the man you are looking for is not one of my men here in Canada, or back at the Vatican.  How he has some of our ammunition, is a mystery that I will personally oversee until we get to the bottom of that, but this man you seek is not one of us."

The three men sat in silence, contemplating their drinks for a few minutes, before Henderson looked over to his partner.  Richards, reading Henderson's mind, gave him a small nod.  Henderson looked back to Hauptmanns and asked, "Do you and your men have anything to do with historical religious documents, like finding them, or recovering them if they went missing or were stolen?" Laughing, Hauptmanns said, "No, we are not librarians, we are a security force, much like the President of the United States' Secret Service, or your own Prime Minister's RCMP Security Services. Why do you ask this, Owen?" "Well, along with the other information I have given you, our man also has in his possession a book. A book we think is a religious artifact of some sort. He stole it from one of the men he killed," Henderson said. "I see," said Hauptmanns, "that is very, how do you say it, particular." "I think you mean peculiar," Richards corrected. "Yes, yes Tyson, that is the word I was searching for," Hauptmanns said with a small smile, "but again, I must stress I do not see how that would tie him to the Guard," Hauptmanns added. "If we can get some fingerprints from his motel room or the car, can we send them to your people to see if they match? Maybe there is someone you have overlooked," Henderson asked. "Oh yes, please Owen, I am more than happy to help you in any way. Please, if you get fingerprints, contact me and I will see that our database is searched immediately," Hauptmanns said. "I must say," Hauptmanns continued hesitantly, "I am becoming a bit concerned. The information you have given me sets off bells. The Pontiff will be here tomorrow and you have a killer loose in this very city." "I was just thinking the same thing," Henderson said. "There seems to be no motive for the first two killings, and then our killer shows up in Ottawa one day before the Pope is to arrive. I don't see how it ties together, but it sets off alarm bells with me as well," Henderson concluded. Richards looked from one man to the other, "Are you two suggesting that this guy is here to try to assassinate the Pope?" Richards asked incredulously. "I don't know," both Hauptmanns and Henderson said at the same time. Henderson continued on, "There are no known mob members, or associates of any significant ranking, that would have drawn him to this location. So it may seem coincidental , but the ammunition and that damn book keep me thinking." "Me as well," Hauptmanns said.

"Gentlemen, I have a big day tomorrow," Hauptmanns said, "the Pontiff will be here at 8:00 am and I must be prepared. If you need me no further, I must get back to my men." Henderson reached his hand across the table to shake Hauptmanns', "You have been great help, Pedro," Henderson said. "I wish I could have been more help Owen, please keep me, how do you say it, in the loop?" Hauptmanns said. "We will," replied Henderson, "thank you for meeting with us and for the small history lesson." Hauptmanns reached into his pocket and brought out a bunch of Canadian money. Richards quickly stood and pushed the man's hand away, "No Pedro, this drink is on us. Thank you for your help," Richards said. Richards too shook Hauptmanns' hand. As Hauptmanns walked away, Richards put some money on the table and he and Henderson left the bar as well.

## Chapter Twenty

When Henderson and Richards got back to their room, Henderson made a call to the sergeant who had met them at the airport, for an update.  "This is Detective Henderson," he said into his cell when the other man answered, "do you have any news?"  He listened for a few moments and then said, "Keep us posted ok?"  Hanging up the phone, he looked to Richards, "They think our guy stole a pickup from the mall parking lot.  One was reported missing around the time they were scouring the lot for him," Henderson said.  "Well, we know then that he is not on foot and could be anywhere," Richards responded.  "Exactly what I was thinking," Henderson said.  "Do you think it's too late to call that guy in London?  I really want to find out if this book has any significance, or if maybe it was just some trophy that the killer grabbed," Henderson added.  Richards grabbed his own cell and scrolled through the messages to find the one his brother sent.  He clicked on the phone number and put the phone between himself and Henderson.  After a bunch of clicks, clacks, and some odd static, the phone began to ring a double ring.  Richards was just about to end the call after half a dozen rings, when a gentleman with a very strong British accent answered,

"Professor Daniel Brown," the distinguished voice said.  Richards nodded at Henderson to acknowledge the call.  "Professor Brown, my name is Owen Henderson, Detective Owen Henderson.  I'm here with my partner, Detective Tyson Richards.  Did we catch you at a bad time, or have we called too late?  We are calling from Canada," Henderson said.  "Detectives you say, from Canada?" Professor Brown said questioningly.  "Yes Sir, we are detectives with the Ontario Provincial Police."  "I see," said the distinguished voice, "and why should I not believe you are just another prankster?" the Professor asked.  Richards jumped in and said, "Professor Brown, this is Detective Tyson Richards, we were given your number by my brother.  I believe you met him a couple of times, Father Wyatt Richards?"  There were a few moments of silence, so Henderson said, "Professor, are you still there?"  There was a bit more silence and Henderson was now reaching for the phone to end the call.  "Gentlemen," the distinguished voice said, "I just confirmed with Father Wyatt through text message that you two are who you say you are.  Sorry about that chaps, I get a lot of crank calls since that author with a similar name published some books."

"We understand," Henderson said.  "When Wyatt first sent us your contact info, we too thought he was playing with us. Is now a good time to talk to you, Sir?" "As good as any Detective," the Professor said. "What information can I help you with, or how can I assist the Ontario Police?" "Well," Henderson said, "I'm not sure if you can or not. We have been investigating a couple of murders, and at one of the murder scenes a book was taken, one we think was an old religious book of sorts." "Why do you think it would be a religious book?" asked Professor Brown. "It had a cross on the front and a vine of some sort wrapped around the cross, and the suspected killer, we believe, is somehow associated with, or was associated with, the Pontifical Swiss Guard. Inside it was more like a ledger than a book. Like something an old accountant would have," Henderson said. Laughing, Professor Brown said, "If I was not of sound mind, I would say you were talking about 'The Rose', or as some have called it 'The Book of Forgiveness', plus many other names it has gone by, but I must say, chaps, that it is a legend. It is folklore. Just one more ancient artifact, or lost book of the Vatican, that keeps the conspiracy theorists going. No one has ever even seen this book," he concluded. "But there is talk of this book?" Henderson asked. "Oh yes, my good man," said Professor Brown, "it has been a mystery for hundreds of years. It has also been said, that if the book were real, that it would, or could, crush the Catholic Church."  "Why is that Professor?" Henderson asked.  "What is in it?  Why if it is real, would it be so important?"

"Do you chaps have time for a bit of a history lesson?" Professor Brown asked.  "Of course, as long as you have the time," Henderson said.  With a bit of a sigh, Professor Brown said, "That is what I have most of these days.  This book, I will call it 'The Rose', was said to have been first used in 1471 by Pope Paul II.  He was a shrewd and crafty old bugger, always looking for ways to increase the Vatican coffers, and, of course, spread the good word.  As legend has it, a nobleman of high standing in Italy, had come to Pope Paul II to ask forgiveness for impregnating his very young maid.  He told the Pope that the devil over took him and forced him to have intercourse with the young girl.  The nobleman said he was crazed by the devil and should not be kept from heaven for this deed.  After some lengthy negotiations, it was decided that the nobleman would donate 50% of his holdings to the Church.  This would absolve him of his wrong doings, and God would forgive him and let him enter into heaven when his time came.  The nobleman, also very shrewd, wanted a guarantee that he would be let into heaven, and that in the event Pope Paul II was no longer Pope, that he would be protected. As I mentioned, Pope Paul II was shrewd and cunning. Sitting before him was a newly crafted accounting ledger that had just been delivered to him by one of his pressmen. He told the nobleman that his name, his sin that would be forgiven, and his donations to the Church, would be entered into 'The Rose', and for eternity it would be known that he was a man of standing in the Church and eyes of God." Richards cut in and said, "And he believed this?" "Oh yes my good man," said Professor Brown, "you have to understand that the Pope was right next to God in those days. He spoke God's words, he was both loved and feared by his devout followers." "So if the book is just a legend, how did you get that story?" Henderson asked. "Pope Paul II died just six months after this first meeting," Professor Brown said, "however, just before his death, he spoke of the book to his aide, who later became the aide of Pope Paul II's successor. The aide told the successor about the book, and the successor also chose to take advantage of the book, using its power to have people give money to the Church in order to have their names entered into the book to absolve them of sin."

"The aide survived longer than this second Pope as well, and told the next Pope, Pope

Alexander VI, of the book, and he too used it to increase the Church's wealth.  This Pope also entered into the book the names of people who helped the Church in other ways."  "Like what?" asked Henderson.  "You need to understand the times, my good chaps," Professor Brown said.  "Some people thought the Church was corrupt and evil, and those people sometimes disappeared.  The people who made them disappear were entered into the book as well.  Their crimes would be viewed as the work of God, to quell the disbelievers, and in turn, secured their place in heaven."  "That still doesn't explain how you would know about the book, Professor," Henderson said.  "In due time my good chap!" Professor Brown said.  "I'm getting to that part.  The aide, who has now served three Popes, started to grow a conscience when he saw that murders were being committed against those who opposed the Church.  He started to write his feelings down.  From his writings, it appeared he was going to send what he knew off to the Cardinals, the more moderate ones anyway.  Unfortunately, he then succumbed to an untimely death.  Death by eating poisoned fruit.  It is documented that Bertrand DeCheviler was testing food for Pope Alexander VI and died after tasting a peach.  Most of the papers he was writing were lost or destroyed, but in 1843 a distant relative found a small trunk on their property, which was also the place that Bertrand DeCheviler had stayed when he served Pope Alexander VI. In the trunk, some of his writings about a book of the devil, or 'The Book of Forgiveness', were found . In one line, he wrote, 'The Book of Forgiveness has become the book of the devil's deeds and all those who lay in it should be damned to hell', along with a bunch of other references."

"That my good men, was just the first reference to 'The Rose'. In 1740, Pope Clement XII, on his death bed, spoke to his aide and said that the book must be destroyed, that it corrupts the holders, and the ones that are written in it are also corrupt. His aide, having no idea of what the Pope was speaking, spent days by his side before he died, getting small pieces of information from the Pope about the book. The aide wrote this information in his journals and described it as the ramblings of an old dying man's delusions. In his writings, he said that the book was now controlled by a group of priests and Cardinals, the 'Brotherhood', was how he referred to them. He went on to say that it was an exclusive group who would vote on who could be put in 'The Rose', what fees would be collected, or deeds be done, to earn a person the right to be in 'The Rose'. He even went so far as to say that the Brotherhood, who were 12 members, each picked their own successor. When one of the Brotherhood would die, his respective successor would assume his spot on the council of the Brotherhood. However, I should point out that this aide also wrote a number of other papers about the Church and other things, and this labelled him as a madman. Most of what he wrote has been discounted and discredited by the Church and other scholars. Even though he was the second to write of this book to that date, no one had recounted what it looked like, or that they had even seen it, therefore, it still remained the fabrication of wild fantasy." Professor Brown then said, "If you will bear with me my good men, I want to grab one last article that was published no less than 20 years ago." "Sure Professor," Henderson said.

Henderson and Richards could hear the old Professor rummaging through papers and cursing someone, or maybe himself. This went on for a couple of minutes, then Professor Brown said, "So sorry, my good chaps. I have so much junk and papers here I forgot where I put the bloody thing. This is the last account of any mention of 'The Rose' that I have been able to uncover, and I doubt anyone else has found more than me. Now, let's see, oh, here we are. This is a transcript that was taken when a German Major, who fled Germany to avoid war crimes, was captured in Brazil. Have either of you chaps heard of Major Hans Bachmeir?" Professor Brown asked. "No," came the response from both Henderson and Richards. The Professor continued, "Well that is not surprising, he was not one of the bigger names associated with World War II. Nonetheless, he was an evil man, and I regrettably should say a bit of a genius as well. Major Hans Bachmeir, Dr. Major Hans Bachmeir, was famous for his work on human limb reattachment after major trauma. Some of his techniques are used today, however, it was his experimentation that caused him to flee Germany. He was later searched for, and found, in Brazil.

The good Doctor felt that with enough time and experimentation, he could succeed at not only attaching limbs that had been amputated in major trauma and war, but also take donor limbs and reanimate them on wounded soldiers. So far, that sounds like a noble cause, except the good Doctor, having an abundance of living specimens to work on from the death camps, experimented on the Jewish prisoners. He would cause the trauma on the prisoners and then try to reattach the severed limbs. He wanted as much realism to his experiments as possible. To simulate real trauma, he would take a prisoner, place their leg in a reinforced cement and mental container, and would then detonate a grenade in the box. When the limbs were too mangled to even attempt reattachment, he would then instruct the guards to hold down the prisoner and have their arm, leg, foot, or whatever, hacked off with machetes or axes. Of course no anaesthetics were used as that would inhibit the experiments. In his own documentations, he wrote that in one day, he severed over 50 hands just to find the right tool to do the job. He was a total beast, Gentlemen, a cruel beast. It gives me chills just to think of the torture those poor people suffered through," sighed the Professor.

"Now, back to how this all ties together," said Professor Brown. "When Doctor Major Hans Bachmeir was finally captured in Brazil, he was totally dumbfounded as to why they wanted to prosecute him. He rambled on that he had paid his dues. He had handed over his family's fortunes, and here is the kicker chaps, he had converted to Catholicism and had his sins forgiven. He rambled on that he even signed beside his sins in the Holy Book that would absolve him. He said his name was sealed with a bloody thumb print in 'The Book of Forgiveness' and he was assured a spot in heaven and could not be prosecuted."

"Incredible," Henderson exclaimed. "So have you spoken to this Bachmeir, Professor?" Richards ask. "No, unfortunately no one ever will," said Professor Brown. "After his capture and the initial interrogation and his ramblings, he ended up hanging himself in his cell down in Brazil. They did not think to remove his shoelaces," Professor Brown finished. "From that I would say, you could conclude the book is real then?" Henderson asked. "On first thought, it would appear so, however it still remains that no one who is alive has ever seen this book. Even with the three stories I have told you, I am still a skeptic. The book you described could be just an old book. No one alive has seen the inside, and now you say the book has been stolen," Professor Brown said. "We have seen the book, Professor," Henderson said. "What?" Professor Brown spat into the phone, "you never said you saw it, you said it was stolen." "It was stolen," Henderson said, "and we found the person who stole it and had a brief opportunity to look through it." "My gawd, young man, that is incredible. You actually had your hands on it?" Professor Brown said in awe. "Yes, Professor," Henderson said, "we were able to flip through a few pages, and then unfortunately, we had to chase a bad guy, and when we returned, the book was gone." "Can you tell me what was in the book?" Professor Brown asked. "It was very faded in most spots," Richards said, "we both thought we saw at least one finger print, an old one on one page, and a few dates, but like Detective Henderson said, we only had a brief look at it."

"Well Gentlemen, from your description, and from the other references to it that I have given you, I might go so far as to say you did find 'The Rose'," Professor Brown said. "As well, from the stories I have told you, you can see how that book would be damning to the Catholic Church and how it would be a very rare and expensive antique. If it ever comes into your possession again, I would not let it from my sight," said Professor Brown, adding, "I would pay handsomely to have just a small peek at it as well." "First, we have to find this guy," Henderson said. "That is our top priority, but if we find him and he has the book, we will consider letting you take a look at it. It will be on us though, for your help." "I would be most honoured Gentlemen," Professor Brown said. "Thank you for the history lesson," Henderson said. "If we have any more questions, may we call you again?" "By all means yes, I am always glad to help the police, in whatever country they are in," Professor Brown said with more of a lilt in his voice. "Thank you again, Professor, it has been a pleasure speaking with you. Good night," Henderson said, hanging up the phone. He looked over at his partner, "This case just keeps getting more and more weird," Henderson said, "but I don't get what DeDominicus would be doing with a book like that, how he would have got it, or how he knew about its significance?"  "And how does this all tie together?" Richards said.  "I'm not sure," Henderson said, "but I need to sleep and look at all this fresh in the morning." "Agreed," Richards said.

## Chapter Twenty-One

The men were all seated around the large table again.  They waited for him to enter the old stone chamber, each eager to hear the news, to hear that the book was finally back in their possession.  He walked in and the chatter ceased immediately.  None of them liked the scorn he would lash out at them if they didn't show the respect that he demanded.  He had his hands folded in front of him, looking more relaxed than he had in months.  He didn't sit in the ornate chair this time, he remained standing.  Again he looked to each of the 11 men seated around the antique table. "Brothers", he almost bellowed, "we have the book.  Our worst nightmare has come to a close," he said, his face beaming.  "When I arrive home on Saturday, I will personally take possession of the book."  An impish man with badly pock marked skin who sat at the far end of the table looked at him, and asked, "And what will you do with the book once you have it?  Will you return it to the archives?"  The man laughed, "Return it to the archives!" he said with deep sarcasm.  "It has never seen the archives.  'The Rose' has always been in the possession of the Brotherhood.  It is not a book for scholars to peruse through.  It is not a book that needs to continue to exist.  I plan on destroying it."

There were gasps all around the table. The same impish man said, "Do you think that is wise? Many people have sacrificed much for that book, should we not just find a safe place for it?" Growing impatient, the man standing at the end of the table said, "There is no safe place for the book to sit. There is no need for it to exist. Let us not fool ourselves and believe that having your name in the book will absolve you of your sins, only God can do that. No, the book must be destroyed so that it can no longer haunt us or hold the Church at ransom. It must be destroyed," he boomed. Some of the men physically shrunk back at the last statement, as if fearing the man standing would lash out at them. All the men around the table started to nod in agreement, looking left and right, each taking and getting acknowledgement from the man beside him. It was the impish man again who spoke, "I think we are making a mistake. It should be placed in the archives. It is not us who have done any of the deeds in the book. We are the newest members of the Brotherhood. The book has not been used for almost 50 years. I disagree with it being destroyed, however, I see that you have all come to the conclusion that it should be." The man standing said in a very compassionate voice, "Brother, I understand your worries and if this were any other book, I would support you, but the public can not have the opportunity to scrutinize and condemn what they do not understand.  This will be the best for all."  There were again nods of agreement around the table.

The man still standing at the end of the table said, "I must take your leave.  I have to get back and receive the book.  The last part of our plan will be completed tonight."  Another man, this time to his right, spoke up, "Is it necessary to continue with the plan now that we have the book?"  "Yes," the man standing said.  Gritting his teeth, he continued, "We have spoken of this many times.  He is old and he is foolish.  He has twice already tried to speak of the book to others.  We cannot have this.  Once he is silenced and the book is destroyed, it will all be over.  Each one of you knows what power he holds over you.  He recruited each of us.  He must be silenced." Again there were nods, now a bit more hesitant, but nods of agreement went around the table again.  With that, the man who was standing turned and left the room.

## Chapter Twenty-Two

Marcus ditched the old pickup truck that he found. He knew that it would be quickly noticed missing and most probably linked to him. He only had a few hours left before the final part of his mission and did not need to be looking over his shoulder for police. He walked to a bus terminal and found a locker. He didn't like the idea of leaving the book in a bus station locker, but knew he could not be carrying it around with him. He made his way over to the final target. Staying in the shadows, he walked the perimeter of the building a dozen times. He saw three guards who rotated on the grounds. Pretty sloppy work, he thought to himself. They were spaced too far apart and their time around the perimeter was within two minutes. That would give him a window of one to two minutes to scale the wrought iron fence, make his way to the side door, unlock it, and get inside before the next guard came by. He had memorized all the details he was given. The lock on the side door was simple, a child could pick it. He was instructed to go in the door, make a quick left, and go down a narrow hall. This would lead to a door that opened onto the chancel. From here, he was told that on the left side if you pressed on the panel, it would open to a rarely used closet, large enough for a man to hide.  He knew it would be uncomfortable to be in the closet for the 12 hours or so, but he had endured other hardships in his life, far worse than sleeping on his feet or staying in a closet for a great length of time.  He did wish there was another way, but there were too many people for him to get into the building without being noticed.  This was the only way.

After his thirteenth trip around the buildings, he wandered off and found a pay phone.  He placed his overseas call and it was answered on the first ring, "Father, it is me," Marcus said into the phone.  "Marcus, my son," said the old man, "are you ready for the final phase?"  "Yes Father, I have scouted the buildings and have found the door you spoke of.  If the rest of your details are as accurate, it will be no problem gaining access.  My concern is getting back out."  "Marcus," the old man said, "have faith in God, he will guide you out when the time is right.  Now tell me what have you done with 'The Rose'."  "I placed it in a locker at the bus station father," Marcus said.  "Very good, and where is the key?" the old man asked.  "I have the key on me Father, but as instructed, I will place it where you told me should I not be able to get out of the building."  "Very good Marcus," the old man said, "but have faith in God, I don't think you will have any problems getting out and then you can bring the book to me." "I would like that very much Father, to bring you the book," said Marcus. "We will talk soon Marcus," the old man said, hanging up the connection.

Marcus walked to the street corner that he had been instructed to. Standing on the very edge of one of the paving stones he saw that it lifted, just a big enough gap to slip a key in, and that is what he did. Now he was prepared. Marcus walked back to the buildings and watched for another hour from the shadows. As the guard rounded the building with his back to him, Marcus started his approach. As soon as the guard was out of sight, Marcus was up and over the wrought iron fence. He quickly made his way to the door. Pulling out a pick set from his jacket, he knelt down and went to work on the old lock. In 45 seconds, the bolt slid back and he was inside. He slowly slid the bolt back in place and stood silently at the door. It was a full two minutes before the next guard made his way to the side door, wiggled the handle and gave a small pull on the locked door. Marcus could hear him walking away, his clumsy foot falls falling noisily on the stone walkway. Marcus turned and went down the small hallway as he was instructed to do. At the end was a door which led onto the chancel. He walked across the small stage and started pressing on the wooden panels.  It was the last one he pressed that sprang back to him.  Pulling out a tiny flashlight, he scanned the interior.  It was big enough for two men his size with nothing more than some old books on the floor and a few cans on a high shelf.  He stepped in and pulled the door closed behind him.  In a sudden moment of panic , not knowing if the door would reopen, he pushed it hard.  The door swung open and was just about to bang the wall when he caught it.  Letting out a long sigh, he composed himself, stepped back into the closet, pulled the door shut, and began to put himself in a meditative state that would help him pass the long hours he must wait.

## Chapter Twenty-Three

Owen Henderson woke with a start. He sat up, at first not knowing where he was, then the events of the day before, the information he and Tyson had learned, started to come back to him. Running his hand through his hair, he still couldn't grab on to what had woken him. Was it another one of the dreams? It didn't feel like it, no cold sweat, no gnawing ache in his stomach, but something woke him, and something was eating at him. Looking at the clump of clothes on the floor, he decided the first thing he needed was a shower, and then he would find something clean to wear.

After getting out of the shower and putting on yesterday's clothes, he decided to find a Walmart. He would grab, at the very least, some clean socks, shorts, and a shirt. When he got out to the lobby, he saw Lieutenant Colonel Pedro Hauptmanns standing just outside the door, smoking a short, skinny cigar that gave off a very aromatic smell. It reminded Henderson of the rich tobacco that the locals were smoking on his and Tracy's last holiday together, the one they took to Grenada just before she was killed. Quickly dismissing the thought, he walked over to the man, "Pedro, I didn't think you were the smoking kind. All your vices are coming out in

Ottawa," Henderson said with a small laugh. "Good morning Owen.  You are up early too I see," Hauptmanns said.  "You could not sleep?"  "I slept, but something woke me and I just can't put my finger on it," Henderson said. "Ahhh, your mind too does not shut off when you wish it would," Hauptmanns said.  "No, I guess it doesn't.  Is that why you are out here at 4:30 in the morning, your brain wouldn't shut off?" Henderson asked.  "Yes Owen, that is exactly why I could not sleep.  I am very concerned about today.  I have thought a lot about our conversation, your killer, the Pontiff being in the same city, it all feels, how do you say?" Hauptmanns said.  "Wrong," Henderson responded.  "Yes, yes, it all feels wrong.  Like we both are missing something.  I have decided to have the detail that is with the Pontiff now, stay on here in Ottawa with us. Normally, I would relieve them and send them home, but I feel I need more men," Hauptmanns said.  "With your men, and the Prime Minister's security detail, I'm sure he will be safe," Henderson said.  "Will you and Tyson be at the church as well?" Hauptmanns asked. "I hadn't thought about it yet.  Would you like us there?" Henderson asked.  "I think it would be good if you can, you are the only two who have seen this man," Hauptmanns said.  "Ok, we will catch up with you later and work out the details, right now I have to go and find a change of clothes. We didn't plan on staying the night," Henderson added. Both men shook hands and Henderson left Pedro to smoke his cigar.

Driving around to find a Walmart, Henderson still could not put a finger on what was eating at him. Was it something he learned from Pedro, or from the Professor? He wasn't sure, but something was sitting in the back of his mind. He knew it would come to him eventually, he was just hoping it wasn't too late when it did. Spotting a Walmart, he wheeled the car in and was able to get a spot close to the front doors. Normally he wouldn't look for clothes at Walmart, but at this hour, he also knew this was the best place to find the basics. He had a small laugh and smile to himself as he thought about Richards' reaction when he found out that Henderson picked him up some clothes at Walmart. It would kill him! He grabbed a couple of pairs of socks, some shorts, and two men's dress shirts, complete with a clip on tie and tie bar. Richards will just flip when he sees this, Henderson thought. At least they will be clean. He paid for his purchase and was walking to the car when it finally struck him. Growing up in the same neighbourhood, he, Tyson and Wyatt all attended the same church, the same church they went to when in high school. The same church that he remembered seeing Louis DeDominicus attend on occasion.  "That's right," he said to himself, "DeDominicus used to attend our church.  He even came back a few times after he moved from Hamilton down to St. Catharines."  Still puzzled at what that meant, he made a mental note to talk to Wyatt and Tyson about this later.

Henderson got back to the hotel to find Tyson Richards still sound asleep.  Henderson put the in-suite coffee maker on, sat down with his pad, and started writing out the facts that he had so far.  With each fact, he would come up with a question to ask either Wyatt or Pedro.  His cell phone ringing startled him and brought him out of the deep concentration he was in.  "Detective Henderson," he said into the cell.  "Hello again, Pedro.  Yes that would be fine.  Ok, we will be there.  You too."  Henderson hung up the phone and saw Richards standing in the door of his room, scratching at himself, and yawning.  Smiling, Henderson said, "You look like shit."  With a sardonic grin, Richards replied, "Good fucking morning to you too, asshole.  Who were you talking to?"  "That was our new friend Pedro," Henderson said.  "He invited us to a meeting with his men to go over the details for today's service with the PM and the Pope.  I saw him outside this morning and he asked if we would go to the service, lend our eyes to him." "How long have you been up?" Richards asked. "Early enough to get you a clean shirt and skivvies," Henderson said, pointing to the Walmart bag sitting on one of the chairs. "Fucking Walmart clothes," Richards said, "man you know I can't wear that stuff. It irritates my skin." His voice changing from sarcasm to concern, he said, "Did you have another one of your dreams?" "No, not at all," Henderson said," something woke me early and I'm still rolling it around in my head. Why don't you shower, we have to meet Pedro and his crew at 9:30 am after the Pope gets settled. There is fresh coffee over there and then we can go over what is chewing at me." "Sounds like a plan," Richards said.

A short while later, Richards emerged from the bathroom, wearing his new Walmart shirt, but opting to keep the tie that was spared by the bullets from the day before. "Does it fit ok?" Richards asked. "You look just fine," Henderson said shaking his head. "So tell me, what woke you so early?" Richards asked. "It took me a while to figure it out, but it finally came to me. When we were in school, and going to church on a more regular basis, do you remember seeing Louis DeDominicus attending Cathedral Basilica of Christ the King?" Henderson asked. "Yea, I remember both him and Vinny going to Mass now and again," Richards said, "but what does that have to do with anything?"  "I'm not sure," Henderson said, "but I wonder if Father Ziggy can shed any light on the two men?"  "It's not Father Ziggy anymore, dude, he is now Cardinal Zigmond Heinz," Richards said.  "Right, I forgot he became a Cardinal," Henderson said.  "Regardless of what title he holds, I wouldn't mind having a word with him to get his take on the two men.  He must have spoken to them over the years.  From what I remember, he didn't seem all that thrilled to have them in his church," Richards said.  "I distinctly remember one time when I was talking to him after Mass, it was about the mark he gave me on my grade 12 religion paper.  He gave me an 'F', said I hadn't even begun to understand the importance of the Ten Commandments.  I was close to begging him to change the mark, it was what stood between me and graduation.  Anyways, Louie came over and just interrupted the conversation as if he owned the church, gave me no regard at all.  Ziggy looked both embarrassed and a bit outraged, but he did dismiss me, and told me to see him on Monday to discuss my mark."  "So maybe he does have a bit more insight into the pair of them," Henderson said.  "I guess it won't hurt to talk with him.  I will check with Wyatt and see where he is," Richards said.  Looking at his watch, Henderson said, "Ok, but for now we have to get up to the tenth floor to meet with Pedro and his men. Father," correcting himself, "Cardinal Ziggy is secondary. I don't think he will be of much help anyways."

## Chapter Twenty-Four

As Richards and Henderson were leaving their room, Henderson's phone rang its familiar bell sound, "Detective Henderson," he said. "Yes Sergeant, we are still in town," he paused to listen to the man on the other end of the call. After a brief moment, Henderson said, "That's great news! Run them and see if you get a hit, and make sure they go into the system so my team has access to them. I'm also going to get a fax number for an overseas police department and send it to you. If you can fax the prints to that number it may help." He paused again to listen, "Ok, that sounds good. Is this a cell? Can I text the fax number to you?" "Ok, we will be in touch," he said and hung up the call. Looking over at Richards, Henderson said, "That was Sergeant Scales, the older cop who met us. He said they found the pickup truck, and they lifted some prints off the roof of the car. Three fingers and a thumb print." "So the guy really does only have three fingers," Richards said. "Yea, I guess that writer, Robert J. Henry," Henderson said in a mocking tone, "did get a good look at the guy's hand." "They are towing the stolen truck in to see if they can find prints on it," Henderson added. "My guess is it comes up clean," Richards said. "I'm thinking that he did not realize he put his hand on the roof of the car, a total impulse move," Henderson said, "or he would have cleaned the outside of the car too."  Henderson then pressed the elevator call button.

When the two men stepped off the elevator on the tenth floor, they were greeted by a tall blonde man, a full two inches taller than Henderson's 6' 2" frame.  Standing in their path, he was wearing the now familiar blue army fatigues that they had come to associate with the Pontifical Swiss Guard.  In perfect English, the tall Guard said, "Gentlemen, this is a restricted floor, I'm going to have to ask you to get back in the elevator."  Producing their badges, Richards said, "We are expected at a meeting with Lieutenant Colonel Pedro Hauptmanns."  Inspecting their credentials, the big man didn't miss a beat, "Yes Gentlemen, the Lieutenant Colonel is expecting you.  Fourth door down the hall," he added, pointing to his left.  "If you are carrying side arms, I have to ask you to leave them here on the table," pointing to a small table setup beside him.  Henderson was just about to go ballistic with this request when Lieutenant Colonel Pedro Hauptmanns came out of a door at the other end of the hall where two more blue clad guards were stationed.  Spotting the two men, he came forward quickly, "Owen, Tyson, so good to see you,"

Hauptmanns said, extending his hand. "I see you have met Captain Amacher, he is one of the very few Swiss in the Swiss Guard," Hauptmanns said. "He takes his job very seriously," Henderson said with a tone of irritability in his voice. With a small chuckle, Hauptmanns said, "Yes, he is a much too serious man. You did not give our hosts a difficult time did you Erik?" Hauptmanns asked the big blond man, smiling up at him. "I was just following my orders, Sir," Amacher said, much too seriously. "Very good Erik," Hauptmanns said. Turning to Richards and Henderson, he said, "Come Gentlemen, we have much work to discuss," as he led them down the hall to the meeting room.

The three men entered the makeshift meeting room to be greeted by another 14 men all dressed in the blue army fatigues. One of the members, in a loud voice, said, "Attenzione," and all the men snapped to attention. Hauptmanns responded with, "A proprio agio tutti, questi sono i nostri padroni di casa, il detective Henderson e il detective Richards." Switching back to English, he said to Richards and Henderson, "If you two had not walked in with me, they would have continued to carry on like I was not here. We take a relaxed approach to things unless we are on display for the public, or our honoured hosts." He continued on, "Some of my men do not speak English very well, so Captain Esposito is going to translate as I speak," pointing to a young Italian man to his left. "I hope that will not be too distracting?" "No, it will be fine," Richards said. "We do appreciate being included in your planning meeting," Henderson added. "No, it is we who appreciate your input, Owen," Hauptmanns said, "forgive me, Detective Henderson." "Let's all just quit with the formalities, Pedro," Richards said. "Ah, yes, very good. Lascia tutto solo relax, abbiamo molto lavoro da fare. I just told them all to relax," Hauptmanns said.

All of the men gathered around a small conference table. Covering much of the 4' x 10' table was a detailed diagram of the Notre Dame Cathedral Basilica, the church where the Pontiff would be giving the Friday evening Mass for the Prime Minister and other dignitaries. There was a bit of elbowing and cajoling from the other men. When Lieutenant Colonel Pedro Hauptmanns started to speak, the room turned completely silent and all the men became the professionals they were. Meeting the gaze of each man, Hauptmanns began, "This here is Notre Dame Cathedral Basilica. It has a seating capacity of 600. We do not expect any more than 300 guests as this is a private Mass by invitation only. As we previously discussed, there are five main entry points into the building."  Pointing to five spots on the diagram, Hauptmanns said, "Here, here, here, here, and here.  Not including the main entrance, which is here."  Directly across from Hauptmanns was Captain Esposito.  Speaking in a quieter tone, he was repeating everything in Italian.  All the men around the table were nodding that they understood.  Looking to Richards and Henderson, Hauptmanns said, "We have had three men stationed at the Basilica for the past 24 hours.  They have been doing a roving perimeter patrol, switching off with fresh men every three hours."  Both Henderson and Richards nodded their understanding.

"We will have two men at each entrance," Hauptmanns continued on, "Detective Henderson and Detective Richards will be at the main entrance with myself.  They have seen the man who I spoke to you earlier about.  When the Prime Minister arrives, his Security Services people with enter with him, and will station four men inside.  One here, one here, one here and one here," Hauptmanns said, pointing to four different spots on the diagram.  "We will continue with the mobile patrol outside, increasing it to four men two hours before the service starts.  That will leave no outside wall of the building unprotected at any time.  Does everyone understand all of this?"  Hauptmanns paused to let the interpreter finish.  He watched each man nod his understanding, some offering a small response of "Understood."  The Pontiff will come over to the Basilica at 1850 and will prepare here, in this room," he said, pointing to a small room off the church's foyer.  "The Prime Minister and his invited guests will start to arrive at 1855.  The Prime Minister and the Pontiff have already had a private meeting, so all of the guests will be seated on their arrival."  Again, Hauptmanns paused to let the interpreter catch up and the men acknowledge the instructions.

Hauptmanns went on for over an hour, describing in detail where each dignitary would be seated, in what order they should be arriving at the church, and finally, what men would be stationed at each of the entrances.  Looking to Richards and Henderson, Hauptmanns said, "Do you feel we have covered all of the details?"  "It sounds like you have everything covered," Richards responded.  "I agree," Henderson added, "you have done a very thorough job and it appears your men completely understand their roles and positions."  "Good," Hauptmanns said, with a curt nod of his head.  Hauptmanns took a sip of water and said, "The Mass will not be a long one, I am told no more than 45 minutes, ending with the Eucharist. It is at this time that I feel the Pontiff and your Prime Minister will be most vulnerable," he added, looking to Henderson. "Why do you say that?" asked Henderson. "The Pontiff will take Eucharist at the cross here, and he will have his back to the church when he does this. Once he has finished, he will rise and invite the guests to take Eucharist. At that point, the Prime Minister and guests will make their way to the front of the Basilica. We will have 300 people standing and moving forward," Hauptmanns said. "If I was looking for an opportunity, that would be the best time. Twenty men cannot be watching the moves of 3oo people all at once." "I see your point," Henderson said, "but these are all invited guests and dignitaries, people who have been vetted." "Yes, and we will have your eyes and Tyson's eyes watching everyone come in," Hauptmanns said, "but if we have missed one thing, something that we have overlooked, this would be the time that I would take my shot."

All of the men stood in silence after Hauptmanns' last comment. They all appeared to be intently studying the diagram in front of them, all with every bad scenario running through their heads. Breaking the silence, Henderson said, "What time will you be going over, Pedro, and may we ride with you?"  "I would like to go over around 1630, check in with each of my men, and go over the building myself.  Yes, most definitely, you can ride over with me.  I would like that," Hauptmanns said.  "We could, what do you say, throw ideas at each other?"  Richards was the first to laugh, then said, "Bounce ideas off each other!  Pedro, man, you need to watch more western TV."   After Esposito finished the translation, all the men in the room broke up in laughter.  With a little embarrassment on his face, Hauptmanns said, "Ok enough, enough.  Everyone go do weapons checks.  Those who should be switching off with the patrol, get yourselves over there."  The crowd of men quickly broke.  The tension being relieved for a short while as there was laughter and more pushing and shoving.  Once the room had cleared, Hauptmanns said to Richards and Henderson, "My appreciation runs very deep for your help.  Let us pray that we are just men that worry too much."  "Yes," Henderson said, "let's pray we are just overcautious.  They found some prints on the car that our man was driving.  Can you still assist us and check your database?"  "Of course, Owen," Hauptmanns responded, "I can do even better.  If you send me the prints, I will use my connections at INTERPOL and see if they too can match them."  "Do you have a fax or email address to send them to?" Henderson asked. Pulling a business card from his jacket, Hauptmanns said, "This is my cellular and fax numbers as well as my email address. The quickest would be if a digital scan can be sent to my email address." "I will have them do that within the hour," Henderson said. The three men shook hands and left the room.

## Chapter Twenty-Five

As the old man left the chamber and the rest of the Brotherhood behind him, he felt as if a huge weight had been lifted from his shoulders.  He now sat in seat 41-A of the Air Canada 737 looking out at Rome as it descended below him.   The flight being under booked left him with an empty seat beside his. This offered him more comfort, as too often, passengers sitting next to him felt the need to unload all of their guilt and problems on him. He really didn't mind helping to console and walk people through their difficult times, but now he just wanted to be left with his thoughts, a few hours of solitude to help organize his thoughts before the hectic days that would follow.  He knew some of his plan would cause talk, and most definitely some chaos.  He was prepared for it, however anxiety still filled him with the thoughts of the coming days.  That will be short lived, he thought to himself, only a few days and then things will start to return to normal, or as normal as they could be.  His thoughts then jumped to the book.  Finally,  to have the book in his possession, and never again having to fear its contents, or those contents being revealed.  The thought of that alone, brought a smile to his face.  His plan so far had gone off flawlessly.  His call to that scum Vinny, posing as Louis DeDominicus and demanding a late night meeting and sending a driver to fetch him, worked without a hitch. The ignorant fool didn't even question the call. Always the follower, Vinny was. "DeDominicus' lap dog," he mumbled to himself, "and DeDominicus, being the greedy bastard that he was, always so eager to see the information I had learned during the confessions of a high ranking politician," he whispered. "What fools they both were."

They both got what they deserved. The years they tormented him, controlled him. If the counsel knew the whole story, he doubted they would be his supporters, but that too was now in the past. With the book in his hands, no one could make him do the horrible things that Louis and Vinny had him do. The lying, the stealing from the Church, and the people they had Marcus make disappear. It was shameful the way they manipulated and controlled him for all those years. Oh yes, they got exactly what they deserved. The last act they made Marcus do was all he could stomach. That poor, poor girl. She died so needlessly, in her prime. He couldn't blame Marcus for that. He understood how it all happened, but what a shame, what a waste of a good person. His thoughts drifted back to the horrible debacle, how he tried to warn people on that one, but what could he do, they always had the book.  It would not only destroy him, it would destroy the Church.  But that was all in the past.  He was sure Marcus would succeed and get away without any problems.  Marcus would be there to meet him when he landed in Toronto, he was certain of that, he thought.  Then he would have the book, and all this would be in the past.  There was just one troubling thought, one decision he still had not come to.  Should he destroy the book or keep it?  Not to use, no, it would never be used again, but for the historical value, for the rich history that was contained in it.  No, it must be destroyed, it must be.  He toiled with this idea for a long time, finally drifting into a light slumber.

He slowly woke as the young female flight attendant gently shook his shoulder saying, "Father, Father, we have begun our decent into Toronto."  Clearing his throat, he sat up straighter in his seat, "Oh my, did I sleep the entire flight?" he asked the flight attendant.  Smiling at him, she said, "Yes Father, you were sound asleep when we served dinner. I didn't want to wake you, you looked so peaceful.  We will be landing before too long.  Can I get you anything Father?"  "No, thank you dear," he said, "and dear, it is Cardinal Heinz, but that is easily mistaken when wearing less formal attire." "Oh forgive me, Cardinal Heinz," she said, offering a slight bow. "Oh there is nothing to be forgiven my dear," Cardinal Heinz said, offering her a warm smile. The captain came on the overhead speaker and in his authoritative voice said, "Flight attendants, please prepare passengers and compartment for final approach." Looking down at Cardinal Heinz, the pretty flight attendant said, "Well it looks like we are ahead of schedule. Make sure you fasten your seatbelt Cardinal Heinz." Again she smiled at him and made her way forward, checking on each of the other passengers as she went along.

Cardinal Zigmond Heinz couldn't believe he had slept the entire flight away. The relief of stress must have relaxed him more than he thought. As he thought about that, he could also feel the anxiety and excitement of his plan finally coming to a close. By now, if Marcus had succeeded, he should be well on his way to the airport to fetch him, if he wasn't already here. He would have the book in his hands in just a few short hours. He would be home before 9:00 am and would have plenty of time to prepare for the day, and the coming days ahead. It is finally over, he thought again. Finally over. He heard, more than felt, the airplane slow, then the landing gear coming out of the bays and locking into place.

Within minutes, the plane was slowly rolling up to the gate.  When the flight attendant finally told the passengers that they could disembark, Cardinal Zigmond Heinz bowed his head.  He said a short prayer of thanks for all his months of planning finally coming to an end.  He was one of the last to stand, opening his overhead compartment, and grabbing his one carry-on bag.

## Chapter Twenty-Six

Marcus slowly opened his eyes.  He had no idea how much time had passed, however, he knew it must be getting close to the time.  His internal alarm clock was steadily pinging.  He reached in his jacket and checked to make sure the yellow rose was still in there.  After doing so, he laughed at himself, thinking where would it have gone to?  It didn't have legs, so it couldn't just walk away!  Reaching into his other pocket, he pulled out his tiny flashlight.  Shielding the light, he clicked it on.  Aiming it at his watch, he saw he had less than two hours to wait.  He thought he would have heard more noise and people by this time.  Maybe the door was thicker than he had first thought and it muffled the sounds better.  Turning his body , he tried peering through the tiny crack where the hidden closet door met the jamb.  He had to shuffle and almost press his entire face against the door to peer out.  Just a thin sliver of light.  An opening, less than the thickness of a dime, was what he was trying to see through.   After a few minutes of jockeying and almost pressing the door open, he was finally in a position to see through the crack.  His tiny view allowed him to see the cross at the very back of the chancel, and the small kneel and communion rail where the old man would receive his Eucharist.

While looking through, he saw a person walk by. It looked to be a member of the cleaning staff, inspecting the area for any last minute cleaning that may be needed. He then heard some faint muffled chatter. He couldn't make out what was being said, just soft muffled voices. He thought one was a woman, maybe the cleaning woman, and the other a man's voice. He was sure of that, it had a deeper baritone sound to it. He felt as if he was underwater in a pool, listening to people speak on the pool deck. Another person now passed in front of him. This one stopped, their back just inches from the door. He held his breath, hoping that they did not lean against the hidden door and it click open. He knew then that his mission would fail and more innocent people may die just so he could escape. The person moved away from the door a few inches, allowing him to hear the person speak more clearly. It was the man, the baritone voice. He said something about a waste of time, or waste of his time. The other voice, too muffled to hear, spoke. The baritone laughed, a loud hearty laugh. The man moved a step closer to the door again, his bulk completely blocking the thin strip of light. He then moved to Marcus' right, now he could see a flashlight dangling off the baritone's belt. Ah, Marcus thought, one of the security people doing rounds inside now, or monitoring the cleaning staff.  No, he thought, the baritone was probably going off shift and flirting with the cleaner.  That was what the muffled conversation sounded like, again some high laughter, then the baritones.  There was a third very faint and muffled voice now.  Marcus could feel the cold sweat running down his spine.  It was not fear of being caught, it was fear of failure.  He had never failed.  Again more laughter and then the voices faded.  He thought he heard a door close.  The room was again silent.  He let out a long slow breath, checking his watch one more time.  Only an hour to go.

Marcus leaned back against the wall.  He removed his weapon, the silencer was already attached.  He hit the release and the magazine ejected.  Running his thumb across the top of the magazine, he could feel the cartridge sitting at the top.  He knew it was fully loaded, the checking was just training, and part of the ritual.  Sliding the magazine back into the butt of the gun, he felt it hit home.  He wouldn't holster his weapon now, he would remain at the ready.  Flicking off the safety, he crossed his arms and rested the weapon on his folded arm.  He closed his eyes.  This time, he would not rest, not try to put himself in a meditative state.  This time, he would count down the minutes in his head. Steadying his racing heart, he took slow deep breaths.

## Chapter Twenty-Seven

As Richards and Henderson stepped onto the elevator to return to their room, they both took out their cell phones and began to dial numbers.  Richards' call was answered first, "Good afternoon, Mrs. Sandhill, it's Richards."  He paused a second, "I know you know my voice, I'm just trying to be polite.  Do you have any messages for me?"  He listened as Mrs. Sandhill listed off his messages.  "Ok, I will return that one shortly.  The rest I think can wait until I get back.  Yes, I have his number.  Ok, we will talk to you later," Richards concluded and ended the call.  He turned to look at Henderson who was quietly listening to what he assumed were voice messages.  This was confirmed after a few seconds when Henderson pressed a button on his cell and then put the phone back to his ear.  The elevator stopped on their floor and the two men walked to their room as Henderson was still listening.  As they reached the door to their room, Henderson finally finished his call.  "Anything important?" Richards asked.  "You first," Henderson said.  "The chief wants an update," with a small sheepish smile he also said, "and his budget reports."  Henderson looked at the smaller man and shook his head, "Now you know why I don't want your job," Henderson said with a chuckle.  "Aww come on buddy, please take it. I hate this part of it," Richards whined. With a wide grin, Henderson said, "No fucking way buddy. Besides, you're way better at that stuff." Turning a bit more serious, he said, "I think the way it is, works just fine." "Fine," Richards snapped. "Now your turn. Anything interesting?" "A call from Danielle saying she is happy about me going back to work. Did you talk to her?" Henderson asked. "I sent her an email. She asked me to keep her up to date," Richards responded. "Aren't you two quite the mother hens," Henderson said. "Also, Cyrsta wants me to call her. She said they have some developments." "Why don't we see if we can set up a conference call with your team and the Chief so everyone can get up to speed together?" Richards said. "Sounds good to me," Henderson replied.

Before Richards could set up the conference call, his cell rang. When he answered it, Henderson could hear Chief Joe Smith's voice booming out of the tiny phone from across the room. "Where the fuck is my budget report and what the fuck is going with this investigation?" Henderson heard. Richards pulled the phone from his ear while the Chief continued with a small barrage of explicatives and other comments. Both men knew the Chief was not seriously mad, but he was trying to get a point across.  That was often the way he did it, with mock anger and very colourful language.  When the sound died down from the phone, Richards returned it to his ear, "Hello Chief," he said.  He listened for a few seconds and then said, "Yes Sir, I do have it complete and had all intentions of getting it to you today."  He paused a few seconds and continued, "As soon as we get back, you will have it."  Again he paused, then Richards said, "Actually Sir, I, or I should say we, Henderson and I, would like to get a telephone conference going with you and his team so we can all get up to speed.  Yes Sir, I can wait."  Pulling his cell from his ear, Richards said to Henderson, "The Chief is at the office.  He going to take his cell into the conference room and get your team in there with him."  Henderson just nodded and went back to looking at his notes.

After putting the cell on speaker phone, Richards placed it on the table between the them.  A short while later, there came some shuffling over the phone, and then the Chief's voice, "Ok Gentlemen, I have Cyrsta and Harry with me now.  Everyone else has moved on to their other cases for now, seeing that you have found your man, or the only suspect we have so far."  Richards said, "Good afternoon," to everyone and then told them that Detective Henderson would fill them in with the details.

"Good afternoon Everyone," Henderson said. A bunch of overlapping good afternoons came back over the phone.  Henderson then spent the next 30 minutes filling everyone in on what they had learned from Hauptmanns, Brown, and their encounter with Mark Able. "Does anyone have any questions?" Henderson asked.  "Do you have any other leads on this character, or where he maybe or going?" the Chief asked.  "No, nothing at the moment," Henderson said, "however, Hauptmanns and I both have a bad feeling about why this guy may be here in the capital."  "Go on," the Chief said.

"Well Sir," Henderson continued, "as you know, the Pope is here in town.  He got in this morning.  He is preparing to give a small Friday night Mass for the PM and some other politicians and dignitaries.  We think our guy may try to take a run at the Pope." "Hmmmm," was all the Chief replied.  There was a bit of silence, and then the Chief said, "What are you basing this on, other than the ammo this guy has been using?"  "I guess it is the book sir," Henderson said.  "If what Professor Brown described is the book this guy has, we think he may be some sort of religious fanatic.  Maybe he somehow knows what is supposed to be, or is in it, and he wants to punish the Pope for it.  Maybe this guy is holding the Pope, just for being the Pope, responsible for the book." "It seems like a bit of a stretch," the Chief said, "but, and a big but, I guess I could buy into that. So you plan on going to the Mass to see if he shows?" the Chief asked. "Yes Sir. We think he has opportunity there. After that, well I guess we are back to square one to try and find him," Henderson said. "I think if he is a no show for tonight, and there is no attempt on the Pope, that you two should return here tomorrow," the Chief said. "But we still don't know where this guy is," Henderson retorted. "True," said the Chief, "but from what we have so far, this sounds like a simple case of a nut job killing two scumbags for an old book. It really doesn't fall into the category of Organized Crime, and that, Gentlemen, is what this department was created to do." "I see the Chief's point," Richards said. "The only reason we are on the case is because of who he killed. If it is just a murder and theft case, we have to turn it over to the locals." A bit hesitantly, Henderson said, "I guess." "Go to the Mass tonight, if he doesn't show, get your asses home. There are a lot of other cases to sink your teeth into," the Chief said. "So nothing else on your end Cyrsta or Harry?" Henderson asked.

Cyrsta Sunland was the first to speak, "We got a partial match on the print you sent us," she said, "but it is a dead end.  There was a print in the database from a baseball bat that was used in a beating 15 years ago, but it has never been matched to a person."  "Where did it take place?" Henderson asked.  "In Hamilton," Sunland responded.  "It was a case of a couple of thugs who picked on the wrong kid.  The kid used his bat in self defence, as far as the report said, it looks like he got a bit carried away.  Eye witness accounts said the boy was being taunted and pushed around.  Then he used his bat to defend himself.  Then he used his bat to punish as well.  They found one print, but never found the kid," Sunland finished.  "Do we have a description of the kid?" Henderson asked.  "Not really," Sunland said.  "He was darker skinned and about 5 feet tall, very skinny.  That's all the description anyone could give."  "No missing digits?" Richards asked.  "Nope, not that the witnesses or the subjects had mentioned."  "So we know he was a kid in Hamilton at one time, and now a suspected killer."  Henderson said.  "And Gentlemen," the Chief cut in, "that still does not make this an organized crime case.  See what happens tonight, and if it leads to a dead end, I mean if he doesn't show, then get home and we can send all we have to the locals."  There were a few little chuckles from the

Chief's unintentional pun, and everyone said their goodbyes.

Henderson looked over to his partner and said, "Yea, I guess the Chief is right. If nothing happens, this really isn't our case. I would have liked to catch the bastard. First shake his hand for getting rid of those two, and second, kick him in the nuts for shooting you." "Aww thanks buddy," Richards said, "so you still do have a heart and care." Smiling at Richards, Henderson said, "Some days it doesn't feel like I have anything left inside of me, heart included. Although being back to work, seeing you and everyone else, having my mind busy on other things, has started to make me feel a little more human. Not whole, but maybe not as empty inside." Seeing his friend's eyes get a little watery, Richards said, "Owen, I know this has been a really tough time for you. I can't imagine what it is like to lose someone you loved so dearly, to lose your best friend. I know it will take a long time for you to heal and for the pain to not be so bad. Over time, it will get better. You had a wonderful life together. Hold on to the happy moments, don't ever let them go, and just work on rebuilding your life. One day the pain will go away, but the memories and the love will always be there." Smiling at the bigger man, Richards said, "Now let's get our shit together, we have a killer to maybe stop." Both men stood looking at each other for a moment. Henderson straightened up to his full height and walked over to Richards, "Thanks buddy, you're a good friend," Henderson said. He then gave him a strangling bear hug.

**Chapter Twenty-Eight**

Richards and Henderson returned to the elevator for the trip down to the lobby to meet Hauptmanns and his men.  When the elevator doors opened onto the lobby, Henderson saw Hauptmanns giving instructions to a few men in dark suits, and a few more men dressed the same milling around the black SUVs parked in the lot.  Walking over to Hauptmanns, Richards said, "Your men look like secret service guys, Pedro."  "Ah Owen," Hauptmanns said, shaking the bigger man's hand, "when we go to Mass or formal outings we wear the suits.  Our casual attire is our uniform.  The two men who will be stationed at the front doors of the church will be wearing the traditional Swiss Guard uniform that you would recognize in many pictures taken from Vatican City."  "Won't that leave them defenceless, if God forbid, something should happen?" Richards asked.  "True, they will not be carrying side arms as the other men will, but all of my men are highly skilled in hand to hand combat," Hauptmanns said.  "As well, they have a small dagger worn on the hip which, I might add, is properly balanced, and all men can throw and hit a bulls eye at 50 paces."  "Have you never heard of the saying 'don't bring a knife to a gun fight'?" Richards asked with a chuckle.  "I think there will be more than enough guns if this turns into a fight," Hauptmanns said with dead seriousness. "Yes, too many guns," Henderson added.

All the men walked out to the SUVs and approached one that had its back door opened. Hauptmanns reached in and pulled out two small black boxes with wires dangling off them. Handing one each to Henderson and Richards, Hauptmanns said, "You know what these are Gentlemen?" "Two way communicators," Henderson responded. "Correct," Hauptmanns said. "Clip the box on your belt at the back. The ear piece runs up the inside of your jacket like this." Taking the black box from Richards, he clipped it on his belt at the small of his back. Hauptmanns then reached up Richards' back and popped the earpiece out by his jacket collar. "The microphone goes down your sleeve and clips onto the cuff." Henderson struggled with both wires, but managed to attach his without Hauptmanns' assistance. Taking another one of the boxes from the rear of the SUV, Hauptmanns, pointing to two dials on the box, said, "This one controls the volume for hearing, and this is for microphone sensitivity. It is voice activated. You turn this one while counting into the microphone. Once you get a response from the team you are all set. Do you not use these in your country?" Hauptmanns asked. Trying to look humble,

Henderson responded, "The ones we use are self contained, all in an earpiece."  "Ah yes," Hauptmanns said, "the newer model."

Once the men had all tested their transmitters and found they were working to satisfaction, they climbed into the SUVs.  Henderson took the back seat of the one Hauptmanns was driving, with Richards riding shotgun.  With great precision, the SUVs pulled out of the parking lot and made their way to the church.  Once the vehicles were travelling down the road, Hauptmanns looked into the rear view mirror and asked Henderson if there had been any developments on the man they were looking for.  "Nothing of any significance," Henderson responded.  "We matched a print to an old one in our database, but no body to go with the print.  I'm not sure if we told you, they found the pickup they think he stole from the mall parking lot, so we have no idea if he is on foot or found another car.  Our boss wants us to head back home if everything turns out ok tonight."  "Let us hope that you will be on your way home soon then, Owen," Hauptmanns said.  "Yea, I guess that will be a good thing," Richards said.  "I will be travelling with the Pontiff to Hamilton tomorrow," Hauptmanns said.  "We will be taking a train.  You are welcome to ride with us, however, it will be a long journey as we will be making a number of stops on the way." "Are all your stops secure?" Richards asked. "Oh yes," Hauptmanns said, "the Pontiff will not disembark the train. We pull into a station and he greets the crowd from his car. He wanted to get off and meet some of the faithful but we have advised against this. Our forward men will arrive at each stop 30 minutes before the train to secure the crowd. We do not anticipate any problems," Hauptmanns concluded. "What about the big Sunday Mass in Hamilton?" Henderson asked. "It is a bit more problematic," Hauptmanns said, "but as you know Owen, we have taken careful security measures there as well. Metal detectors were installed today at the entrance, and two men have been inside the church since we arrived. There will be no Eucharist at this Mass. Well not a traditional one. There are just too many people."

"How will you do it?" Richards asked. "Your brother, and a few other priests from Hamilton, will help with those duties, and have set up a communion rail far back from the chancel. They removed a few rows of pews from the front of the church for this purpose," Hauptmanns said. "This also helped make room for a few large TV monitors so that no one is straining to see his Holiness." "That is why there was so much hustle and chaos when I went to see Wyatt?" Henderson said questioningly. "Yes. Father Wyatt was going over the plans and giving instructions that day you came to visit," Hauptmanns said. The three men sat in silence for the rest of the ride to the church, each deep in his own thoughts. As they rounded a corner, they were stopped by a police barricade set up by the RCMP. Hauptmanns rolled down his window and produced his identification and the one Richards handed him. Henderson too rolled his window down and handed out his ID. After the scrutiny, they continued down the short street. Hauptmanns said over his shoulder, "The RCMP have been gracious enough to keep the crowds well away from the church. This should help with our security measures. I must tell you, the Pontiff was not very happy with these arrangements." When they pulled into the short drive, the other SUVs where already unloading. Three men pulled short automatic rifles from the back of one of the vehicles. Henderson, pointing at the men who slung the compact guns over their shoulders, asked, "How did you get them into the country?" "We have diplomatic immunity in all countries and they do not search our luggage," Hauptmanns said with a wink. "We did not intend to take them from the plane. They are protection for some of the more questionable stops on our trip. However, under the current circumstances, I told my men to bring them when they arrived with the Pontiff. "

Standing at the front of the church were two Swiss Guards, dressed in their fanciful and brightly coloured parade uniforms. The official dress uniforms, that are so familiar in tourist pictures, stood starkly against the drab grey of the old stone church. The blue, orange, red, and yellow colours gave them an old renaissance appearance. Their wooden and iron staffs stood at perfect angles. The sword on one hip had highly polished golden handles that gave off sparkling glints from the sun. On their other hip, in rich brown leather scabbards, sat the deadly daggers that Hauptmanns had mentioned. Both men stood ridged and stern faced, facing out to the road with their straight backs looking like they were made of stone. Henderson studied them for a few moments. He noticed that it appeared they were not even breathing, then there was the smallest movement of eyes as they scanned a car that drove past in front of the church. Heads not following the path, just a small eye movement. Henderson nodded towards the men and said, "They are very impressive, Pedro." "Yes, yes, it takes much dedication and training for the men. They will stand like that until the Pontiff has exited the building and his car leaves the property,"

Hauptmanns said. "They are to appear as statues, but let nothing go unnoticed. Come with me," Hauptmanns motioned as he walked towards the two guards.

As they approached the two guards, Hauptmanns reached into his pocket and pulled out a small coin. He then tossed the coin at the closest guard. It gently bounced off his cheek, about a half inch from his eye. The guard did not duck, nor did his gaze move, or his eyes blink. Hauptmanns said something in Italian to the guard. Without changing his gaze, the guard responded in Italian with two words. Looking at Henderson and Richards, Hauptmanns said, "I asked him what coin I tossed at him and he responded with 'Canadian nickel'." Richards bent down and picked up the nickel from the ground and showed it to Henderson. Both men were very impressed. Hauptmanns said, "They miss nothing. They can tell you the licence tag from the last 20 cars that have passed by, and if a car has passed by more than once." "Very impressive," Henderson said with great admiration. With a small grin, he added, "It is a 1972 nickel, and the last car was a blue 2005 Honda Civic, Ontario licence plate ABBZ 091." Smiling at him, Hauptmanns said, "You too are very impressive, Owen. I could use a man like you on my team." "I don't think I could stand still for hours though," Henderson said with a small chuckle. "We can train you," Hauptmanns said. "Come, come, let us go inside and start our rounds. The Pontiff and guests will start to arrive shortly."

**Chapter Twenty-Nine**

The three men went into the old church, immediately started doing assessments, and scanning for security breaches, each going in their own directions and following their own methodologies. After 45 minutes, they were all satisfied that everything was well under control, and the building was as secure as it could be. The three men had met up back in the foyer of the church, and were discussing the logistics of what was about to happen, when their earpieces came to life with some Italian. Hauptmanns translated for Richards and Henderson, "The Pontiff is arriving first, so he can prepare. His car has just passed the RCMP check point. He should be pulling in the drive now." At that moment, they heard the cars turn off the street onto the short drive up to the church. "Gentlemen," Hauptmanns said, "if you would take your positions now, I will be with you shortly." Richards and Henderson straightened their ties and adjusted their ear pieces. They walked over to the front doors, one on either side, about five feet back from the opening. Hauptmanns raced down the stairs to greet the Pope's car as it stopped at the front doors. Looking over at Henderson, Richards had a big grin on his face, "Ok dude, this is show time. Put on your game face, the man who has God's ear is about to walk in the door." Henderson just smiled at Richards as he adjusted his jacket, he was feeling a little underdressed in his casual pants and Nike running shoes.

With Lieutenant Colonel Pedro Hauptmanns on his one side, and Archbishop Pietro Parolin on the other, Pope Francis bounded up the steps of the church with the vigour of a man 30 years younger than his current 76.  He paused as he reached the two Swiss Guards standing at attention on the outside of the church.  Turning to each man, he spoke to them in a soft gentle voice.  Each man, with their stern faces now showing expression for the first time, offered the Pontiff a small bow and then resumed their positions.  Henderson noted the little smile and glint in Hauptmanns' eyes as he too nodded at each of the men.   At that moment, Henderson thought to himself what proud men they were, what proud dedicated men.  Henderson's thought was quickly interrupted as the Pontiff came toward him.  He was not an imposing man, standing maybe 5'8" with a grandfatherly face, grey hair balding on the top, soft, warm brown eyes behind simple silver rimmed glasses that showed not only intelligence, but compassion.

 He was dressed all in white.  The material appearing to Henderson to be cotton and not silk.  A simple outfit, showing his humility.  Pope Francis looked down at Henderson's shoes. He then looked at his own black leather shoes. When he looked up to Henderson, he had a warm, gentle smile. In clear but heavily accented English, he said to Henderson, "My son, you are the smartest man in this room, wearing shoes for comfort and not for show." He then took Henderson's hand and offered him a small handshake as he moved in the direction he was being guided by Hauptmanns and Parolin. Henderson straightened a bit more and looked over to Richards. Richards just stood there, a goofy grin on his face, shaking his head, in a whispered voice Richards said; "Only you could impress the Pope with your Nikes!"

After a few minutes of silence, Hauptmanns returned to the two men. "Ok Gentlemen," Hauptmanns said, "our guests will be arriving shortly. Our job is to just greet them and direct them inside the church. Your Prime Minister will be first, and the rest will follow within minutes." As soon as the man had finished speaking, there was chatter over their headsets. Hauptmanns translated that the cars were coming through the check point. Over the next 20 minutes, there was a bustle of activity as first, the Prime Minister and his family arrived and were seated, next came the rest of the invited guests. Richards and Henderson scrutinized each of the familiar and unfamiliar faces as they entered the foyer and made their way into the church proper. The last guest, the Deputy Prime Minister, arrived in a rush. All three men appeared to relax somewhat as the heavy wooden doors to the church were closed. "Let us take our places for the Mass," Hauptmanns said to the two men. They made their way into the church, each taking up their assigned positions. The doors behind them opened and Archbishop Pietro Parolin entered carrying a cross and walking in a slow measured pace. Music started up at the front of the church, a hymn that Henderson remembered, but could not place. With that, Pope Francis entered, a broad smile beaming on his face as the parishioners in the church rose, and he made his way down the aisle.

**Chapter Thirty**

When Marcus heard the music start up, he slowly opened his eyes. He had heard the comings and goings of people and foot falls near and far. He had steadied his nerves and was now at complete peace with himself and the task that lay before him. He let his arms fall to his side to let the blood circulate and flow into his stiffened joints. Flexing his one hand a couple of times, he passed his weapon to his free hand and began flexing the other hand. He took in long slow breaths, further bringing his body under his control and placing his nerves at ease. He shifted a bit so that he was now facing the door that was carefully hidden within the panels on the chancel walls. He let himself think of the task ahead and this caused his heart to skip a beat, some anxiety welling up in him. Again, he took in long steady breaths, closing his eyes so he could concentrate on the service, knowing exactly when he would emerge and finish his assignment.

As he stood there straining to hear the service, he contemplated all he had done over the years. Knowing this would be the last of his assignments, the last of his deeds to cleanse his soul and he would be free. He heard the hymn, the last one before communion. His thoughts cleared for the task ahead of him. His mind and body were still at ease. He had calmed his racing heart.  He was now God's assassin, doing God's work.  He brought his weapon up, again ejecting the magazine to check its load.  This time, it slipped from his hand as it popped from his weapon.  His heart raced as he felt the cold steal slip from his fingers.  He heard the hymn coming to its end as the magazine was falling to the floor.  He knew the sound would be heard, if not in the entire church, at least on the floor of the chancel.  For the half a second it took for the magazine to fall to the ground, his heart had stopped its beating.  He felt the dread of failure, and then he felt the magazine thump on his shoe.  He took in a deep breath, cold sweat covering his body, and reached down between his legs with trembling hands to retrieve it. As he stood, he peered through the tiny crack and saw the old man kneel at the rail.  He slid his magazine home as he watched the old man take the small wafer that represented the body of Christ.  The old man reached to his side.  Taking the silver chalice, he wiped the cup where his mouth would touch it with the golden cloth that was draped over his arm.  When the old man raised the cup to his mouth, Marcus pushed the hidden door open onto the chancel.  He didn't wait to see if it banged against the wall.  He strode over to the kneeling old man, brining his weapon up to aim.  The old man paused, with the chalice at his mouth. The movement from his right side caught his attention. He turned his head, recognition washing over his face as he saw Marcus take three long strides towards him. He opened his mouth in shock, knowing what would happen next. He spoke his last words, "Marcus, why?"

**Chapter Thirty-One**

Hauptmanns came over the radio set and spoke a long couple of sentences in Italian. Richards and Henderson looked to each other waiting for the translation.  In English, Hauptmanns repeated his command, "Look sharp.  There will be one more hymn, the Pontiff will first take communion, and then offer it to the guests.  Please keep your eyes peeled.  Another voice spoke over the headset, this time it came first in English followed by Italian, "All is clear outside, Sir. We have had no cars pass and the grounds are secure."  The organist started up the final hymn, and Pope Francis began the preparations for Eucharist.  He first said a prayer or blessing, then removed a golden cloth that covered a tiny tray with thin white wafers on it.  He blessed the wafers, telling the congregation that this was the body of Christ, He who gave His life for our sins.  Walking to a small carafe and silver chalice, he blessed the vessel and the wine.  Pouring a small amount into the chalice, he blessed it and said to the congregation "This is the blood of Christ, He who gave His life for our sins."  Pope Francis placed the small tray and chalice on a shelf that stood over the kneel and communion rail that sat below the heavy cross, it bearing a too realistic Christ hanging from it.

Kneeling at the communion rail, the Pontiff bowed his head. He looked up to the cross above him, crossed himself, and said some words that only he himself could hear. All the security men in the room were on high alert, each man slowly scanning the crowd for any signs of abnormal behaviour. One by one, each man said one word over the radio. Henderson took it as a sign that all was clear. When there had been no words spoken over the radio for several seconds, Henderson scanned his area of the church and quietly said into his own microphone, "Clear." Several seconds later, he heard Richards repeat the same word. The Pontiff said a small prayer and placed one of the small wafers in his mouth. He bowed his head for several seconds. He then reached to his side. Taking the silver chalice, he wiped the cup where his mouth would touch it with the golden cloth that was draped over his arm. When the old man raised the cup to his mouth, he paused, and said a few words to himself. As if he heard a sound or saw movement to his right, the old man looked that way. At once, all the security men saw this gesture and they too turned to see what had interrupted the Pontiff.

## Chapter Thirty-Two

Marcus saw the look of recognition wash over the old man's face. He also saw the shocked look, horror, and then saw the man's face take on the look of complete peace, understanding of his imminent fate. Marcus aimed and pulled the trigger in one fluid motion. The silenced weapon erupted a small pfft, the bullet striking the old man in the center of his chest. The instructions given to Marcus for the final assignment were one lethal shot to the heart, a head shot was not necessary. The old man felt the impact, surprisingly, he did not feel any pain. He sucked in a final ragged breath. His body relaxed and he slumped to his side. Marcus walked the final few feet to the old man, watching as his chest expelled his final breath, his hand went limp, and the sliver chalice chimed a long lasting single note as it struck the floor. The deep crimson wine, the blood of Christ, slowly mixing with the deep crimson blood of the old priest. The ringing of the chalices last note hung in the air as Marcus pulled the yellow rose from his pocket, and placed it gently on the priest's lifeless body. He slowly looked up to the cross, he said a small prayer, "Forgive me Father, my sins have been for you, please accept my spirit into your Kingdom."

Marcus straightened up, and heard a gasp of shock from someone behind him. He turned and looked into the crowd, not one person had moved, mouths stood in slack aww, while others with pressed lips were quivering. He saw an old woman. He looked directly into her milky blue eyes, a small tear had escaped and was running down her paper thin skin. Marcus turned, quickly walked to the door at the rear of the chancel, and made his way down the short hall to the door he had entered just the night before. There were no shouts, no screams of panic, or racing feet that he had expected. He unlatched the door, stepped out into the cool evening, and quickly made his way to the iron fence. As he reached up to hoist himself over the fence, he heard the first sounds of panic and chaos coming from the tiny chapel. The door he had entered burst open and a portly security guard, with a radio to his mouth, was yelling as Marcus bound over the fence. He never looked back. He forged ahead as there were more shouts from behind him. Rounding the first corner he came to, he picked up his pace and began to jog.

Taking off his yellow windbreaker, he stuck it into a bush as he ran past it. Coming to another corner, he no longer heard shouts, no racing feet behind him. As he took the second corner, he saw the car he had parked there the day before.  He unlocked it and took in three long slow breaths.  He now looked over his shoulder to the corner, still no one had caught up to him.  He turned the key in the ignition and the engine caught.  He rolled down the window, placed the car in gear, and calmly drove away.  As he approached stop light, he saw an ambulance race through.  A police car, with lights and sirens going, followed shortly after.  Marcus signalled his turn to go in the opposite direction, and calmly drove out of the city.

## Chapter Thirty-Three

The Pontiff paused for a long moment, staring off to his right.  A look of grave concern, of sadness, could be seen on his face.  He turned back and looked up to the cross before him.  He hung his head.  His lips were moving as if speaking to someone or saying another prayer.  He brought the chalice to his mouth and took a drink of the blood of Christ.  Still kneeling, he said another final prayer and stood to face the crowd in the church.  Henderson had slowly made his way over to Hauptmanns' side.  As the Pontiff was inviting others to take communion, Henderson whispered to Hauptmanns, "What was that about?  It was like he saw a ghost or something."  "I am not sure," Hauptmanns responded, "I will try to speak with him later about it."  The two men parted and went back to scanning the crowd, as pew by pew they rose and made their way forward for communion.  Henderson and Richards had eased their way forward as the guests began to rise, looking at faces again, then towards hands.  Nothing set off any alarm bells as the guests shuffled by.  As the crowd was slowly making their way back to their seats, a feeling of great relief was slowly washing over the security personnel.  When the last person had returned to their seat, there were a few sighs of relief over the transmitter as the tension started to drain from each man.  Henderson, Richards and Hauptmanns had moved further back, and were now at the entrance to the church when the Pope said his final prayers and thanked everyone for coming this evening.  A hymn was struck on the organ, and the Pope stepped down from the chancel, and approached the Prime Minister and his family for a final handshake and goodbye.

The old grey stone church emptied out just as quickly as it had filled.  It was Friday night, and most of the people probably had other functions and parties to attend, the service just the first in their busy political lives.  Henderson and Richards were standing outside as the Pope's car and escorts drove away.  They could hear small cheers and applause coming from up the road as the procession turned onto the main street.  Hauptmanns spotted the two men and walked over.  Patting Henderson on the back, he said, "I guess our hunches were unfounded, which is a very good thing, yes?"  "Yes, it is a very good thing," Henderson responded.  "It was a nice service.  The Pope has a way of speaking that keeps you engaged.  He is a gentle man and he is, how they say, the people's Pope.  He is very down to earth," Hauptmanns said.  "Yes, very genuine," Richards interjected, "reminds me of my brother." "Yes, indeed Tyson. He is very much like your brother," Hauptmanns said. "I admit, I was startled when he looked off to his side as he was about to drink from the chalice," Hauptmanns added. "I think everyone was, well at least the security men. I even saw one of the PM's security get a little tense," Richards said. "You will ask him about that?" Henderson asked, looking at Hauptmanns. "Yes, if I have the opportunity to bring it up, I will," Hauptmanns said. "Now Gentlemen, I suggest we go to the hotel and you join me for a cocktail in the lounge." "I think that is the best idea anyone has had all day," Richards said.

By the time the three men had finally climbed into the SUV to head back to the church, full darkness had fallen. When they approached the corner that had the RCMP checkpoint, there were only a few city workers clearing away garbage cans and trash that was left behind by the crowd of worshipers eager to catch a small glimpse of the Pope as he drove by them. Henderson was staring out the window watching the cityscape drift by him, not really focusing on any one thing. His thoughts bouncing from the service and message the Pope had just given, to his own life and recent past. The adrenaline from the days of being on the heels of a killer was draining from him and he could feel the cold grip of his depression slowly tightening around his chest.  He knew he couldn't let it get hold of him, that he needed to move forward, but without an active and engaging case, he was not sure if he could.  Richards looked in the side mirror and caught a glimpse of his partner's face.  He had seen that look too often over the last few months.  He knew what was most likely playing on his partner and best friend's mind.

## Chapter Thirty-Four

Hauptmanns jolted both men from their thoughts and silence when he said, "Ok Gentlemen, we are here. I must go and change and will meet you in the bar shortly. Do you mind if a couple of my men join us? They are eager to hear stories of real crime fighting police," Hauptmanns chuckled. "I'm not too sure if we can tell them anything too exciting. I would think your stories of dashing around the world with the most recognized man on the planet are more exciting than ours," Henderson said. "Oh, I'm not too sure about that," Richards interjected, "we could tell them about the time you emptied two clips on a pickup truck that was 40 feet away and didn't land one shot on it!" Richards laughed. "That's not fair," Henderson shot back, "I had sand in my eyes and it was pitch black out." "Ok," Richards said sarcastically, "that's the official story, so we will go with that!" The three men got out of the black SUV, all now in jovial spirits, bantering back and forth as they made their way into the lobby of the hotel. Hauptmanns headed for the elevator as Richards and Henderson made their way to the tiny bar to round up a couple of tables for their new international friends.

The room was empty, so Richards and Henderson commandeered three tables at the far end of the long, but tiny bar, close to the single dart board and pool table that took up the far end of the room. As the two men were about to sit, Hauptmanns and four of his men came through the entrance, all in high spirits, and now dressed in their more casual blue paramilitary uniforms. Once all of the men were seated around the tables, the middle aged barman came over to take their drink orders. Hauptmanns was the first to speak and ordered pitchers of beer and baskets of chicken wings for the tables. He gave the barman his room number and showed his pass key, telling him that the bill was to go on his room account. This put the men in higher spirits with many thanks and pats on the back for his generosity. Once the beer and wings arrived at the tables, the men dug in eagerly. The conversation became very animated, with laughter that could be heard out in the lobby of the hotel. When the pitchers of beer had been drained, Hauptmanns waved at the barman for more beer. With this, his men beamed with delight, all knowing this would be a night of relaxation and fun.

It was nearing 11:00 pm. Hauptmanns and Henderson were the only two left seated at the tables. The other men had taken Richards to the dartboard and were showing him the finer art of knife throwing, using the dartboard as their target. Richards was getting the hang of it, being able to hit the dartboard nine out of ten times, but his accuracy was not quite that of the Swiss Guards. Even with a couple of drinks in them, all the men had deadly accuracy, each taking turns showing off and hitting the bulls eye multiple times. When the barman returned again to the table, both Henderson and Hauptmanns ordered water for themselves and more beer for the men at the dartboard. Hauptmanns looked over to Henderson, who, although watching the antics at the dartboard, appeared to be deep in thought over other matters. "What seems to be troubling you, Owen?" Hauptmanns asked. "This case," Henderson responded, without really looking at the man. "But things have worked out ok, have they not?" Hauptmanns said. Turning now to face his new friend, Henderson said, "Oh yes, it worked out well that our assumptions about the Pope were wrong. I'm very thankful for that. I'm just trying to make sense of the whole case," Henderson said. "With the Pope being safe, we will now be pulled off the case because it does not appear to be anything to do with organized crime, which is our specialty." "I see," said Hauptmanns, "but you do not feel this way? Or you do not like to leave loose ends?" "Both actually,"

Henderson responded, "the two victims were both big names in organized crime and you just don't go chopping off the head of a dragon like that. Ten more will now try to pop up. What's puzzling is that there seems to be no other links to organized crime, other than the two dead men. I feel as if I'm missing something, and yes, you are right, I don't like to walk away from a case that is still open and active. I don't like the loose ends."

The room had taken on an eerie silence and both Henderson and Hauptmanns looked over to the men at the dartboard. They saw that all of the men, including Richards, were staring in their direction, but up over their heads. Swivelling in their chairs to see what had caused the hush and stares, Henderson and Hauptmanns saw the television screen the men had been looking at. The sound was muted, but the scroll across the bottom of the screen spoke it all, "An unidentified man shot and killed an elderly male early this evening at St. Joseph's," it said. Getting the barman's attention, Henderson asked if he could turn the volume up on the television. The sound slowly rose and filled the tiny room. The announcer was recapping the breaking news. In a sombre, yet authoritative voice, the announcer said, "Earlier this evening, a lone gunman entered the chapel at St. Joseph's, the rest home and religious centre on the east side of town, run by the Catholic Church. He shot and killed an elderly male in the tiny chapel. Police have released few details, other than a partial description of the suspected killer. He is described as having short dark hair, standing between 5' 6" and 6' 3" tall with a slight build, non-Caucasian with tanned skinned. The victim's name has not been released pending notification of next of kin. Sources close to the scene have said that it was an elderly priest who was performing Friday evening mass for residents of St. Joseph's. We will follow up with this story as more details are released. Henderson looked at Hauptmanns and asked, "Do you know this St. Joseph's place?" "Yes, I do," Hauptmanns said, "it was an old monastery for many years. It has, in the last 15 years or so, been converted into more of a rest home for aged and retired clergy and nuns. As well," Hauptmanns continued, looking somewhat embarrassed, "it is a treatment centre for," he hesitated, "for clergy who have done things that I do not wish to think of." "I think I understand what you are trying to say," Henderson said.

"Do you think this is connected? That this is your man?" Hauptmanns asked. All of the men had returned to the tables, their moods now turning sour. Henderson scanned all of the faces before he answered, "I am almost positive it is our man. How it all ties together, I do not understand." Looking at Hauptmanns, Henderson asked, "Do you know who the priest would have been who was killed?" "No, I am sorry, Owen. There are many retired priests there, as well as others seeking treatment," Hauptmanns said. Richards spoke up and said, "I still don't think this will tie the guy to our division, Owen, and I doubt the Chief will think so either." "Yea, I don't see a link either," Henderson responded. "I still want to talk to Father Ziggy though, just to see if there was any link to all three murders. I can pass any information he may have on to the locals, if he can help at all." "Who is this Father Ziggy?" Hauptmanns asked. "Oh, Father Ziggy was the priest at the church that Owen and I attended as teenagers," Richards said. "I don't think he would like to be called that anymore. He is now Cardinal Zigmond Heinz." "Yes, I know Cardinal Heinz," Hauptmanns said. "He is the

Cardinal for the parish that your brother's church belongs to. I have met him a couple of times in Rome. How do you feel he can assist you?" "Well, the two mob guys who were killed, used to attend that very church when we were kids," Henderson said. "Father, sorry, Cardinal Heinz, was the priest there, and both Tyson and I

remember those two at church on occasion. Ty even recalled the Cardinal and Louis DeDominicus having a conversation one Sunday after Mass." Seeing the confused look on Hauptmanns' face, Richards added, "DeDominicus was the mob boss. He was the second one killed."

"Yes, I understand now," Hauptmanns said, "so you want to know if Cardinal Heinz can tell you how these three men could be linked together?" "Even if they are linked together," Henderson said. "It's a far stretch that a retired priest living in an old age home could be linked to two Canadian mobsters. This is starting to sound more and more like a nut job who has gone on a killing spree. He could very well have been associated with one of the two killed, knew of this book he stole, and what was in it. If it is this 'Rose', or 'The Rose', that Professor Brown spoke of, maybe he is on some sort of religious revenge thing. However, like Tyson and our Chief said, it is not the type of crime our unit works on. I will see the Cardinal when we get home tomorrow, if he is available, more just to ease my mind I guess," Henderson said, the last part almost as if to himself. "Well it can't hurt to have a chat with him," Richards said. "Maybe he can give a link to the last killing, or maybe he can offer information that would point to the killer. He knows a ton of people." "Yea, that's true," Henderson said. The conversation had slowed to a standstill and one of Hauptmanns men stood. He extended his hand to Henderson, and in accented English, said, "Thank you for a good evening. I wish you the best in your investigation, Detective Henderson." All of the men started to stand as if on cue. Handshakes and well wishes were extended around the table. Richards, Henderson, and Hauptmanns were the last to leave the bar, taking the elevator together. As Richards and Henderson were getting off at their floor, Henderson said to Hauptmanns, "Thank you for the drinks and company, Pedro. Give us a call when you get in to town tomorrow. If you have time, I would like to return the hospitality." Shaking Henderson's hand, Hauptmanns said, "I will. I would like that very much." Wishing the man safe travels tomorrow,

Richards and Henderson returned to their room.

## Chapter Thirty-Five

As with their flight to the Capital city, the return flight was quick and uneventful.  The two men quickly de-planed and were in Richards' car within minutes.  Traffic on a Saturday morning heading out of Toronto was light and they were making good time getting back to their offices.  It was a good 20 minutes before either of them spoke.  It was Henderson who spoke first, "I think that was the oddest and quickest case that I have ever worked," he said to his partner.  "I was thinking the same thing," Richards responded.  "Are you still going to talk to Cardinal Heinz?" he asked.  "I think so.  I can't see how it will hurt any.  It might actually answer some of those nagging questions that we both have.  Plus, it may be able to help the locals in their investigations on tracking the guy down, or building a motive for the killings, besides that damn book," Henderson said.  "For the life of me, I can't see how two mob guys and an old priest are tied together, and why anyone would want to kill an old priest," Richards said.  "Yea, that one has really put a twist in it," Henderson said.  "The only conclusion I can draw is that this 'Brotherhood' that the professor talked about, maybe the old priest was a member of it, and our shooter knew that."  "Well, this is my take on the whole situation...I think our shooter is some religious fanatic who learned of this book somehow and found out where it was. He was going to use Vinny to get at Louie, but killed him for not being cooperative.  Then he went to Louie's, killed him, stole the book, and offed the priest because that is how he learned of the book."  "You know how to close up the loose ends!" Richards said.  "That would give a reason as to why he was in Ottawa.  The Pope being there was just coincidence."  "So you think that the Ottawa Police will be the ones to find the guy and solve it all?" Henderson asked.  "Yup, I think that is as solid a theory as you're going to get," Richards said confidently.  "I guess it makes sense," Henderson said, "but for some reason it still doesn't sit one hundred percent with me."  "You just don't like me to be right! You want to be the one who solves it!" Richards said jokingly.  "Yup, that's it exactly," Henderson said condescendingly.

The pair had drifted off to other topics of conversation by the time they pulled into the parking lot of their offices.  They were still sitting in the car talking, when Cyrsta Sunland saw them and tapped on their window.  Rolling down the window, Richards, in a drunken slur, said, "Sorry Ocifer, was I speeding?"  Shaking her head and smiling, Sunland said, "You're a dink, Richards.  Are you two going to sit out here all day?" Not losing a beat, Richards responded, "We were thinking of making this the new conference room. Do you have a problem with that?" Sunland shrugged, and said, "Nope!" She then opened the back door and climbed into the car with the other two. Looking at Richards, Sunland said, "Should I call the rest of the team and get them out here for this meeting? I'm not sure we will all fit!" Henderson looked at the two, and said, "You two are odd. How did you even make it onto the police force? Well, I'm going to my office to check messages and then I'm going to head home." "Are you going to see Cardinal Heinz?" Richards asked. Sunland piped in, "Who is Cardinal Heinz? He sounds important." "Cardinal Heinz, or as I like to call him, Father Ziggy, was our priest when we went to school. He has now become a Cardinal," Henderson said. Sticking her nose in further, as she was very known to do, Sunland asked, "So why are you going to see him?" "Aren't we just the nosy one?" Richards said. Laughing, Henderson said, "Vinny and Louie used to go to the same church as us when we were in school. Father Ziggy was the priest back then. I just wanted to have a chat with him to see if he could add anything to the investigation." "But are we not off the investigation?" Sunland asked. "Technically yes," Henderson said. "It's not technically," Richards said, a little too forcefully, "we all heard the Chief. If there were no incidents last night, then we are done, and it goes to the locals."

"Ok," Henderson said, "yes, we are off the case, however, we know Father Ziggy, and I just wanted to get what I could from him and pass any information he may have on to the locals." "Plus," Richards said, "something is nagging at the old guru here and he needs to see this through a little further. He doesn't like my theory so he needs to push a little further." "Oh this sounds like so much fun," Sunland said laughing. "Are you two lovers having a lovers' spat?" "Ha Ha," Henderson said, "Ty has a good theory, but I just want to ask a few questions. Who knows, maybe the Cardinal can shed some light." "Can I go with?" Sunland asked. Henderson looked to Richards, who just shrugged at him. Turning in his seat to look at Sunland, Henderson said, "I guess, but you have to behave. This guy is a Cardinal. I don't think he will put up with your smartass remarks." "I thought you said he was a 'Father Ziggy'. Any dude with a name like that has to have a sense of humour," Sunland said with a sly smile and twinkle in her eye. "I mean it Cyrsta, no shit or you can't go," Henderson said. Sticking out her bottom lip, and offering her best scorned look, Sunland said, "Yes Detective Henderson, I will be a good little girl."   All three broke up in laughter after the look and last comment.  As the three got out of the car, Henderson said, "I still have to see if he is in town and if he will see me.  I'm going up to my office.  I will call Richards' brother and find out.  Are you going to stick around or were you on your way out?"  "I was just going to grab something to eat.  I won't be too long.  Did either of you want anything?" Sunland asked as she strolled towards her own car.  "No thanks, I'm fine," Henderson replied.  "I'm good too.  Thanks for asking," added Richards.

The two men made their way to the upper part of the building, parting ways as they both went into their own offices.  As Henderson was rounding his desk, he noticed a stack of telephone call slips.  The top two were from Wyatt Richards.  Snatching the desk phone from its cradle, Henderson returned that call first.  It was answered on the second ring, and Father Wyatt Richards' smooth professional voice came over the earpiece.  "Wyatt, it's Owen," Henderson said, "I see you called me a couple of times."  "Owen, how are you doing?" came the response from Father Wyatt.  "I'm good.  Your brother and I just got back from Ottawa and I'm just catching up on my phone messages," Henderson said.  "So you know about Father Canelli's murder?" Father Wyatt asked. "Who is Father Canelli?" Henderson asked. "The priest who was shot and killed last night at St. Joseph's," Father Wyatt said. "Oh, sorry. I didn't know his name," Henderson said. "We are no longer on the case, so I had no specifics. The only thing I know about it is what I saw on the news last night. So do you know this Father Canelli? And how do you know his name? They never released it?" "Yes, I know him," Father Wyatt said. "He is, or rather was, a close friend of Cardinal Heinz. The police called the church last night because Cardinal Heinz is listed as next of kin," Father Wyatt said. "What? They are related?" Henderson asked. "No, not at all, but Father Canelli was like a father, or more like a mentor to the Cardinal. They have been close friends since the end of World War II," Father Wyatt said.

"How did the Cardinal take the news?" Henderson asked. "He doesn't know yet," Father Wyatt responded. "He is on his way back from the Vatican. He has been there for the last week. I expect him here sometime today." Henderson simply responded with, "Hmmmmm." "What do you mean by that?" Father Wyatt asked. "I'm not totally sure," Henderson said, "but Father Ziggy knew each of the people who were killed. He is a common associate of all three." Father Wyatt responded a bit tersely, saying, "Cardinal Heinz was not an associate of DeDominicus or DeLatrota," with great emphasis on the 'Cardinal', "they were members of the church. He knew of them. What are you insinuating, Owen?" "Easy Wyatt, I was not insinuating anything," Henderson said. "I was pointing out the simple fact that Cardinal Heinz knew all three of the murder victims. I was thinking more along the lines that he might have an idea of who the killer could be, or how all three are linked. I can't imagine that these are random. Somehow the three are linked. If I can find the link, then I have a better chance of finding the killer." "I thought you said you were off the case?" Father Wyatt asked. "I am," Henderson said bitterly, "I meant if I can pass on the link to the locals, then they will have a better chance. Do you know when Cardinal Heinz is due back?" "He may be back now," Father Wyatt said. "You called me at the church office. The manse has its own telephone line, and the entrance to it is off the side street, so he could be back now. He was expected today in preparation for the big Mass tomorrow." "Do you think he would have time to talk to me?" Henderson asked. "I'm sure he will make time, in light of all that has happened," Father Wyatt said. "You're going to inform him of his friends death?" Henderson asked. "Yes, I think it would be best coming from me," Father Wyatt said. "When you do, can you ask him if I can stop by for a few minutes? I won't take up much of his time. Call me back, or text me, and let me know what time would be good," Henderson said. "Sure, sure. I will speak with him and let you know. And remember, it's Cardinal Heinz now, ok?" Father Wyatt added. "Yes Wyatt. I remember," Henderson said.

## Chapter Thirty-Six

Marcus had ditched the car he stole to get himself out of Ottawa just ten minutes from the Toronto International Airport. He was now approaching the arrival doors for international flights in the Church's Lincoln Town car. It was an older model, but he still loved the feeling of driving it, the comfort of the ride, and the power under the hood. Not that he would be needing any power for getaways, or anything else for that matter. It was still a comforting feeling to him. He had debated all the way to Toronto what he would tell the Father about his encounter with the police at the motel in Ottawa. There had been no mention of it in any of the newspapers he had purchased, and nothing on the radio. Even the news of the old priest who was killed didn't indicate any links between the two events. He felt confident in his decision to keep that little mishap to himself. As he navigated the big car around the final bend in the long road to the arrivals, he could see Cardinal Heinz standing patiently at pillar J, just as he said he would be.

Marcus eased the car to the curb. He was about to get out and open the door for the Cardinal when the old man did it himself. "Relax Marcus," Cardinal Heinz said as he climbed into the car, "I don't have that much pomp and circumstance that you need to open the doors for me." "It is good to see you Father," Marcus said, looking at the old man in the rear view mirror. "Ah, it is good to see you too my son, and good to be back home," Cardinal Heinz said. "Everything went ok for you last night I see," he added. "Yes Father, just as you had said it would. I fulfilled the final part of the assignment and was out on the streets with no one even trying to stop me," Marcus said. "You have the book, Marcus?" Cardinal Heinz asked. "Oh yes, Father, sorry I did not give it to you first." Marcus hefted the large velvet encased book off the front seat and offered it to the Cardinal, with his apology. The Cardinal held the large book in his hands for a few moments, a small smile of satisfaction crept across his face. He untied the gold braided cord that enclosed the one end. A waft of dusty old book, ancient mould and mildew, escaped as he pulled the book from its protective satchel. He ran his hand across the cover, feeling the deep carved grooves of the intricate and detailed leather. He felt a small shiver of excitement run up and down his spine. "Finally, you have come home to me," the Cardinal whispered to himself. He slid the ancient book back into its velvety sleeve and very carefully, slowly, re-tied the braided cord as if he was showing a youngster how to tie their shoes for the first time. He sat the book on his lap, rested both hands on it, and gazed at the stark contrast of his aged and pale hands against the deep blue of this mystical book of secrets.

Pulling himself from deep thoughts, the Cardinal looked at Marcus in the mirror and asked, "Did anyone get a good look at you?" "No, Father. The descriptions in the newspapers were very general and could describe hundreds of men. Here, you can read for yourself," Marcus said, handing the Cardinal several newspapers. The Cardinal took the newspapers and started reading the front page stories of the murder of an elderly priest in Ottawa, as Marcus pulled the big car from the curb and entered the stream of traffic. "I see they have not yet released his name," the Cardinal said. "No, Father, even the radio news has not mentioned who he was," Marcus said. "So you had no problems then, nothing that will compromise you?" the Cardinal asked. "Looking up in the mirror to catch the Cardinal's eyes, Marcus said, "No, Father. I stayed at the motel as you instructed. I then monitored the compound for several hours, all with no incidents." The two men held eye contact for a few seconds until Marcus broke the gaze to look at the traffic in front of him. "Very good, Marcus. As I told you, this would be the easy part," the Cardinal said, going back to the stack of newspapers beside him.  Marcus looked back to the mirror and said, "Father," pausing for a second, he continued, "Father, this is the last assignment as you said, correct?"  Cardinal Heinz sighed heavily, "Yes, Marcus.  That was the conclusion to this whole mess.  You will never be called upon to do any of those evil things again.  Your work for God, for the Church, ended last night."  Marcus smiled and focused his attention back on the road.

"You are not going to leave me now, are you, Marcus?" the Cardinal asked.  "No, Father," Marcus almost shouted, "I wish to stay.  I still want to serve the Church, if you will allow it."  "Of course, Marcus.  I was hoping that you would stay on and help with the Church, and all the wonderful work you do with the gardens, and keeping the cemetery clear of vandals," the Cardinal said.  "Maybe we can even find some funds to fix up the garden cottage to make it a bit more comfortable for you."  "That is not necessary, Father, it is a sound building.  It's clean, free of wind and rain, and is more than any one man deserves," Marcus said humbly.  "I, and the Church, owe you a debt of gratitude for all the work you have done, Marcus.  If there are some things you need, to make it more comfortable, more liveable, more your permanent home, you only need to ask," Cardinal Heinz said. "No, Father, it is quite comfortable and it is I who owe you and the Church. If it was not for you, I would surely be in prison, or worse, dead by now," Marcus said. "Your debt has been paid, Marcus. You owe no one. You are a blessed child and one day you will meet our maker and have a seat at his grand supper table," the Cardinal said.

The two men sat in silence for the rest of the ride home. Marcus concentrated on driving and giving the Cardinal the smoothest ride home he could. Cardinal Heinz sat reading each story out of the five newspapers that Marcus had given him. Something in Marcus' gaze earlier had put a small knot of concern in the pit of the Cardinal's stomach. He re-read every article about the killing several times to be sure he had not missed anything, had not overlooked a detail in the description of the killer, that would point to Marcus. He had finished reading the last paper for the fourth time, when he felt the familiar bump in the road as Marcus steered the car around the sweeping drive that led up to the church's manse. The old stone house, that would usually be occupied by the current residing priest of the church, was built with the same large stones as the church. Father Wyatt, the current presiding priest of the church, preferred to live in a house that was left to him by his grandmother. This left the manse free for the Cardinal's residence. The house sat to the rear of the church and off to one side. It had a crop of evergreens that separated it from the big stone church on the one side, and a row of cedar hedges on the other. This gave the building a sense of being in the middle of a forest. The stone structure was humble, yet it held an old world charm to it. There were two stained glass windows on the front of the house, separated by a large oak door. The windows had a similar design to the ones on the front of the church. Two more tall narrow windows sided the front door. They too were of stained glass. The heavy oak door had a hand carved cross in the middle, that took up the majority of the door. To the back of the house, stood the old and meticulously kept cemetery. Marcus' small cottage, the original groundskeeper's house, sat at the far end of the cemetery. The one room house was also surrounded by ancient pines and built from the same stone. It had a high steeped roof and several small windows on either side.

Marcus eased the car up to the front door of the house, turning in his seat, he said to the Cardinal, "Do you need me to help open up the house, Father?" "No, Marcus. I will be fine, but after you park the car, can you come back and make us some lunch? I didn't get a chance to eat on the plane and I'm feeling famished," the Cardinal said. "Yes, Father. I will park the car and put my things in the cottage. I will be back up in 30 minutes to make some lunch. Will some soup and sandwiches be agreeable to you, Father?" Marcus asked. "That would be splendid," the Cardinal said, as he exited the car, grabbing his carry bag and the velvet encased book. Just as Marcus had held the book close to his chest when he left Louis DeDominicus' house, so too did the Cardinal as he entered the large front door of the manse.

The Cardinal entered the small foyer. Passing his coveted treasure from arm to arm, he struggled from his overcoat and hung it on one of the brass hooks to the left of the door, not once putting the book down. Opening the interior door, he stepped into his familiar dwellings and dropped his carry bag at the bottom of the aged wooden stairs that led up to the single bedroom. He carried on down the short hall. To the left, was a set of double doors that led into a large sitting room parlour combination that took up the one side of the house. Opposite those doors was a large single door, which led into his office and study. Opening the door to the study, he walked in with more of a bounce in his step, the stress of the last few years finally lifting from his shoulders. The study was a beautiful room, paneled in rich dark woods. One wall was covered with a floor to ceiling book shelf. His desk sat in front of the book shelf, with two old heavily used and luxuriously stuffed winged chairs facing the desk. The front wall of the room looked out to the front drive, the stained glass obscuring any view, but casting a beautifully coloured pattern on the polished hardwood floor. Sitting behind his desk, he placed the book in the centre, and breathed a great sigh of relief.

He was startled when his desk phone chimed its muted ring. He also heard the echo of the extension in the kitchen with its louder ring. He cleared his throat and picked up the phone, "Hello, this is Cardinal Heinz," he said. "Cardinal, you are back," Father Wyatt's voice came over the ear piece. "Yes, Wyatt, I just got in this very minute," the Cardinal said. Adding more cheer to his voice, he continued on, "How are things? Are we all prepared for the Pontiff's arrival tonight and the Mass for tomorrow? This is all very exciting for our little church, don't you think Wyatt?" "Yes, Sir. It is very exciting," Father Wyatt said, his voice not expressing much excitement at all. "You sound glum, or burdened with something, Son. What troubles you?" the Cardinal asked. "Well,

Sir, I'm afraid I have some terrible news," Father Wyatt said. "I wanted to speak to you in person, Sir, but unfortunately, I am tied up, and felt the news could not wait." "You have me worried, Wyatt. What is it?" the Cardinal asked. "Sir," Father Wyatt stumbled a bit, not knowing how to get the words out, "Sir, Father Canelli was murdered last night," he spat. The phone was silent for a long minute, "Sir, are you still there?" Father Wyatt asked. He heard a long haggard sigh come from the other end of the phone, "Yes, Wyatt. I am here," the Cardinal said. "Cardinal Heinz, I am so very sorry for your loss. I know what he meant to you and how close the two of you were." "Thank you, Wyatt," the Cardinal said with as much grief as he could muster in his voice. He continued on, "Do you have any details, Wyatt?" "I do," said Father Wyatt, "however, Owen Henderson wanted to speak to you and I'm sure he can give you more information than I can." This news caused the Cardinal's heart to race, thinking to himself why on earth would he want to speak to me. His voice a little shaky, he said, "Why does Owen wish to speak with me?"

Mistaking Cardinal Heinz's shaky voice for grief, and not the fear that the man was feeling, Father Wyatt said, "It doesn't have to be now, Sir. I can have him wait. I understand what you must be feeling right now."  You have no idea, the Cardinal thought.  Father Wyatt continued on, "What I can tell you, is that they feel the same man who killed Vincent DeLatrota and Louis DeDominicus, may have been the man who killed Father Canelli.  Owen just wants to know if you may have any idea how the three would be connected, if they ever could be connected, and if you have any idea who the killer may be."  "Why would he think I know who the killer is?" the Cardinal said, with heavy concern in his voice.  "He doesn't actually think you may know the killer," he said, "he just wants to ask some questions about the three men to see if he can find a link.  You knew Father Canelli very well and for a long time, plus the other two had been members of the church years back.  You know what Owen is like, everything is a big puzzle to him," Father Wyatt said.  With a small chuckle, the Cardinal said, "Yes, I do remember that about him."  Feeling a little more at ease, Cardinal Heinz asked, "When did he want to meet?"  "Today, if possible," Father Wyatt said.  The Cardinal's nerves were settling even more as he thought it through further, "That will be fine, Wyatt.  Tell him around 2:00 pm, if he can make it.  He need not knock, I will be in the office all day, so he is welcome to come in."  "Thank you, Sir.  I will pass that on to Owen.  And Sir, I am very sorry for your loss," Father Wyatt said. "Thank you, Wyatt. That means a great deal to me." "Goodbye then." "Goodbye Cardinal." Both men hung up their phones.

Cardinal Heinz sat staring at his trembling hands for a few seconds. He then placed them on top of the blue velvet that encased the book. He felt an inner peace come over him, thinking to himself there is no way Henderson can connect those dots. No, Marcus was never seen, and really, no one knows who he is. He felt confident that he could answer any questions and would be able to steer the inquires away from him and Marcus. It made sense that since he knew all three, Owen would want to question him. Yes, it was unnerving, but nothing to get alarmed about. All the loose ends were now closed and Henderson's question period would amount to nothing. Feeling more satisfied, Cardinal Heinz removed the old book from its protective coverings, and placed it in front of himself, gazing at it as a child would look at a favoured Christmas gift just as it was unwrapped.

## Chapter Thirty-Seven

Henderson received a text from Father Wyatt shortly after 1:00 pm telling him that he could go and visit Cardinal Heinz at 2:00 pm that very same day.  He found Cyrsta Sunland working in her office and the two set off for Cathedral Basilica of Christ the King at 1:40 pm, leaving them plenty of time to make the short trip.  Sunland, being her perky, chipper self, had babbled non-stop for most of the ride.  Henderson paid little attention to her as he was deep in his own thoughts.  He offered the occasional grunt, or 'you wouldn't say', at the appropriate times.  When they pulled into the long drive that would take them to the Church's manse, Sunland said, "So what do you think?"  "Think of what?" Henderson responded.  "Of what I just said," Sunland scoffed.  "Have you not heard a word I said to you this entire time?"  "Well, umm," Henderson stumbled, "well, sort of," he paused, "no I guess I haven't.  Sorry.  I was lost in thought.  Did you want to start again?"  She just stared at him, with eyes that could melt glass, "Oh just forget it," Sunland said in a gruff, folding her arms over her chest.  She just sat stone faced looking through the windshield.  "Look, I'm sorry," Henderson offered, "this case has me baffled and I was just deep in thought over it.  I didn't mean to ignore you. Once we leave, we can go grab a beer and you will have my full attention." "You promise?" Sunland sulked. "Promise," Henderson responded, "now let's go play detective and see if the great Cardinal Heinz can shed any light on all of this." "I prefer Father Ziggy," Sunland giggled, "Cardinal just sounds too stuffy." "Me too," Henderson chuckled.

Henderson parked the car at the front of the Cardinal's house and the pair walked to the front door. Henderson reached for the door knob and Sunland put her hand over his. Looking at him, she said, "Don't you think we should knock?" Henderson smiled at her, "It's ok, Sis, he is expecting us. My instructions were to let myself in and go to his office." Sunland released his hand, looking a little sheepish, she said, "Sorry. I thought maybe you were still in your deep thought dreamland." "No worries," Henderson responded. He opened the door and the pair stepped into the foyer. The door to the main house was slightly ajar. "See," Henderson said, "we are expected." As soon as Henderson approached the familiar office door, many memories from his school days came flooding back to him. He had often been summoned to Father Ziggy's office, as had many of the other kids in his school.

Sometimes it was a lecture on why your religion paper was graded so poorly, and other times it was for some sort of scolding for some stupid thing you had done at school. Henderson grappled to find one memory, in any of the years, when he had been asked to Father Ziggy's office for something good. Nothing came quickly to mind. Knowing the protocol, he gave a solid double rap on the door and waited. The two stood staring at each other for a few moments, Sunland periodically sticking out her tongue, or making some other strange facial gesture, to get a rise from Henderson. He didn't take the bait and was about to knock again when the door opened. There stood Father Ziggy. A much older man than Henderson had remembered, but still the same man.

Extending his hand, Cardinal Heinz gushed, "Owen, it's so good to see you. It has been far too long." Henderson took the older man's hand in his and replied, "It is good to see you to Cardinal Heinz." Moving his gaze to Cyrsta Sunland, Cardinal Heinz continued, "Who do we have here?" Sunland extended her hand and Cardinal Heinz grasped it in both of his, a small smile crossing his face. "This is Detective Cyrsta Sunland," Henderson said. "Pleased to meet you, Cardinal Heinz," Sunland said. "The pleasure is all mine,

Detective Sunland, or may I call you Cyrsta? What a lovely name that is," the Cardinal said. "Please, yes, call me Cyrsta. It is Guyanese," Sunland added. "Oh how lovely. Won't you both please come in. Have a seat," the Cardinal motioned into his office. Following the two in, the Cardinal rounded his desk and asked them to sit. "Would you care for something to drink?" he offered. "I'm fine," Henderson said, as he sat in one of the wing backed chairs. "Tea would be nice, if it's no trouble," Sunland responded. "Of course it's no trouble. I could use a bit of tea myself," Cardinal Heinz said. He picked up his desk phone and pressed a button on it. After a short pause, he said, "I have some guests. Would you be so kind as to make us some tea and bring it to the study?" He hung up the phone and studied the pair in front of him. His expression turned more serious and he focused his attention on Henderson, "So Owen, is it true that it was Father Canelli who was shot and killed last night at St. Joseph's?" "Yes Sir, I am afraid it is true," Henderson said. Cardinal Heinz lowered his gaze, resting his head in his hands for a short moment as if he was saying a small prayer. The Cardinal looked up from his small vigil. To Henderson's surprise, his eyes did not have the glassy look you might expect from one who had just lost someone in their life to a violent crime. There almost appeared to be a look of hope, maybe even joy.

"He was a very good man, such a waste," the Cardinal said, shaking his head. "I have known him for most of my adult life. It was he who first showed me my true calling. It was he who brought me to the Church, to God. What a shame. What a waste," the old man sighed heavily. "Well, I'm sure you have not come here to see an old man grieve his losses, Owen. What questions did you have, or how may I help you and the police?" Something had caught Henderson's eye. Something in the room felt familiar and he couldn't quite put his finger on it. He had been in this room many times as a student and wasn't sure if that was what was pinging in his head, or if it was something else. He shook the thought from his head and looked into the Cardinal's eyes. "Well, I don't know if you can help, Sir. This is a puzzling case. First we had two of Canada's most prominent crime bosses murdered, and then, from what we can put together, we had an old priest killed by the same man," Henderson said, "and oddly enough, the only connecting piece to the puzzle is you, Sir. You are the common denominator in all three murders." Henderson's voice was taking on a bit of an edge. He noticed it himself and was just as perplexed by it as the Cardinal appeared to be. "That sounds," the Cardinal said, pausing to find the right words, "well that almost sounds accusatory, Owen." Sunland also had a quizzical look on her face as she turned to face Henderson.

"What I am saying, Sir," Henderson continued, "is that you had acquaintances with all three murder victims. As investigators, we always look for the missing link, or the line that connects all the dots. You are that line, Sir. I am not accusing you of anything, I am merely pointing out the facts as I see them, and you cannot deny that you knew all three victims." Henderson now paused. As an excellent investigator and interrogator, he knew the human condition. You state facts and then you pause to see if the person you are speaking with will fill in any blanks, state facts, add to the discussions. Reporters do that all the time when they ask a question, or state a fact. They will pause for a long time, baiting the questioned to volunteer information, or to expand on their answer. Nine times out of ten, the questioned will start to fill in the silence with more information. The Cardinal was no different than anyone else. "Well," the Cardinal stammered, "it is true. I knew all of them, but I had nothing to do with any of it." Henderson studied the old man's face, his eyes, searching for clues as to what direction he should take now.  "Sir, please do not misunderstand me," Henderson said, his voice now becoming calmer, more soothing.  "As I said, I am not accusing you of being involved.  No, Cardinal Heinz, you misunderstand.  I am seeking information from you to see if you can add information.  If you knew all three victims, then maybe you also knew the killer, because he also knew, or knew of, the three men."  Henderson was still studying the man's face, his mannerisms, something was still pinging in the back of Henderson's mind and something about the Cardinal's behaviour was not calming that ping.  "Can you think of anyone else who would know the three men, any other way that all three could be connected?"  Henderson asked.  Now the Cardinal's eyes went from Henderson's gaze over to Sunland, who was still looking at Henderson.  When the Cardinal's eyes came back to Henderson, they seemed to be holding a different look, almost a look of superiority.

The Cardinal sat up a bit straighter in his chair, squared his shoulders some, and looked sternly at Henderson.  "Owen, I know many, many people, however, I know of no one who would associate with the criminal world that Vinny and Louis lived in."  The use of the first names of the two crime bosses turned

Henderson's ping up to full blast. First names indicated familiarity, indicated more than a passing acquaintance, or of past members of a church. First names indicated that Cardinal Heinz may have had more recent contact with the two men. Henderson slouched a bit in his chair, offering the Cardinal false security, indicating that he felt inferior to him, that he was the school boy in for a scorning. Sunland was still staring at Henderson. She almost appeared to be fascinated with how the conversation was going, and with the changes she saw in Henderson. "Please forgive me, Cardinal Heinz, I was not suggesting you associated with people in the criminal world," Henderson said. "I am grasping at loose ends, Sir. Please forgive me." "I should hope that you are not suggesting that, Owen," the Cardinal said sternly. "No Sir, that was not my intention at all," Henderson said, "I am here to seek help from you, as I have in the past, to help guide me in the right direction so I can find the killer and put that person behind bars. I'm sure you would like to see the person who killed your dear friend behind bars, wouldn't you Cardinal?" "Well of course I want to see this person behind bars, Owen," the Cardinal said. "It is preposterous to suggest otherwise, but I really don't see how I can be of any assistance to you." "As I previously said, I know you know of no one from the criminal world, other than Vinny and Louis," Henderson said.  "Well, that is just semantics, Owen," the Cardinal said tersely.  "I knew of them, and yes, they attended this church over the years."

"I remember a conversation that Tyson Richards and I had a few days ago," Henderson said.  "It has been sitting in the back of my mind.  I guess you could say it has been nagging at me.  It is, in fact, one of the reasons I came here to see you."  "And what would that be, Owen?" the Cardinal asked, with a tone of arrogance now in his voice.  "Tyson was telling me a story of when we were both in school.  It was our last year of high school," Henderson said.  "Ty came to you to discuss his grade on the final religion paper.  He told me that when he was talking with you, Louis DeDominicus barged into the conversation, and you dismissed Ty to speak to him."  "And your point, Owen?" the Cardinal said, clearly becoming agitated.  "My point, Sir," Henderson said with a condescending emphasis on the 'Sir', "is why would you dismiss a student of yours to speak with someone from the criminal world, as you put it?"  "Um, well, you see," the Cardinal said, clearly stumbling and frustrated, "well that was a long time ago.  How should I remember what the conversation was about?"  The Cardinal shuffled uncomfortably in his chair, and that is when Henderson finally made the connection to what he had seen earlier, what had caught his eye, and had given him that sense of seeing something familiar.  Perched on one of the book shelves behind the Cardinal, over his left shoulder, sat a very familiar looking deep blue velvet bag with a braided gold cord neatly tying the one end closed.  The shape of the object was unmistakable.  Henderson said, "Are you sure you can't remember?  Or is it that you just don't want to share that with me, Father Ziggy?"  The use of the boyhood name, the name that all of the students called the man then known as Father Heinz, caused the Cardinal's face to take on an amber tint, and his eyes to grow cold.  Sunland, still staring at the exchange, let her mouth drop open.  There was a light rap on the door, Cardinal Heinz said, "Yes, Marcus, come in."  Henderson immediately stiffened in his chair at the use of the name.

## Chapter Thirty-Eight

Henderson wasn't sure why the name caused his senses to go on high alert.  Was it the similarity to the name Mark Able, he wondered, the man he had been chasing, the man who shot at him?  The name and the very familiar deep blue cloth bag sitting behind the Cardinal could not be coincidental.  Henderson didn't believe in coincidence.  He believed in that nagging ping in his brain, his so called sixth sense, which was now sounding like an alarm bell, pounding on his forehead from the inside.  The man the Cardinal called Marcus, came in the door behind Henderson and Sunland.  His step was quiet and confident. Eying the Cardinal, Henderson noticed no expressions of alarm, no odd reactions or eye twitches.  The three, who were seated, were all silent as Marcus, Cardinal Heinz's house boy, or man servant, or secretary, brought in the tea that was requested.  As the man came around the left side of Henderson, carrying a wooden tray with an old tea pot, cups, and small containers of sugar and milk, Henderson's eyes immediately noticed the peculiar bulge in the man's sport coat, under his right arm.  He gripped the arms of his chair so intently, his knuckles began to turn white. Henderson followed the length of the man's arm down to the coffee coloured wrist and hand that was gripping the wooden tray. At first, he noticed nothing out of the ordinary, just a coffee coloured hand steadily gripping the side of the tray. Marcus leaned forward slightly and placed the tray on the edge of the Cardinal's desk. As his hand let go, Henderson continued to stare at it. The pinging in his head was so loud he felt everyone could hear it. He counted off the fingers, one, two, three. He counted again, one, two, three. Marcus nodded a curt nod to the Cardinal. As he straightened, he turned his head slightly to acknowledge the Cardinal's guests.

Henderson had brought his head up from observing the man's hand and was still counting, one, two, three, in his head. When he reached three for the third time, Henderson and Marcus' eyes locked. An eternal second passed before the recognition finally washed across the face of the coffee coloured man's face. Henderson saw the look of recognition. He then saw the look of panic that swelled in Mark Able's eyes. Sunland and the Cardinal, both reaching for tea cups, had not noticed the exchange of looks between the two men. Mark Able reacted first, plunging his left hand into his sport coat, reaching for what Henderson now assumed to be a gun in a shoulder holster under Able's right arm. In an instant, Henderson, using the coiled power in his legs and arms, sprung from the chair, not even attempting to go for his own weapon.  He was intent on stopping Able from pulling his gun.  The lack of noise, and the sudden moves by both men, startled the Cardinal and Sunland, causing the Cardinal to drop his tea cup and Sunland to freeze in mid-motion.  Henderson wrapped his arms around Able.  A loud grunt and rush of air escaped Able as Henderson's power and bulk slammed into him.  The two men crashed into the bookshelves behind, and to the right, of the Cardinal.  As the bodies were careening to the floor, Able's feet came up off the floor, one toe catching the edge of the serving tray, sending hot tea, cups and the likes, sailing through the air.

Both men crumpled to the floor.  Both of Henderson's arms were pinned behind Able, who had his left hand, his gun hand, pinned between the two men.  As Henderson struggled to free one or both of his arms from under the man, Able viciously punched, clawed, and hammered, at Henderson's head.  Able was struggling to free his left hand, which was now securely wrapped around his automatic weapon.   Henderson turned his head slightly, allowing Able to land a solid punch to his left eye.  This caused Henderson's vision in this eye to blur, then fade to black. Using his considerable strength, Henderson hefted his weight to the right, and managed to free his left arm. Trying to fend off another blow, or land a blow of his own, Henderson brought his arm up ready to strike. From his right, Henderson heard a shrill cry come from what he figured to be the Cardinal, "No! Leave him alone! Don't hurt him! Get off him!" Henderson ignored the screams and cries that sounded as if they came from an old woman and not the Cardinal. As Henderson's balled fist was about to come down and land a blow on Able, the Cardinal leaped on his back, pounding and screaming to leave Marcus alone. Sunland, who had been sitting slack jawed in awe of the few seconds that had just passed, leapt at the Cardinal, tugging and pulling at him to get him off Henderson. To her, he felt like a bag of old bones in a cloth bag. His strength at this moment, however, was uncanny, as he wrenched back on Henderson's outstretched arm. With Sunland yanking at the Cardinal, and the Cardinal tugging at Henderson's arm, it left Henderson more exposed to Able's blows than before. Able's fist slammed into Henderson's nose. Feeling a slight pop, and then the warm rush of blood, Henderson knew that his nose was now broken.

Henderson reeled back against the blow, sending the Cardinal and Sunland clattering into the Cardinal's desk chair.  With all of the weight finally off him, Able yanked his hand from his jacket, bringing with it his Glock automatic pistol.  Scampering to get away from the tangle of bodies on the floor, Able swung his gun hand back, aiming for the bridge of Henderson's broken nose.  Henderson saw the attack coming and narrowly turned his head in time to have the butt of the gun scrape down the side of his scalp.  Able got to one knee and was just standing when Henderson shot out his foot and caught the man on the side of his left knee.  There was an audible crack, and a scream from Able, as he again crumpled to the floor.  Falling on his back, with his left knee at an odd angle to his body, he brought up his weapon and was tracking for a target.  Sunland had gained the advantage over the old Cardinal and was pinning his arms to the ground.  His shrill cries were still calling out to stop all this and leave Marcus alone.  Able was steadying his gun on Sunland's back when Henderson dove on the man.   Holding Able's gun hand away and aiming it helplessly at the bookshelves, Henderson lashed with a number of powerful and quick blows to Able's head and face. It appeared Henderson now had the advantage, when Able snuck in a punch to

Henderson's nose, causing even more blood to gush from it. Stunned, Henderson lost his balance, and was thrown on his back by Able.

With his vision clearing slightly, Henderson saw the gun baring down on his face again. With both hands now free, Henderson was able to block the blow and land a punch that threw Able to the side. Henderson was quick to pounce on him and was struggling to gain control of Able's gun hand. He was surprised with the slight man's speed and strength as the two wrestled. Henderson slammed his knee into Able's shattered knee, causing him to scream in pain, which relaxed his left arm slightly. Henderson struggled to free the gun, but was only able to get the weapon pinned between the two men. Henderson was now on top again with only one free hand. Simultaneously, both men continued to try to land blows while fending off the other. Henderson had finally wrapped his much larger hand over Able's gun hand and was pushing the weapon into Able's stomach. With a look of terror, Able began to vigorously squirm, attempting to get free and get the upper hand. Able's free hand began to pound relentlessly on Henderson's head, most punches careening off and causing no damage. Able wildly bucked his hips in an attempt to throw Henderson off. Henderson heaved his trapped hand one more time. He looked Able square in the eyes, a small smile crossing his face, "Say your prayers, Asshole," Henderson said. A small muffled pop was heard and the room went silent.

Henderson let out a small moan, and from sheer exhaustion, slumped on the dead man. Sunland shot a look towards Henderson, "Owen, Owen, are you ok?" Sunland asked frantically. Henderson moaned another time and rolled off the dead man, "Yea," Henderson said, "my face and head hurt, but I will live." Feeling the struggle finally drain from the Cardinal, Sunland let out a long sigh. Releasing her grip from the old man, she pulled herself from the floor. Walking over to Henderson, who was laying on his back pinching the bridge of his nose, Sunland looked down at the big man and said, "Gawd, your face looks like shit. Well, more like shit than it usually does," she added with a giggle. Henderson extended his hand, "Help me up, please," he said. When he stood, the entire front of his shirt was covered in blood. His own blood, mixed with the blood from Able, whose body lay lifeless, eyes blankly staring at the bookcase. Henderson reached both of his hands to his face and firmly placed his off kilter nose between his two thumbs. There was a faint pop, when with a small twist of his hands, the broken bone found its natural place.  Another small trickle of blood ran down his face.  Sunland looked at him and said, "Ewwww!  Did you have to do that?"

The Cardinal slowly crawled over to the lifeless body.  His sobs were loud, as if he was crying for a lost child.  He cradled the dead man's head in his lap.  Through his sobs, the Cardinal said, "Oh dear God, please bless this child, please accept this child at your table tonight."  He gently placed the dead man's head on the floor and struggled to his feet.  He stood shakily, staring down at the lifeless man.  Swatting at the tears that rolled down his cheeks, the old man hobbled over to his desk.  Henderson walked over to the man's side.  Steadying him with one hand, Henderson righted the overturned desk chair.  The old man poured himself into the chair and sat hunched, sobbing into his hands.  Henderson just stood there, staring at the man he at one time had great respect for.  Now he was unsure of the feelings he had.  He turned and took a long look at the dark blue velvet bag with the intricate crest stitched into it, and the gold braided cord keeping it closed.  "Is this what it was all about?" Henderson asked, still looking at the object on the shelf.
Henderson's voice was now growing in volume and anger.  "All of this was over some old

fucking book?  You send out your own personal hit man, death squad, for a fucking religious artifact?"  He reached for the bag, hefting it in both hands.  Turning, he let the book drop from his hands onto the desk in front of the Cardinal.  It made a loud thud, the sound only slightly muffled by the thickness and cushioning of the velvet bag.

## Chapter Thirty-Nine

The Cardinal slowly raised his head from his hands.  The sound didn't startle him.  It was as if he had not heard it.  His face had aged and sagged noticeably.  His eyes, sunken and milky, were rimmed in red and stared blankly at Henderson.  He wiped at his eyes with the back of his hand, blinking as if coming from a deep sleep.  "Why did you kill poor Marcus?" the Cardinal croaked, his voice raspy, like that of a long time smoker.  Henderson didn't respond to the question, he just glared at the old man.  Henderson sighed, shook his head, and rounded the desk.  He slumped in the chair he had occupied just moments earlier, before the chaos, before he had put all the pieces together.  "I asked you, did you have those people killed just because of this book?" Henderson said.  This time it seemed that the Cardinal did hear what Henderson said.  "It's not just a book," the Cardinal mumbled.  "You disgust me," Henderson said, "you are no better than DeDominicus was.  Just a thug, a common criminal, only you tried to keep your hands clean by using him," Henderson said, pointing to the dead man.  "What is so important in that damn book that you killed people over it, killed your own dear friend?"

The room was eerily quiet, so quiet you could hear the three breathe.  Sunland broke the silence by asking, "Do you want me to call this in, get forensics over here?"  Henderson sat slumped over, pondering his hands; hands that he noticed were steady, even with all the adrenaline flowing in him.  "No, not just yet," Henderson responded, "I want some answers first."  Sitting up a bit straighter, Henderson looked at the old man sitting across from him.  "I want some answers from you.  I want to know what is so important in this book that you killed at least three people for it.  No, correction, four, including your butler there lying on the floor."  "I didn't kill Marcus," the Cardinal spat, "you did that.  You killed poor Marcus."  The old man began to sob again.  "Just stop with the grieving act, Ziggy," Henderson said.  The use of the name made the old man glare at Henderson, who just continued to stare back.  "You wouldn't understand it, Owen," the Cardinal said, "you lost your faith in the Church a long time ago so you would not understand the damage this can do to us."  Stroking the velvet bag that encased the book, he continued on, "What is written in here can further damage the Church.  With all the scandals, the infighting, and today's society, the Church would crumble."

"Why don't you enlighten us then, Ziggy," Henderson taunted. "Stop calling me that," the Cardinal bellowed, "my position in the Church demands more respect than that. You of all people should understand that, Owen." "When you killed four people for a book, you lost that respect. You are nothing but a killer, and I will treat you as such," Henderson snapped back. "I killed no one. You have no proof, and you have no way of proving anything. You killed the person responsible for the murders right here in my office. Your partner can even verify that." "No Ziggy, you killed all of them. You may not have pulled the trigger, but it is pretty clear you are the one responsible for it. I don't see any jury in this country that would see it any other way. Do you Cyrsta?" Henderson asked, looking over to Sunland. She shook her head and said, "Nope, looks pretty cut and dry to me. This guy," pointing to the Cardinal, "ordered his butler, or whatever he is, to kill people to get that book that is sitting in front of him. Once forensics gets their hands on the book, they will probably find prints from all the dead men, and the Cardinal there, all over it." "No," the Cardinal shouted, "you can't let the book get into the public's hands. It must be returned to the Church. It is not for public consumption. I will not allow it. It is property of the Church. I hold high ranking and great authority in the Church and I will not allow it."

Henderson spoke up, with strength and authority, and said, "I don't think you understand, Ziggy. You are going to be placed under arrest for three murders and probably numerous other charges. Once that happens, you will surely be stripped of any authority you hold in the Church, most probably, totally defrocked and excommunicated from the Church. They will not want to get their hands dirty in this sordid affair. Then you will be tried, found guilty, and sentenced to spend the rest of your sad, pathetic life in prison. That is exactly how it will go. The book will get turned over to us as evidence, and who knows what information in it will come out. And frankly, I don't give a shit what is in the book, or who sees it. The 'Rose' is nothing more than a bunch of fiction and entries of old rich people trying to buy their way into heaven." With the use of the book's moniker, the Cardinal shot Henderson a look. "Oh yes, Ziggy, I know all about the 'Rose'," Henderson said. "There is a very knowledgeable Professor in England who gave me the entire history on it, how it was first used, how the Brotherhood finally ended up taking control of it, and how most had thought it just a fable. I guess now we all know it is a real thing. I'm sure the Professor will get great delight in having the opportunity to browse through its pages.  Maybe he will even write a book about it, you know, one of those scathing exposés."

The Cardinal looked to Henderson; his face appeared to have sunk even further.  His skin had a pale ashy look.  The bags under his eyes seemed to droop even further.  "You don't understand," he almost whispered.  Henderson, near total exasperation, the adrenaline from the last few minutes starting to ebb some, just glared at the old man.  He then cleared his throat, shook his head slightly, pulling as much compassion as he could into his voice, he said, "Cardinal Heinz, you keep saying I won't understand, why don't you explain it to me so I can understand."  Almost as if in a trance, the Cardinal began in a slow monotone, not really looking at Henderson, more looking through him, "They stole the book years ago."  "Who?" interjected Henderson.  "Vinny and Louie," the Cardinal said, still trance like.  "It was years ago.  At first, nobody knew how it disappeared, or where it went.  It was shortly after the war, lots of things changed then, lots of things went missing.  But it was them who stole it, right from under his nose."  Henderson opened his mouth as if to ask from under whose nose, but the Cardinal kept speaking.  "Right from under

Father Canelli's nose. He didn't even notice it was missing for months. By then I was back here in Canada studying at the seminary. He didn't even tell me it was missing for years after that. I think he was embarrassed that it had been taken from him. But none of that really matters, they were the ones who took it, we found that out soon enough. They did not hide the fact they had it, no, they waved it right at us, taunting us."

"I remember the day very clearly. It was a Wednesday. Father Canelli was here visiting me, and both Vinny and Louie showed up at the door, both very pompous. They had the nerve to bring the book with them. At first, both Father Canelli and I thought they had somehow come across it and were here to return it to its rightful place. That joy was short lived. Louie made it very clear that he knew what was in the book, what it meant to the Church, to me," he finished in an almost whisper. Both Henderson and Sunland just looked at the old man who appeared to be fading and aging in front of them. The Cardinal sighed and continued on, "At first, their demands were petty. Do a few favours for them, simple tasks they said, and the book would be returned. The first thing they asked was for Father Canelli to take some papers back to Rome with him, a passport and other identification. It seemed simple enough; take the documents to an address in Rome. When the Father got to the address, he found that the passport and identification were for a man who was wanted for 15 murders all across Europe. The passport looked like an original Canadian passport with this killer's face on it. This went on for a number of years, either taking documents or passports to Rome, or bringing them to Canada."

"We tried to stand up to them, but they always had the book and threatened to send it to one of the gossip papers, or worse, '60 Minutes'." The Cardinal slumped in his chair a bit further. He folded his hands in his lap. At first Henderson thought he was finished speaking, but then in a whimpering voice, he said, "Then they started demanding money. They would give me fake invoices to submit for repairs to the church, or for supplies that were never received. When I became a Cardinal, they had people in Rome lobby and bully others to get me on certain committees, ones that oversaw larger amounts of money, money that they extorted. By this time, the Brotherhood was frantic and sharply divided. Some said to just go along with it. Others wanted to just end it, let them reveal the book, and let the chips fall where they may. I protested heavily. I asked the Brotherhood to give me time and I would get the book back. I told them the Church would not be able to withstand another attack and that I would come up with a plan to bring the book home. That is when Marcus came into the picture, oh the poor child." The Cardinal began sobbing again. He recovered, blowing his nose into the hanky he pulled from his pocket, "He really was a good boy. He just wanted to serve the Church."

"He came to me after getting into a fight with some local hooligans. He was scared and had no family here. He was small for his age at the time, nineteen years old and he looked to be twelve. This local group of thugs started to pick on him, pester him, and wanted to rob him. He was on his way to his dorm after a game of baseball. He was a student from Spain, studying at McMaster, and was alone in this country. When they wouldn't leave him alone, he swung the bat to keep them at bay. This just got the group angrier and they came at him. He swung again and hit the closest one in the head. It all happened just around the corner. There was so much blood coming from the boy he hit. It was all over the ground. Marcus thought he killed the boy. He came here to the church for protection, so I took the boy in. I listened to the talk around the streets. The police even stopped by and asked if I had heard anything. It was then that

I learned that the boy who was hit was ok. He only suffered a minor concussion and was released from the hospital the next day. I was in this very room explaining to Marcus that we had to go to the police. If we told them what really happened, we could get his name cleared and stop the situation from getting worse. That was when Vinny showed up. He wasted no time. He knew the police were looking for a young, darker skinned boy. He quickly put two and two together. Vinny pushed and prodded at Marcus until Marcus confessed. Oh the silly boy. I tried to tell him to keep quiet, but he was scared, and Vinny was a relentless bully.

Vinny got in touch with Louie and the pair of them started telling me that I was harbouring a fugitive. They said things wouldn't look good for a Priest with my past, to be harbouring fugitives." Henderson's brows knitted together. He looked at the Cardinal quizzically, "What past is that, Cardinal Heinz?" Henderson asked. It was like the Cardinal didn't hear the question; he just kept talking in his trance like monotone. "That is when they started to use Marcus for things, bad things, hurting people, setting fires, intimidation. They told him it was his penance for killing the kid in the street with the baseball bat. I tried so hard to tell Marcus that they were lying, but he wouldn't believe me. He kept talking about all the blood from the boy he hit, how the boy just fell limp to the street.  Then they had Marcus kill a man, and that changed everything.  Marcus was now a killer, one that I kept here at the church.  I was just as guilty as him.  Oh my.  What a waste.  What have I done?  I had to stop them," he mumbled, "I had to end this.  And then Pope Benedict stepped down, and there was a vote.  I got 17 votes in the first round.  Can you believe that?  I was actually considered in the first rounds of voting to become the next Pope.  I knew then that I had to get the 'Rose' back.  Get it back to save the Church."

The Cardinal went silent for a long minute, staring down at the book.  Speaking as if to himself, he said, "Surely if I was the one to return the book, it would put me in high standing.  Then, next time, more would vote for me.  Oh Dear Lord, what have I done?"  The Cardinal began sobbing again.  He looked first to Henderson, then to Sunland.  He gave her a warm smile, "Are you a believer in Christ, my dear?" he asked her.  "Umm, I guess, well at times," Sunland stammered.  "And you, Owen, do you still believe in our maker, or has your life hardened you, have you lost your way?"  Henderson just glared at the old man.  "Well, I believe in our Lord.  I believe that he will see that what I did, I did for the greater good of the Church. I did it in his name." The Cardinal leaned to his right, pulled open the desk drawer, and again looked to Sunland, then to Henderson. "I will eat at the Lord's table tonight," the Cardinal said. When he pulled his hand from the desk drawer, it contained a small calibre handgun. He placed it to his temple and pulled the trigger. Sunland gasped, and then said, "Oh shit!" Henderson leaned back in his chair, a look of astonishment on his face. The only word out of his mouth was "Fuck!"

## Chapter Forty

Sunland and Henderson both sat in silence for several moments.  Henderson had leaned forward, his elbows resting on his knees, his hands covering the lower half of his face.  He just stared blankly at the dead man in front of him.  Sunland had turned a bit in her chair and was studying Henderson.  Sunland broke the silence, "So, do you think I should call this in now?"  Henderson turned his head slowly towards her, gazing at her blankly, "What?" he said.  "I asked if you wanted me to call it in, now?" she repeated, punctuating the sentence with 'now'.  "Oh, yea, I guess we better call it in," Henderson said, straightening in his chair.  Sunland had pulled out her cell phone and was scrolling through the numbers.  She was about to hit the green button to make the call, when Henderson suddenly said, "No, wait, wait, don't call just yet!"  Sunland lowered the phone to her lap, "Why?" she asked.  "What more can we get out of them?  You do realize," Sunland said sarcastically, "that they are both dead?"  "Yes," Henderson said, "I do realize they are both dead.  I'm just thinking of the best way to handle this."  "I don't understand what you mean by 'handle this'," Sunland said.  "Sitting in front of us is a priest, and not a good priest, I may add, who has just saved the government a shit load of money by ending his own life.  We won't have to waste money on a trial, or his prison sentence."  "He did us all a favour," Sunland added.

"Yea, I get all that," Henderson said, "it's the rest of it that I'm thinking about."  "Rest of what?" Sunland snorted.  "The rest of the fall out that will happen," Henderson said.  "What fall out?" Sunland asked incredulously.  "Oh, I don't know," Henderson said, "maybe the fact that we had a high ranking Cardinal ordering hits on people.  Not to mention whatever is found in that damn book, for starters."  "That's not really our issue, is it?" Sunland asked.  "We are cops.  We prevent crime, or arrest people who commit crime.  We don't worry about the fall out of criminal's actions."  "Oh come on, Sunland," Henderson said, sounding annoyed with her succinct outlook of the events, "this is a bit bigger than just a murder and a priest turned bad.  This involves organized crime, international organized crime.  Not to mention what it may do to the entire Catholic Church."  "What?" Sunland scoffed.  "Since when did you become so religious that you are worried about the Catholic Church?"  Henderson shook his head, "It's not that," he said, "it's not that I have found religion, that's not it," Henderson sighed, "it's hard to explain," he said.  "Well you need to explain it to me!" Sunland said.  "As far as I can tell, this needs to be called in now.  What are you thinking, hiding the bodies?" she said with a nervous chuckle.  "No!  Don't be stupid," Henderson said, shooting her a look.   Henderson took in a long breath, relaxing a bit he said, "I guess I just feel a bit different about the Church since I met the Pope.  He is different than other Popes."  "So you are a Pope expert now?" Sunland said sarcastically.  Ignoring her comment, Henderson continued, "He just seems more human, more like a real man.  Just look at some of the things he has been saying in the press lately.  I," he paused, "I just think this scandal will chop him off at the knees before he gets a chance to make a difference."

Again the pair sat in silence, this time both looking into each other's eyes, searching them to find the answers.  With sincere compassion, and no sarcasm in her voice, Sunland said, "So, what do you want to do?"  "You don't have to go along with this," Henderson said.  "If you're not comfortable with this, we can say you were in the car."  "Comfortable with what?" Sunland asked hesitantly.  "With maybe altering some of the details of what went on," Henderson said.  "Let's just pretend for a moment that our buddy Marcus there was the mastermind behind all of what happened."  "Ok," Sunland said again, very hesitantly.  "If

Marcus burst in here," Henderson said, standing and walking towards the door, "burst in and caught us all off guard," Henderson paused, scanning the room and moving a bit closer to the desk. "So, he burst in, caught us off guard, and rushed over to the Cardinal." "I'm not buying this, Owen," Sunland said. "Yea," Henderson sighed, "me neither." Henderson scanned the room for a moment, looking at everything, yet looking at nothing. "No," Henderson said slowly, "he was here when we got here. We walked into the room and he was already here. He had his gun out, the small one, and was aiming it at the Cardinal when we walked in. He was yelling and screaming at him, we are not sure what it was he was saying. He saw us, and pulled the trigger, killing the Cardinal. I dove at him, and his pistol when flying. You went to secure the gun as I tackled him, and he pulled a second weapon. We fought, and I managed to get the gun pointed at him and pull the trigger. What do you think?" Henderson asked.

Sunland shrugged, "I guess it sounds plausible," she said. "You sure you want to run it this way? And how does the book play into it?" she asked. "Hmmm," Henderson murmured. "Are you ok with it playing out this way?" Henderson asked. Sunland studied Henderson for a long moment, "Do you think he can make a difference, change things?" she asked. "He's different, Cyrsta," Henderson said, "I feel he is going to make everyone stop and think. If we let this play out like it did, he won't get that chance. He is a different man." Sunland was still studying Henderson, looking deep into him, finally she said, "I trust you. I will call it in. You clean the Cardinal's prints off the other gun." Henderson took a step forward, placing a hand on Sunland's shoulder, he asked, "Are you ok with this?" "If you are, then I am, Big Brother," Sunland said, smiling up at him. Sunland picked up her phone and made the call as Henderson walked around the desk to where the Cardinal was slumped in his chair. He pulled a pair of latex gloves from his pocket and picked up the small hand gun that had fallen from the Cardinal's hand. Pulling some tissues from a box on the desk, he wiped the gun down. He walked over to the dead man on the floor. Crouching down, he stared at the man for a few seconds. Lifting the fingers that were still wrapped around the bigger gun, Henderson pulled the hand away. Working one finger into the trigger, Henderson closed his hand around the dead man's. As he was dabbing the dead man's fingers on other parts of the gun, he heard Sunland speaking to dispatch, she was asking for a full forensics team and coroner.

## Chapter Forty-One

It took slightly more than 30 minutes for a pair of local detectives and their forensics team to arrive.  They came without lights and sirens since any crimes that had been committed were long over.  Both Henderson and Sunland knew the two detectives, having worked cases together when there was a joint investigation between the OCU and Hamilton Police.  One detective paired with Henderson and the other with Sunland.  Since this needed to be treated like any other crime, they were taken into separate rooms to give their statements of what had transpired.  Once that was done, the two detectives asked Sunland and Henderson to wait in the other room while the pair compared notes.  As Sunland and Henderson were sitting, there was a small commotion that erupted at the front door. Henderson recognized Wyatt Richards' and Pedro Hauptmanns' voices.  He was about to get up from his chair and go to the front door, when both men appeared at the door. "Is it true? Cardinal Heinz has been murdered?" Father Wyatt asked.  Getting up from his chair now, Henderson let out a long heavy sigh, "Yes, Wyatt.  I'm sorry to tell you that the man we had been chasing murdered Cardinal Heinz tonight."  Hauptmanns placed a hand on Father Wyatt's shoulder, saying, "I am so sorry, Father." Father Wyatt was silent. He just looked at Henderson, as if reading the bigger man's eyes and face. He cleared his throat, and without taking his eyes off Henderson, said, "Was it quick? Did he suffer? What of this killer you were chasing, what happened to him?"

Sunland was the one to speak, "Henderson tackled the guy, but was not quick enough to stop him from shooting the Cardinal. Once he had him on the ground, the bastard pulled another gun. There was a pretty good struggle and I think one or two shots got off before Henderson got the weapon turned on the gunman, and, well," she paused, "Henderson was able to pull the trigger." Sunland and Hauptmanns were looking at the two men, neither seemed to have blinked during Sunland's summary. Father Wyatt asked, "So, he is dead too?" Henderson finally spoke, "Yes, he is dead as well." "Can I see Cardinal Heinz? Offer him a prayer?" requested Father Wyatt. "I'm not sure you can, or that you would want to," Henderson said, "It's not a pretty sight. The two men broke off their gaze when the pair of Hamilton detectives walked in. The older of the two detectives looked at Father Wyatt and asked, "Are you Father Wyatt, the Priest of the Church?" "I am," Father Wyatt said. Looking at Hauptmanns, the detective asked, "And who are you?"  Hauptmanns pulled out his identification and handed it to the detective.  I am Lieutenant Colonel Pedro Hauptmanns with the Swiss Guard.  The detective scanned the identification and then asked, "And why are you here?"  "We are the security for the Pontiff.  He is presiding over Mass tomorrow.  We, Father Wyatt and I, were in the church going over final preparations."  "Did you hear anything coming from here?  Gun shots maybe?" the detective asked, looking from Father Wyatt to Hauptmanns.  Both men shook their heads, and in almost perfect unison said, "No, we did not hear anything."  Father Wyatt continued on, "The Church is almost 300 metres away and both buildings are made of thick stone blocks.  Even if we had our ears against the wall of the Manse, we wouldn't have heard a thing."

"Well it doesn't really matter anyway," the detective said.  His partner cut in, and said, "We have two very reliable witnesses here who saw it all go down.  The coroner placed the TOD at around the same time as Detective Henderson said they arrived.  So it seems pretty cut and dry.  We were just hoping there was a third witness to confirm times."  "I'm sorry, Detective," Father Wyatt said, "we can be of no help, like I said, the walls are very thick. If it helps any, I did set up the appointment for Detective Henderson to see the Cardinal today." The detective asked, "What time was it set for?" "It was set for 2:00 pm," Father Wyatt responded. The younger detective looked to his partner and said, "Well Jim, sounds pretty straight forward to me. What do you think?" "Yea, I agree," said the detective named Jim. "The shooter matches the description of the guy everyone has been looking for, and once we compare his prints to the one they found on the car in Ottawa, I would say we both have our man, and the case is closed." The detective named Jim looked to Father Wyatt and said, "I know this may be tough, Father, but nobody knows who this guy is. Can you take a look at him and see if you recognize him? It's not a pretty scene, but it would help if you could." "I will go with you if you want, Wyatt" Henderson said. "Yea, that's fine," the detective named Jim said, "Detective Henderson can accompany you. Forensics is done in there. We are just getting ready to transport the bodies to the morgue." "Yes, I will take a look at the man," Father Wyatt said. "I'm sure I have seen worse. I would also like to see the Cardinal and say a prayer for him." The younger of the two detectives said, "It's not a pretty sight, Father, you sure you want to do that?" Father Wyatt looked at the younger detective and studied him for a moment. "Detective, have you ever gone to an abandoned warehouse to find a youth who you had been counselling on drug abuse only to find that they had overdosed and been laying dead for a week, in the middle of the summer, in a hot warehouse?" Father Wyatt asked. "Um, no, Father, I haven't," responded the detective. "I have, and that is not pretty. I'm sure I can handle what is in the next room," Father Wyatt said with authority.

The two Hamilton detectives, Henderson, and Father Wyatt, all walked across the hall and into the Cardinal's office. One of the detectives asked Father Wyatt if he recognized the man lying on the floor. Father Wyatt looked at the man on the floor and let out a small gasp. "Oh my goodness, that's Marcus! He looked after the property and was like a personal assistant to the Cardinal," he said, shaking his head. "Why would he kill the Cardinal? Why would he do this?" Father Wyatt asked, to no one in particular. The detective named Jim said, "We don't know. From what Detectives Henderson and Sunland have said, they think it was over some religious book. Maybe he went off the deep end, or got involved with some cult or something. Whatever the reasons, he most likely killed the priest in Ottawa as well." "I never spoke to him much," Father Wyatt said. "He kept mostly to himself and would make himself scarce when I came around." "Umm, do you think maybe they were, you know, maybe involved, and had a falling out?" said the younger detective, sounding embarrassed. Father Wyatt shot the younger detective a look that could melt ice, and with restraint, said, "Detective, contrary to your limited understanding, not all priests are homosexuals and pedophiles." "Well, I was just saying, you know, I have to ask the question," the detective said apologetically.

Father Wyatt stepped over the dead man, and walked over to where Cardinal Heinz was still slumped in his chair. Henderson looked at the two detectives, "Why don't we give the Father a minute alone," he said. "Yea, that's fine," the older detective said, "we are done in here." With that, the three men left Father Wyatt kneeling beside the Cardinal, his head bowed, saying a quiet prayer. The three men crossed the hall and joined Sunland and Hauptmanns, who had been quietly sitting in a set of chairs. The older detective looked to Henderson, and said, "Well, you are free to go. As I said, this looks pretty cut and dry. Your description of the incident matches up with what Sunland told us. The ballistics will confirm what bullets came from what guns, and both your weapons check out. So I think that sums it up." The older detective looked to his partner, and said, "Do you agree?" "Yea, I think we have spent more time here than we needed to," said the younger detective. Everyone in the room turned then as Father Wyatt entered the room. He looked tired and his face seemed to have paled some. "Are you ok, Father?" Hauptmanns asked him. "Yes, I am ok. This is all such a shock," Father Wyatt said. "I will speak to His Holiness and tell him tomorrow's Mass will be cancelled. I'm sure he would want that with all that has happened," Hauptmanns said. "That won't be necessary, Pedro," Father Wyatt said. "The Cardinal would want the Mass to take place. His Holiness has traveled many miles to speak to the faithful. Things should go on as planned." "As you wish, Father. I will speak to the Pontiff when I go back to the hotel and tell him what happened. He may wish to see you later," Hauptmanns said. "I am always available to speak to His Holiness," Father Wyatt said.

## Chapter Forty-Two

Father Wyatt, Sunland, Henderson, and Hauptmanns were all standing around Henderson's car, watching as the two detectives drove off and the technicians loaded the bodies in to the back of their black van.  None of them spoke; they just stood there observing the technicians work.  As soon as the driver had closed his door and started to drive away, Father Wyatt turned to Henderson and said, "So what of this book?  I didn't see any rare religious books in the Cardinal's office."  "We're not sure," Henderson said, "that Marcus fellow must have stashed it someplace.  Your brother and I saw it in Ottawa, so your guess is as good as mine."  "Do you think he had help, like an accomplice or something?" Father Wyatt asked.  "We don't think so," Sunland said, "all of the information on all the killings points to a lone gunman at the locations, and he was the only one here with the Cardinal when we showed up.  I agree with Henderson, I think he has stashed the book someplace and now that he is dead, it will be lost unless someone stumbles upon it."  "That is a shame," Father Wyatt said.  "All this killing over a book, or because of a book, and now we will never know what was in it, or what could have driven Marcus so mad that he would kill over it. "

Father Wyatt let out a long sigh, "Well, I need to get back to the Church.  I will have to start to make arrangements for the Cardinal's funeral and finish preparations for tomorrow," he said.  "Father Wyatt, I will contact the Vatican.  They have people who will take care of the funeral.  This is something that you do not have to worry about," Hauptmanns said.  "Of course, you are right, Pedro.  What was I thinking?" Father Wyatt wondered aloud.  "What of Marcus?  Who will take care of his funeral?"  "I wouldn't worry about that either, Father," Henderson said, "he is now the City of Hamilton's responsibility.  If you know of any next of kin, you can let them know.  If not, then just let it go."  "I guess you are right," Father Wyatt said, sounding almost a little defeated.

The three police officers watched as Father Wyatt walked the path towards the church.  Henderson turned to Sunland and said, "Can you give me and the Lieutenant Colonel a minute, Cyrsta?"  "Sure," she said.  "I will go and wait in the car."  As Sunland walked away, Hauptmanns said to Henderson, "What is it, my friend?"  "Walk with me a bit," Henderson said, leading them away from the Manse and Sunland.  The two men strolled through the cemetery, talking in quiet voices.  Every now and again, they would stop and take in their surroundings. Often it looked as if Hauptmanns was questioning Henderson, using his hands to talk, as well as his voice, as you sometimes see with Italian or other European people. It was 20 minutes before the two men wandered back to the car where Sunland was sitting, reading emails on her Blackberry. Hauptmanns extended his hand to Henderson. Taking the offered handshake, Henderson said, "So you will be in touch with me then?" "Yes," said Hauptmanns, "I am heading back to the hotel now. I will inform the Pontiff of all that has gone on here today and give you a call early this evening." Releasing Hauptmanns' hand, Henderson said, "Ok, I will wait for your call." Climbing into the car and starting it, Henderson looked to Sunland and said, "You ok?" She turned to look back at him, "Yes, I'm fine. I agree with you. This was the best way to handle it. It's done now, right?" Sunland said. "Yes, it's done," Henderson said, putting the car in gear, swinging it around the looped drive, and heading to the street.

## Chapter Forty-Three

Henderson received the telephone call at 7:30 pm that evening; he was asked if he could come to the Crowne Plaza Hotel in downtown Hamilton for 8:30 pm. Traffic from his house to the hotel was surprisingly light for a Saturday night, Henderson thought, as he made his way down Main Street. He figured the light rain and cooler temperatures that evening contributed to the lighter traffic. He arrived at the hotel at 8:25 pm and was not quite sure where he should park his car. As he eased his way in front of the main entrance, he saw Pedro Hauptmanns wave at him to stop the car under the portico. As he was getting out of the car, one of Hauptmanns' men came up to him, and said in his broken English, "It will being my pleasure to park car if you so wish." Smiling at the broken English, and the man's genuine attempt at being both polite and professional, Henderson said, "Thank you, that would be great." He reached over and hefted a small duffle from the passenger seat and stood back as the man drove his car away. Hauptmanns was now standing on the top step of the classy hotel. "Owen," Hauptmanns said extending his hand, "thank you so much for coming this evening." "No, thank you, Pedro, for arranging this, and making time for me," Henderson said, also extending his hand.

"Come, come inside before this damp weather seeps into your bones," Hauptmanns said, turning and leading Henderson to the big brass doors of the hotel.

Henderson had never been inside the Crowne Plaza. It was something that he and Tracy had talked about doing, coming to the hotel to celebrate a birthday or an anniversary, just another of the things they had wanted to do, and now he knew they wouldn't. This brought a pang to his chest and a moment of sorrow. Hauptmanns quickly picked up on the bigger man's change in stride and mood. "Is something wrong, my good friend?" Hauptmanns said. "Oh, no, I'm ok. Just had one of those thoughts float through my head," Henderson said. "This hotel brings you bad memories?" Hauptmanns asked. With a small chuckle, Henderson said, "No, there are no bad memories from this hotel. Actually, this is the first time I have ever stepped foot in here." Feeling very comfortable with Pedro Hauptmanns, Henderson continued on as they strode through the grand lobby, "My wife and I had always wanted to come here to celebrate something. You know, have a nice dinner, maybe go dancing, then retire to one of the plush rooms," "Ah yes, I understand, one of the many things that will never be," Hauptmanns said with compassion. "Yes, that is it exactly," Henderson said, "one of the many things that will never happen now." Hauptmanns punched the button for the elevator and the two men stood in silence, staring at their reflections in the polished brass doors of the hotel.

The doors opened and the two men stepped inside. The walls of the elevator where covered in large mirrors, making the small cubical look as if it went on forever and ever with multiple Henderson's and Hauptmanns'. Henderson looked into one of the mirrors and straightened the tie he had put on. Hauptmanns chuckled and said, "You did not have to dress so formal, Owen." "So I can take this damn thing off?" Henderson said, yanking at his tie. "Yes, like the Swiss Guard, when the Pontiff is not on display, he tends to dress more casually," Hauptmanns said. "He really is a Pope of the people, as I'm sure you will soon see." The doors opened as Henderson was cramming his tie into the pocket of his sport coat. They exited the elevator onto the top floor of the hotel. As with the hotel in Ottawa, there was a man standing at the elevators. This time he just gave a curt nod to the two men as they stepped out. Hauptmanns led Henderson down the hall to a set of double doors at the one end. A placard on the wall beside the doors announced this room as the 'Queen Elizabeth Suites'. Hauptmanns turned to Henderson, and said, "Please wait here for a moment, Owen. The Pontiff had another meeting this evening and I am not sure if he has concluded it yet." "Yes, of course, no problem," Henderson said, almost tripping over his words. Hauptmanns smiled at the bigger man and stepped into the room. Henderson, now standing in the hall by himself, was both perplexed and surprised at how he felt so nervous about this meeting. He had already spoken to, and shook hands with the Pope in Ottawa, however, for whatever reasons, he had nerves right now.

The door opened, startling Henderson, and bringing him back from his self evaluations. Hauptmanns stood at the open door. Extending his arm into the room, he said much too formally, "Please Detective Henderson, come in." Henderson smirked and raised an eyebrow as he passed Hauptmanns and entered the Queen Elizabeth Suites. Hauptmanns closed the door behind Henderson and said to him, "Please wait here, Detective. His Holiness will see you shortly. He is just finishing up a meeting." "Thank you, Lieutenant Colonel," Henderson said, feeling awkward with the sudden formality. He stood in the large foyer that looked to be bigger than any hotel room he had ever been in, wondering how big the suite was if this was just the foyer. He heard some muffled voices growing a bit louder. They were coming from behind the double doors that Hauptmanns had gone through. A moment later, the doors opened, and a man stood with his back to Henderson. The man was offering his respects and saying his goodbyes to whoever was in the room; The Pope, Henderson figured. The man in the doorway turned, facing Henderson, and the double doors were closed behind him. "Fancy meeting you here, Detective Henderson," Father Wyatt said. "I could say the same about you, Father Wyatt," Henderson said, extending his hand to his close friend.

As the two men shook hands, Father Wyatt said, "Remember when you came to the church to see me, and I told you that the Pope had read my paper?" "Yea, I remember that," Henderson said. "Well I'm not sure if I told you, but it had been mentioned that His Holiness wanted to have a private word with me about it," Father Wyatt said, beaming now. "Well, I have just spent the last hour discussing my paper, along with a number of other issues, and," the Father paused, "the incident that took place today. Henderson patted his friend on the shoulder, "I'm sorry about today." Quickly changing the subject back to something more positive, he continued, "How was the rest of your discussion, the part about your paper and the other stuff?"   As Father Wyatt was about to speak, the double doors opened again and Hauptmanns came through them.  "Sorry to interrupt you, Gentlemen," Hauptmanns said, "His Holiness would like to see you now, Detective."  Henderson turned to Father Wyatt, "We will catch up when all the excitement dies down," he said.  "Enjoy your visit," Father Wyatt said.  "Me, you, Tyson, and Pedro here, can all go for beer and chicken wings tomorrow night."  "Sounds good," Henderson said, hefting his duffle and following Hauptmanns through the double doors.  Father Wyatt watched as the two men walked down the short hall, looking at the bag Henderson was toting.  He wondered to himself what Owen would be bringing to the Pontiff.  Was that this book everyone was talking about?  He shook the thought from his head as he heard the double doors close.

## Chapter Forty-Four

Henderson was surprised when he walked into the room behind Hauptmanns to see the Pope standing there to greet them wearing an oversized Roots sweat shirt over his more usual smock.  With vigour and a confident stride, the Pope walked over to Henderson and took his outstretched hand in both of his, "Detective Henderson, it is so good to see you again, but I wish the circumstances were much different."  "Thank you for meeting me, Your Holiness, and I too wish it was under better circumstances," Henderson said.  "Please, let us dismiss with the formalities for now, if that would be ok with you?" the Pontiff asked.  "Please, I am a simple pastor Detective, Father is fine with me or Francis is you wish." He said with a chuckle. "May I call you Owen?"  "Of course," Henderson stumbled, "um, yes, please call me Owen."  "I would like Pedro to join us if that is ok, Owen?" the Pontiff said, sitting on an overstuffed chair and smiling up at Henderson.  "Sit, please, you are much too tall for me to look up at and talk to."  Henderson composed himself and sat in a chair to the left, and facing the Pope.  Hauptmanns took the chair on the right, and was also facing the Pope.  "Now, this is better," the Pope said, "I have been on my feet all day and I don't have those comfortable looking shoes that you wear, Owen." Henderson smiled, "I will get you a pair, Sir, just tell me your size." The small bit of humour relaxed the room and Henderson started to feel more himself.

"Pedro has filled me in on the details of the events of today, and what has been happening over the past week," the Pope said. "I find it so troubling that Cardinal Heinz was not only part of this, but it appears he was the one who orchestrated it from the beginning. This is truly shocking." "I have known Cardinal Heinz for many years," Henderson said, "he was the Priest of our church as we were growing up. He presided over my wedding, 21 years ago. No one is more shocked that I am, Sir." "Tell me, Owen, why did you lie to the police this afternoon? Why did you cover up what really happened?" the Pope asked. Henderson didn't answer directly; he sat studying the duffle lying between his feet. Henderson looked up at the Pope; he had a look of resignation on his face. "Sir," Henderson began, "11 months ago, I was involved in a very large drug case. It spanned from Mexico to here in Canada, probably the biggest drug case this country has ever seen. Nearing the end of the case, when we were preparing for trial, I began to get death threats. These threats were against me and my family." Henderson paused, as if organizing his thoughts. "I was so wrapped up in the case, and the notoriety that it would give me, how it could help my career, that I ignored the threats. I felt no one could harm the great Detective Owen Henderson. I thought only about me and what this case would mean to me." He hung his head, "I didn't think about my family."

Henderson sucked in a huge breath. "I lost my wife, and almost lost my daughter, because I was selfish, because I thought of me. I didn't stop to look at all of the people who were being affected. Because of my actions, no sorry, that's wrong, because of my inactions and arrogance, I caused the death of my wife, my best friend." Henderson cleared his throat and wiped the tears that had welled in his eyes with the back of his hand, "Sir, I wanted to do the right thing this time. I stopped and thought of the bigger picture and how this could, or would, affect other people. I thought of you. I thought of Father Wyatt. I took myself out of the equation and did what I thought would be best for everyone." "But Owen," the Pope said, "if others found out, you could lose your job; your career would be over for what you have done." The three men sat in silence. Henderson had his head hung low. The Pope and Hauptmanns were watching him. The room was silent and still. A small ping could be heard coming from the antique radiators that the room still had. Henderson lifted his head, he looked directly into the Pontiff's eyes, "Sir, my career is very small compared to the damage the truth and this book would cause," Henderson said. He unzipped the duffle at his feet, reached in, and pulled out the heavy book still encased in its heavy blue velvet bag. He stood, walked the few feet to the old man, and placed the book in his lap, "I think this belongs to you, Sir," Henderson said. Returning to his chair, he sat and faced the man who was staring down at the large book in his lap.

The Pontiff looked up from the book on his lap, so this is what has brought on all this death and deceit, he asked Henderson. As far as I can figure out, this is what it was all about, Henderson responded. There was one comment that Heinz did say. He made comment to getting 17 votes in the last ballet, so he had aspirations for your job as well. Ah, yes, the Pontiff said, nodding his head. I remember the first round, 11 of us divided the votes. Did you know about the "Rose", Henderson asked. The Pontiff did not answer right away, he left the question hanging in the air for a long minute. This is a very old institution, the Catholic Church that is, and there are many rumours, many stories and many conspiracies. To an outsider it sometimes looks as if we are hiding secrets, the Pontiff said. As well there are many different ideologies, and many different interpretations of the Bible. One cannot believe everything he hears and sometimes not even what he sees. To answer your question Owen, I had heard the rumours and I did read some of the writings of Bertrand DeCheviler. But I as many others dismissed the notion that something like this existed. What about this so called Brotherhood, Henderson asked. Now that one is more difficult, the Pontiff said. As I said there are many varying opinions within the Cardinals, often there will be groups of them that have similar views on matters. To think that a group would find extortion and murder acceptable is very hard for me to imagine Owen.

I thank you for turning over this book to the Church Owen, the Pontiff said. What will be done with it now, Henderson asked. I would think careful review and interpretation of the writings in it will be the first thing. I don't think we can hide from our past, over time the public will become aware of it and we will have to deal with the consequences, however, the consequences will be less difficult without the scandal today would have caused. Pedro and his men will follow up on any criminal activity that is found and deal with that in a lawful way. Are you sure you want to turn this over to the Church Owen, I will not stand in the way if this is needed for evidence in any criminal case. No, it should go back to Rome with you, that 's where I feel it belongs. The Vatican archives are the safest place until the Church is ready for the public to see it, Henderson said. Did you look in the book before you brought it here, the Pontiff asked? Henderson didn't answer, he just looked back at the Pontiff. The older man rose from his seat and placed the large book on a table to his side. He looked down at Henderson, placing his hand on the top of Henderson's head the Pontiff said a small prayer and then blessed Henderson. When he was finished Henderson looked up to the older man and said, Thank you Father. Henderson and Hauptmanns both rose from their chairs and Henderson extended his hand and said, I won't take up anymore of your time Sir. Thank you Owen for stopping by to see me, I hope that you will come to Mass tomorrow, the Pontiff said. Henderson just smiled and gave a short nod to the older man.

Hauptmanns escorted Henderson out of the sitting room, closing the double doors behind him leaving the Pope to himself. His Holiness is very grateful for you returning the book to the Church, as am I Owen , Hauptmanns said. I feel if it was found at the murder scene today it would have caused irreparable harm to His Holiness and the Church. This way when the time is right His Holiness can let scholars view it and the public will become aware of it without the scandal of assassinations and mob connections. I am curious Owen, I know the Pontiff asked you if you looked at the book, you did not answer him. Will you answer me if I ask the same question? Henderson gave his new friend a long look, Yes Pedro, I looked to see if there was an entry that would explain why Cardinal Heinz acted the way he did. And you are now satisfied, Hauptmanns asked? I wouldn't say I was satisfied, but now I do know how all the puzzle pieces fit, Henderson replied. The two men shook hands as the elevator doors opened, if you wish to come to the Mass tomorrow please call me and I will leave word with my men so you do not have to stand in the line up to enter the church, Hauptmanns said. As the elevator door started to close Henderson said, Thank you Pedro, I will be in touch. As Henderson was riding down in the silent elevator he thought back to one of the final entries in the "Rose", February 15, 1949 ~ Corporal Zigmund Heinz ~ Canadian Army...

## Chapter Forty-Five

### *February 14, 1949 D-Day + 1714 Days, Rome, Italy*

The young Corporal had been sitting alone at his table and was half way into his 5$^{th}$ pint of the strong Italian beer. That and the 3 shots of Ouzo had him close to seeing double. He wasn't used to drinking this much but he though, Hey what the heck, when in Rome. He chuckled to himself as he whispered the phrase out loud, When in Rome. He liked this tiny little bar, he wasn't sure if it was the very pretty girl serving the beer or how they treated the military people that stopped in here. If you stayed for two drinks you usually got two more paid for by the owner. The squat little Italian man was barely five foot tall, but he was always so happy to see any of the remaining military men stop in for a drink. He would scoot out from behind his bar when you walked in, escort you to a table and make a great show of cleaning it off, putting on a fresh red and white checked cloth. Patting you on the back and in his broken English would say, You so kind come save my country, you welcome always in my bistro. Seet, seet, I bring you beer yes, or you want good Italian wine. I make myself, you try some. It was always the same lines, then he would place a basket of fresh breads on the table. Tonight though it was the pretty young waitress that had been serving him. He felt things stir every time she would bring another pint, the way she bent over in front of him, giving him a small peek down the slopes of her peeks.

He leaned back in his chair, almost too far and had to swing his arms wildly to stop from toppling right over. Again he giggled to himself. He looked around the smoky room, there were few people in here tonight. He thought it would be packed with it being Valentine's Day. There was one couple canoodling in the back corner, their laughter would drift over his way now and again. A couple of enlisted men sat at a table behind him. It wasn't a big place, maybe a dozen or so tables, most with seating for four, some smaller ones just made for two. When you walked in it seemed to pull you back in time. The old wooden bar that sat at the back of the room, candles stuck in chubby old wine bottles, sweet Italian music coming from an old radio perched at one end of the bar. It had a hallway that ran down beside the one end of the bar. Down the hall the first doorway led into the tiny kitchen where you could always here pots and pans clinking and clanging. An old woman, most likely the bartender's wife, was always in there making something. He had stumbled in there once or twice looking for the bathroom which was further down the hall. The old woman would laugh and shoo you out of her kitchen and steer you further down the hall. Always laughing and muttering something in Italian. The kitchen always smelled so good with aromas of fresh herbs, chopped onions and garlic, fresh bread.

He motioned to the pretty waitress, she smiled at him and came over to the table. She said something to him in Italian, he wasn't good with Italian, German and English were his languages. Something about my eyes, she said. She must be complimenting me on my eyes he thought. One more pint dear he slurred out. No, no, the pretty waitress said to him, you go sleep now. Oh I would like to go sleep now with you he thought, smiling up at her. Just one more for the road, he slurred again. She shook her head and walked to the bar, Papa, he heard her call out, her voice was drowned out by the laughter from the enlisted men from behind him. The old bartender bellowed something in Italian to the girl as she reached the bar, this or some other funny thing caused the enlisted men to burst out in laughter again. The old bartender brought the pint over to him, I apologize for daughter, he said. She not understanding what bravery you did freeing our country. Setting the pint in front of the corporal and patting him on the back. She no understand, he said again as he walked away. He caught a glimpse of the pretty waitress carrying a mop and bucket down the hall. The young corporal thought to himself, that it wasn't his bravery that saved the little Italian mans country. He missed all that by a couple of years, but he was happy to get free drink and cordial service on behalf of the men that came before him.

Sitting there sipping his pint of beer the thought of the bucket went through his head, this made him think of water. Oh, that's it I have to pee, the corporal said to no one. Standing up to quickly his head swam, he took a stumbling step back and bumped into one of the enlisted men sitting behind him. Easy Mate, one of the men at the table said. So sorry chaps, the corporal said facing them. I got up to quickly and I have to pee. He giggle again. Maybe time to hit the barracks, another one of the men said. He wasn't sure because the room was spinning a bit now. Soon, soon, the corporal slurred out as he ambled his way along the wall towards the hallway. Dragging one hand along the wall to keep his balance he made it past the kitchen with the great smells wafting out of it. What could she be cooking that smells so good he said out loud. He reached the door to the bathroom and nearly fell through it. The pretty waitress was on the other side and she shrieked as he crashed into the room. She put her hand on his chest, No, no, is closed now for cleaning, the pretty waitress said in broken English. She then said something in Italian, he looked at her perplexed and she tried to repeat it in English. He didn't understand and shook his head. She held up her hand all five fingers spread out. Waving her hand in his face she said, uno minuti, again waving her hand at him. Oh, yes, of course, he said, holding out his hand 5 uno minuti, cinque minuti yes. Si, she said to him, Si, yes, cinque minuti. He turned and walked into the door, Oops, He said laughing. She shook her head and didn't join in his laughter.

He stumbled out of the bathroom and was leaning against the wall in the hall way. Ooo I have to pee, he said to himself. Spying the door at the end of the hall he remembered that it led out to the allyway that ran behind the building. He launched himself off the wall and smacked into the one opposite, easy does it old chap he muttered to himself, laughing again at himself. He stumbled to the old wooden door and fiddled and fumbled with the knob until it finally turned and a whoosh of cool night air hit him as the door swung open. He stepped out into the cool night, his shoes echoing off of the narrow corridor. He turned to his right when he exited and leaned his one shoulder against the brick wall. Finally being able to relieve himself he let out a long slow moan. When it echoed off the walls he first jumped almost pissing on himself, then he giggled realizing it was his own echo. When he was finally finished he tucked himself away and leaned his back against the wall, taking in deep breaths of the cool night air that cleared his head some. He pulled his pack of cigarettes from his breast pocket, shaking the packet to get one out he ended up dumping half of them on the ground. With one finally in his mouth he took out his matches and wasted 5 trying to get the cigarette lit. Taking in a long drag he leaned his head back against the wall and let out a long stream of smoke. The air was still and the smoke hung just a foot in front of him, a blue cloud that slowly drifted up. The young pretty waitress stepped out of the open door carrying her bucket. She turned her head and saw the young corporal standing there and said something in Italian to him, il bagno e libero ora  or something he thought. Sorry, he slurred, I couldn't wait, had to use the wall.

She tossed the dirty water from the bucket down the alley and walked closer to him. Placing a soft warm hand on his cheek she said, avete bevuto occhi. Si doverbbe dormire adesso. (You have drunken eyes, you should sleep now) Again he thought, she said something about my eyes. He slid slightly on the wall and was losing his balance; she caught him under the arm. She tugged him a bit towards the door and said, We sleep now, yes. Nodding her head up and down. We sleep, the corporal repeated to her. Si, yes we sleep now, here, she said pointing to another door just past the one they came out of. Stumbling along he leaned on her as she led him to the door. She opened the door and a faint whiff of cat urine and mildew wafted out. It had a lumpy looking bed tucked in the one corner, a single bulb on a wire hung from the ceiling. She placed her hand on his cheek again and said the phrase in Italian avete bevuto occhi. Si doverbbe dormire adesso, something about his eyes. We sleep now, Si, she said pointing to the lumpy bed in the corner. Now he understood her completely, she was telling him he had nice eyes and they were going to sleep together right here and right now. As drunk as he was he still felt himself stir with the thought of being with this pretty Italian girl. He had never been with a girl, this was exactly what he needed on Valentine's day he thought.

Taking her face in both of his hands he swayed a bit then leaned in to her and kissed her full on the mouth. She struggled away from him. She laughed, No, no, she said shaking her head. She patted the bed, We sleep yes, she said. Yes, we sleep he said, but we kiss first, then we sleep. Again taking her face in his hands he kissed her hard, she struggle to pull away and he wrapped an arm around her waist pulling her tight to him. Leaning his head back a bit he said you like yes. She reeled back and slapped him hard on the face, pushing to get away from him, speaking rapidly in Italian. The slap sent shockwaves through his clouded head, without thinking his free hand swung and he struck her hard on the face with the back of his hand. You like it rough eh, he grumbled at her. She didn't cry out but tears had welled in her eyes and she brought her hand up to gently touch her red and slowly swelling cheek. Oh don't cry dear he said to her, we are just having fun. He bent to kiss her again and she struggled to get away from him. Quit squirming, he shouted to her. He forced his mouth on her, cramming is tongue in her mouth, stifling the scream she was about to let out. She bit down on his tongue, drawing blood and he reeled away from her. She turned quickly for the door, he reached out and snagged her by the back of her dress. A loud tear was heard, revealing the young girls naked back. She struggled to free herself from his grip, holding tightly to her dress that was now almost falling off of her.

She turned slightly and was about to scream again when he slammed into her, his hand coming up to cover her mouth. Sshhh, shhhh, No need to make extra noise my sweet he whispered to her. She tried to turn her face from his sour drunken breath. He had beads of sweat on his forehead and a look in his eyes that frightened her further. She relaxed some, thinking that if she didn't struggle maybe she could talk her way out of here. He pressed his groin into her and she moaned in fear. He liked this, see I do know what you want, just like to play rough do you. Holding her tight to his body he turned the two of them so her back was now to the bed. She was shaking her head no, beating at his arms to no avail as he pushed to two of them on the lumpy bed. All the air escaped her as they slammed on the bed, she struggled under him to catch a breath, his hand was so tight over her mouth and nose. He yanked at the front of her dress exposing her naked breasts. Squeezing and pawing at her he didn't even see the panic that was welling in her eyes, tears streaming down her cheeks. He was enraged, as if he was possessed by an entirely different person. He tugged and tore at her clothes. His hand slipped from her mouth briefly and she drew in a long breath, a small scream escaped her mouth and he quickly covered it again. He took the look of terror in her eyes as pleasure as he roughly entered her. More tears spilled from her eyes as she squirmed to be free, squirming to be free of the pain. She went still as he finished and rolled off of her. See dear you liked too, I could tell by the way you moved. She said nothing in return to this comment. He struggle to one elbow to look at her, she stared blankly at the ceiling, Oh come on it wasn't that bad was it he slurred. She again didn't respond to him. Hey stop fooling around he said a bit panicky. He reached over to turn her face towards his so he could look in her eyes when he spoke to her. Her head just lolled to the side.

He felt panic swell in him as he looked at her. He gave her a slight shake and there was no response, it was like shaking a rag doll. Oh my god, what have I done, oh my god. He sprang from the bed, he stumbled and fell as his pants tangled around his ankles. He shuffled away from the bed, leaned against the far wall, his knees pulled tight to his chest. Oh my god what have I done. The fear and panic consuming him, he began to weep like a child. I have to get out of here he thought, I have to go now. He struggled with his pants, standing and swaying against the wall he nearly fell on top of her. He got his pants done up and lurched for the door. Yanking it open he burst into the alley without looking and ran straight into a large man who was coming down the alley. Hey, Hey dove vai cosi di fretta. Whoa, Whoa, where are you going in such a hurry the large man said to him in Italian. He looked up at the bigger man, his shoulders and chest were broad, his face almost square but gentle looking. He stumbled a bit and the bigger man righted him, the big man said  English. The corporal nodded yes, Yes I am Canadian. In English the man repeated where are you going in such a hurry? I, I am late, must get back to the barracks, the corporal stuttered. What were you doing in there, the big man asked pointing to the small door the corporal had stumbled from. Oh just confused, got lost, I have to get going now, he turned to leave but the bigger man had a firm grip on his arm. I thought I heard a girls scream come from there, the big man said.

No, no, it was just me, a, a rat startled me, the corporal said panicky. Pulling the smaller man to the door the big man peered in. After a long moment  of looking in the door the bigger man turned, in a soft gentle voice he said, is she dead? The corporal began sobbing, it was an accident, she wanted me, she led me in there, I don't, I don't know what happened. She wanted it, she was begging me. The bigger man had let go of the corporals arms and stood staring at him. The corporal was now weeping loudly into his hands, mumbling that she wanted it, over and over. The bigger man shook him, listen to me, listen to me he said more firmly. The corporal lifted his tear streaked face up to look at the bigger man in front of him. You must get out of here now, if they come looking for her and you are found here you will go to prison for a very long time. The corporal looked at the big man dumb founded, what, what did you say. You must leave, leave at once, come, come with me. The bigger man tugged at the corporals arm and started dragging him, pulling at him to follow. This way the big man said, pointing to the end of the alley. Hurry, we may not have much time. Confused, his head swimming, the corporal stumbled after the bigger man, going deeper into the alley, away from the dead girl. They reached the end of the alley and the big man fumbled in his pocket, he pulled a key ring from it. Selecting the right key he jammed it into the door facing them. When he opened the door he looked around the alley and shoved the corporal inside, quickly the big man said to the stumbling corporal. He pulled the door closed behind them and tuned the lock.

## Chapter Forty-Six

The two young Italian men had just exited the back door of the jewellers shop with their loot when the young corporal had run into the bigger man. Staying back in the shadows they watched and listened to the exchange between the big priest and the smaller man in the military clothes. They strained to hear what was being said, not wanting to move or get closer. When the priest, practically dragging the drunken army man, had passed where the two were hiding they peered around the corner and watched as the priest entered the back of the church. The older of the two started to make his way over to the door where the priest and army man had been peering into. Louis, what are you doing his partner hissed. I want to see what happened, Louis hissed back, waving his partner to stay put. He peered into the door and saw the young girl, her dress was tore open exposing her naked flesh, she staring blankly at the wall. He pulled back from the door, he said some sort of prayer and crossed himself. He snuck back to his partner waiting in the shadows, he had a blank look on his face when he arrived. Well, what did you see his partner asked. It was young Silvia from the bistro, Louis said, she's dead, looks like the army guy raped and killed her. Vinney, we got to get into the church and see what that priest is up to. Why Louis, lets just leave now before someone finds her and blames us. No, this could be good, follow me, Louis said heading down the alley towards the door the priest and army man went into.

Louis gently tried the door and found it locked. He reached into his coat and pulled out two pieces of thin polished metal. Sliding both into the lock on the door he fiddled with them for a few moments while his partner Vinney kept watch down the alley. After about 3 minutes there was a small click and the sound of oiled metal moving as the lock slid open. Opening the door slowly Louis peered in the small opening. Vinney hissed, are you sure we should do this. Waving his hand to quiet his partner he nodded yes and slipped around the door, Vinney followed close behind. They entered into a hallway at the rear of the old darkened church. One end of the hall was black, the other end had a faint glow of light flowing through it. The two men crept towards the light and heard a faint voice speaking. Peering around the door Louis saw candles burning on the altar and another door at the far end of the church. The doorway was illuminated in awash of light, voices or one voice clearly coming from within that room. The two men had been in this church many times over the years and knew that to be the priest's office. Creeping over to the far wall they made their way down the length of the church. As they got closer to the door they could hear the priest talking to the army man.

I'm sure it was an accident, yes she probably tried to seduce you as you said. Maybe she was a whore and did this to all army men, the priest said. Yes, yes, said the young army man, she was a whore and tried to seduce me and take my money. I was protecting myself from the whore of a woman. What is your name son, the priest asked. Heinz, Zigmund Heinz, Corporal Zigmund Heinz, the young corporal said. Ahhh, you are German, yes, the priest said. No, I am Canadian, see here, the corporal said pointing to the Canadian insignia on his uniform. Ahh yes, I see said the priest. I think I can help you with your problem, the priest said. Maybe offer you an alibi if the authorities should come asking around. But they will know it was me the corporal said, hanging his head and weeping some more. I'm sure I can help the priest said. I could do it as a favour to you, and maybe sometime if I am in need you will be there for me. You would lie for me, the corporal asked. I wouldn't call it a lie young Zigmund, I am just taking your word for what you said happened. The priest reached into the bottom drawer of his desk and pulled out a large old book. He scrawled something in the book and turned it towards the corporal. Here Zigmund, you sign here. What is this, the corporal asked, his body now weaving heavily. It is nothing but a book of promises, the priest said. See I put your name here and the date and you sign it showing that you were here and it is then I am your alibi. Oh, sure, yea that will work, the corporal said extending his shaky hand to grab he pen the priest held out to him. He had to close one eye to be able to focus on the pen and grab it. His body swaying he leaned over the book and signed his name to where the priest pointed. Very good Zigmund, now you rest, the priest said, walking around his desk towards the corporal. The young army man said yes I should rest and leaned back in his chair, closing his eyes. The priest grabbed an old blanket and tucked it around the snoring corporal.

Leaving the office the priest closed the door behind him, standing facing into his church he wondered if this stupid young man could be of any use to him. Time will tell he said out loud. He made his way to the back of the church and out the door he had come thru less than 30 minutes earlier. He stood in the cool air and looked down the alley. No one seemed to be prying around, if he acted now he could clean up the entire mess and no one would know what happened. Maybe they would think the young girl ran away with an army man. Walking quickly down the alley he reached the partially opened door where the young girls body laid. He stood looking down at her for a long time, she was such a pretty girl he thought, her beautiful voice will be missed in his Sunday choir. He sighed and wrapped the young girl with the blanket that was on the bed. He hefted her body over his shoulder, barely 100lbs he thought. Pausing at the door he looked both ways down the alley, he saw no one and moved quickly from the door towards the street entrance of the alley. Staying to the shadows and the late hour of the night he encountered no one as he made his way to the river. Again looking in all directions to make sure the way was clear, he said a long prayer for the girl and gently slid her lifeless body into the river. He stood there watching it sink and disappear as the strong current took her downstream. He stood there a long time, hands stuffed into his coat, he just watched the river flow, wondering if he had done the right thing.

## Chapter Forty-Seven

The two young Italian men, Louis and Vinney, stayed in the shadows until they heard the back door close. Vinney was about to get up when Louis grabbed his coat and hissed to stay put. I will go look in the office and see if the army man is asleep. Standing slowly, Louis crept to the office door, light still oozing out from under it. He tried the knob and it was unlocked. He turned the knob slowly and eased the door open. He saw the snoring army man curled up in one of the chairs. He immediately spotted the large book that sat on the desk, looking over his shoulder to make sure Vinney or the priest were not sneaking up on him he silently crept to the desk. He turned the book so it was facing him. He was impressed with the intricacy carved leather that bound the book. He opened the cover and shook his head at the unfamiliar scrawling. Flipping the old pages he found the last entry near the middle back of the book. The ink barley dry from where the army man had signed his name beside the priests inscription. "February 15, 1949 ~ Corporal Zigmund Heinz ~ Canadian Army ~ Rape and Murder of the Virgin Child, Silvia DeSalva" . My god Louis thought to himself. Closing the book he spun it back around to the way he found it. The Corporal Zigmund Heinz of the Canadian Army stirred, turned in his chair and resumed snoring. Louis just stared at him.

He left the office with the book and the corporal as he found them. Sneaking back over to Vinney who was still hidden in the shadows he said come on, lets get out of here. What did you see Louis, Vinney asked him. Nothing, just the drunken army man asleep in a chair, nothing worth stealing. What was that talk the priest said about signing something, Vinney asked. I don't know Louis said angrily, now can we get out of here before the priest comes back. Sure Louis, you don't need to snap at me, Vinney sulked. The two men made there way to the back of the church and eased out the door into the shadows of the alley. When they neared the door that had the dead girl behind it they saw the priest stick his head out and look down the alley in both directions. Lucky he looked away from the pair first so they had time to step back into a door way without being spotted by the priest. Easing out a fraction Louis saw the priest come out of the door with the girl over his shoulder, poorly wrapped in an old grey blanket. The pair followed the priest as he made his way from shadow to shadow, eventually stopping at the river's edge. When the priest finally slipped the girl into the water Louis turned to Vinney, come on lets go we don't need to see any more.

## Chapter Forty-Eight

The young army corporal was awoken the next morning by the insistent shakings from the big man. What, what, Corporal Heinz said, where am I? Who are you? The big man leaned in closer, Zigmund, it is me your friend from last night, Father Canellii. Do you not remember me. The Corporal rubbed at his eyes, he slowly looked around the old church office. Um, I think so. Yes, the alley. Oh my god, the alley, the Corporal said. A tear spilling from his eye and running down his cheek. Oh my god, he said again as the nights events came rushing back to him. What have I done. He went to get up from his chair and his body swayed, his head thumped, he sat hard back into the chair. His face was pale and sunken, barley able to look the other man in the eye he said, Who are you? With an empathetic look the large priest said, I'm Father Canelli, Zigmund. You remember me helping you last night? Yes, you remember coming here? Oh my head, it hurts so bad, the young corporal said. Holding his hand out with two small tablets the priest said here take these, they will help with how you feel. With shaky hands the corporal took the two pills and the offered glass of water. Now just relax Zigmund, the Priest said. Everything has been taken care of.

Corporal Zigmund Heinz just sat in his chair, his eyes blankly staring at the larger man for a long moment. Finally he croaked out what happened. Well my new young friend, you had a run in with a girl last night. Do you remember that, the Priest asked. The corporal sat in silence for another long moment staring at his feet. Yes, he finally said. Yes, that whore from the Bistro tried to seduce me and take my money and then, then, oh my. He let out a long heavy sigh. Then I think I may have accidentally killed her. The big priest stared at the smaller man for a few moments, he cleared his throat and the corporal looked up at him. He notices for the first time that the big man was wearing a black shirt with the white priest collar. The corporal said, you are a priest? Yes Zigmund, I am Father Canelli, I am the priest for this beautiful old church that we sit in, Basilica of San Nicola. We met last night do you remember? Do you remember running into me last night as you came out of the shed in the alley. Yes, I think so, the corporal said slowly. You brought me here, you help me out. Said you would take care of things for me, give me an alibi for what happened with the whore. I signed your directory or visitors book or something right, for my alibi, yes I remember that now. Yes, you said you would help me out, isn't that right? The big priest sighed. My young friend I think you remember your words but not mine. I don't understand, said the corporal, a perplexed look covering his face.

The big priest reached down and opened a drawer, he pulled out a large intricately carved book and carefully placed it on his desk. You signed in here my friend, the priest said. You signed in the book of promise, the "Rose" as some have come to know it. The corporal looked to the priest then at the large book on the desk, the "Rose" , the book of promise, he asked? To help you with your sins, to offer you penance my son, the priest said. Sins, he paused, penance, again another pause. I don't understand the corporal said perplexed. I'm so confused, my head hurts so bad. I don't know. The young corporal lowered his head and began to sob. Placing a hand on the corporal's shoulder the priest said, please do not trouble yourself, all has been taken care of. You have signed in the book of promise and all will work out. I, I don't understand. The priest opened the large ornately carved leather book, he slowly flipped the aged pages, the smell of mildew and age wafted from the pages as he carefully turned them. He stopped two thirds into the book, ran his index finger along a line of writings and mumbled something then looked at the corporal, here it is. Right here, February 15, 1949, Corporal Zigmund Heinz, Canadian Army, asks for forgiveness and pledges his life to the church of Christ, the Roman Catholic Church and Vatican City, the Holly See for the deed of rape and murder of the Virgin Child Silvia DeSalva age 17 on the night of February 14, 1949.

Corporal Zigmund Heinz sat stone still, his face turned the colour of fresh fallen snow, tears ran freely from his eyes, his mouth hung agape. Twenty seconds passed and he finally stirred, quickly reaching for the metal trash can that sat beside the big priests desk. He cradled it and emptied what little contents he had in his stomach into the receptacle. With spittle still dripping from his chin he looked up to the big priest sitting across from him, No, it's not possible, I couldn't have. The large priest turned the book, pointing his sausage sized finger to the scribbled signature of Zigmund Heinz. I am sorry my son, but you did confess to me last night and you did sign here. The corporal pawed at his chin with the back of his hand, attempting to clean the vomit from his chin. He leaned forward and stared at his signature on the last line of the book.

## Chapter Forty-Nine

By the time Owen Henderson had made the drive to his house the skies had cleared. It was as if the rain of the night had cleansed the skies, cleansed the roads and cleansed his soul. He stepped out of his car and took a deep breath of the clean air that hung in the night. His house sat dark, as it often did these days without his beloved Tracy. When she was still alive neither of them would ever come home to a dark house. Whoever arrived first always had lights or candles burning, warm inviting glows always spilling from the windows. Owen sighed as he felt that loneliness creep over him as he walked to the house. Opening the front door he stepped in and wanted to call out "Honey I'm Home", a quirky little thing that both he and Tracy loved to do when they got home. Always whoever was the last to arrive and call it out was to be greeted with hugs and kisses. It was silly, but it was just one of the things they did to keep their love true, young and alive. Tonight Owen knew that yelling out "honey I'm home" would only add to his feeling of sadness and loneliness . Dropping his sport coat on the back of the Lay-Z-Boy he walked over to the stereo and hit the power button. After all the components clicked to the on position the Boss started wafting from the speakers. This caused him to pause as the song was again one of their favourites. He looked around the living room, the cold fire place, the pictures on the mantle. Maybe time for a move he whispered to himself.

Flicking on lights as he made his way to the kitchen he had not only the feeling of loneliness but a small sense of closure. Back on the job for only a week after nearly eleven months of absence and he had been involved in a high profile murder case that eliminated two people that he had been trying to put behind bars for years. He had also more closely connected with his daughter, someone he felt he alienated in his bout of self pity, self remorse. He grabbed a tumbler from the top shelf of the cupboard and held it under the ice dispenser of the fridge. When he was satisfied with the ice in his glass he opened another cupboard and pulled out the dusty bottle of Sailor Jerry's Spiced Rum, the last bottle of rum that he and Tracy had purchased. Pouring in a generous shot he then looked in the pantry for a can of Dr. Pepper. Knowing there had to be a couple cans he got frustrated moving things until he finally found the last few cans at the back. Finished making his drink he placed it on the counter and went back to the living room to switch the speakers to the outdoor speakers he and Tracy had installed out by their dock.

With his drink in hand and his tattered old Roots sweatshirt on he ventured out on to the dock. The night air was cool, not cold. It held that just rained smell, the smell of ozone that you normally found in an early spring rain. The sky was clear without a single cloud. The stars hung clear and bright as if someone had just placed a brand new string of twinkle lights from the trees. Using the sleeve of his sweatshirt Owen cleaned the rain from his chair and sat down. He felt a pang strike his chest, a feeling of sadness, of missing the past. He let out a long sigh and then took an even longer swallow of his drink. He gazed over their tiny lake, the bright stars reflecting off the glass surface. Instinctively he reached his right hand out towards Tracy's empty chair. For a brief moment he felt her soft, warm hand embrace his. He could smell her perfume, feel her gaze on him. Tears spilled from his eyes and ran down his chilled cheeks. He was sure he heard her say "I love you babe".  An old Bruno Mars song came to him at that instant, it made his heart race, he whispered the last couple of the last lines of the song, "Goodbye my lover, Goodbye my best friend".

***---- A sneak peak at the new untitled Owen Henderson novel. Coming to a fine book store in 2015 ---***

## Chapter One

It was always the same feelings, the same emotions, washing over him as he stood there watching. It was as if time had slowed, like watching that dramatic moment unfold in a movie. His arms crossed in front of him, almost hugging himself. Fists clenched tight, heart racing. His right foot constantly tapping to some hyped up beat that he only heard.

The squeak of a sneakers on polished hardwood as each player positioned themselves for the inevitable. He held his breath momentarily as he watched it unfold. His stomach clenching, waiting, waiting. The ball still hanging in the air as if being guided by an unseen hand. The two girls squaring off both with an inner knowing of what is about to happen. Only one can be the winner, the taller girl planting her feet for the jump. A knowing smile spreading across her face as she sizes up the tiny girl across from her. A wicked smile as she sees the broken nose happening as she slams the ball down. And then it happens, the shortest girl on his squad jumps just at the precise second. Achieving the un-achievable, this tiny girl of a meagre five feet 3 inches raises herself off the ground with a kangaroo like spring in her legs. Surprising the taller girl across the net from her as her jump puts her almost 2 and a half feet off the floor. Her hand connecting to the ball at just the precise moment and the perfect spike is achieved.

The crowed, what little one there is, goes nuts as they watch this little seen unfold. A smile washes over his face as the goosebumps crawl up his back. It always moves him to see his team come together in a game. It still amazes him to see that beautiful tiny girl just dominate the game. He knows because of her height she will never get a volleyball scholarship, but does she ever play like she is working for one. She as well knows her spike will not get her a nod from universities but she loves the game.

This was going to be his year, this was the team that would finally win the Provincials for senior girls volleyball. What a great way to finish his career. A shit load of money, a winning team and his name would be on that trophy as coach for everyone to see for years to come. "Great spike Allie", he yells to his tiny secret weapon. She turns her pretty face towards him, pony tail flopping in the air, and beams at his compliment.

Less than 30 seconds to go in the game with his team leading this set, it was a sure win for him and his team. Their opponents look exhausted and are slowly giving up hope of even tying this set. The buzzer goes off and his girls erupt in a frenzy of hugs, screams, and bouncing pony tails. The other team just turns and heads to their bench.

Brian Stomrich jumps down from his perch on his team's bench and walks over to the other coach. He extends his hand to Dave Cover, "Great game Dave. I thought you had us in the second set. That was a shitty call from the ref." Dave Cover, english teacher and senior girls volleyball coach for St. Mary's Catholic high school from Ajax, extends his hand as well. "I'm not so sure about that Brian. Your girls really had command of the court all night. Great game and congratulations of moving on to the quarter finals." Smiling, no beaming, Brian Stomrich says his thanks. Nodding towards Cover's bench he says "Are those twin sisters you have on your team." "Yea, they are fosters, they came to the school about 6 weeks ago. Mother and father killed in an auto accident and they have no other family." Cover says.

"Wow, that's not how we normally get the foster kids." Stomrich says. "No, I know what you mean. Usually broken families, abuse, runaways. The troubled ones", Cover says. "Yeah, it's sad the way some of these kids are treated. More like pets than children" Stomrich adds. "Ha, the pets are usually treated better than any of the fosters I have seen." Sighing Stomrich nods his head and says "Yea, your right. They look like nice girls." "Oh, they are. Just as nice and beautiful on the inside as on the outside. It's a shame."

Stomrich extends his hand again, "Great game Dave, see you around sometime." They shake and both move back to their respective benches to get their teams moving. "Ok girls, that was an awesome game. Now we have to pick it up a notch because next week we start playing the really hard teams in the quarters." They were barely paying any attention to his little speech as they downed their water and bounced around. It really amazed him how they could still have spunk and energy after the games they played. "Ok, lets get our stuff and hit the road. I will meet you all on the bus."

As the girls started to pack up their stuff Stomrich headed to the exit and pulled his phone out. He knew he received a couple text messages during the game, he felt the vibration. He never pulled out his phone during a game, he felt it showed disrespect to his team. He punched in his password and brought up the text message screen. The first message was from his wife. "Hey hnny, wnt b home wen u get here. Grls nite out. Xoxo." Yea, girls night out, sure, more like date with the guy from accounting. Bitch, he mummbled under his breath. And why the fuck could she not spell out the words like normal people. We had unlimited texting for fuck sake, we don't pay by the character he said to himself.

Not giving a shit where his whore of a wife was going to be he deleted the message and started reading the second one. He stopped in his tracks the guy who was right behind him ran smack into him, his phone lurching out of his hands as he stumbled forward. The man apologized for the blunder as Stomrich recovered and snatched his phone out of the air before it the floor. He gave Stomrich a small pat on the back, "Sorry about that Mr. Stomrich, you stopped so quickly." Looking up from his phone somewhat of in a daze, Stomrich replied, "Hmmm, Oh, sorry, sorry Mr. Sail." Shaking his head and clearing his throat "I'm sorry, that was totally my fault. I shouldn't have been reading text messages while walking. Big no, no." he chuckled.

"Are you ok Mr. Stomrich, you look kind of pail." "Ok, sure, ya." Stomrich gave his head a shake. "Just the text message caught me off guard. I'm good." He said regaining his composure and smiling. Tucking his phone back into his coat pocket, Stomrich put his hand on the back of Mr. Sail and walked him out the door giving him compliments about his daughters game.

## Chapter Two

He sat at the back of the school bus, staring out the side window. He could hear the driver talking to him, it just didn't register. It sounded like he was talking about the game. At this point he didn't care. His mind was elsewhere. The bus bounced and came alive as the first couple of girls started to board. Giggles, screeches, and the occasional curse word started filtering down to him as he pulled himself to the present. He turned to look at the girls boarding and she was standing right there, not 10 feet from him. His heart stopped, how could it be, she cant be here. He gave his head a quick shake. "You ok Mr. S? You look like you saw a ghost or sumpin" the girl in the aisle said. Smiling at the young girl with the chocolate skin "No, no sorry Becky. I was thinking of someone and you just startled me." He said. "That's cool Mr. S, I hope she was as beeeeautifulll as me." The girl said, really drawing out the be, smiling at him she tucked herself into an empty seat.

"No one is as beeeeautifulll as you Becky" he responded back. He tried to focus on the girls, bringing himself into the present. He would find out what the text message was all about when he got these girls back to the school. It wasn't the first time he got a cryptic text message from him. In fact he got them all the time. This one though was like non he had ever gotten. It chilled him and scared him. It some how changed everything. They wanted a refund, or new product in 5 days. He had never been under pressure to deliver. It was always on his timetable. He sent a message and would tell them he had product to deliver and give them a date and time. He couldn't just pull product from the air. It took time, planning, careful planning. This was so out of the norm. He needed to find out what went wrong with the last delivery. There was no way he was giving the money back. The product was good when he delivered it. Everyone was happy when he dropped it off and the payment was in his bank by the time he got back in his car. So what went wrong.

He didn't even realize the bus had started moving until the bus pulled up to the front of the school. One by one all the parents cars started up. School policy was that kids ride the bus to and from all extracurricular activities. Even though half of these parents were at the game the girls still had to ride the bus back to the school then go with their parents. It all went back to a missing girl 2 years ago. There were so many conflicting reports on if the girl got on the bus or left the game with a boyfriend or girlfriend, no one was quite clear.

She was found 3 months later, her body badly mutilated, no one was ever charged. However, the school board had ultimate responsibility for the girl and the lawsuit was staggering. So even though it was a royal pain everyone had to go back to the school and be counted and released to a parent or guardian.

Stomrich said good night to the last girl, checked her off his attendance list and headed for his car. The last in the lot. As he reached for the handle his phone did a small little ticklish dance in his coat pocket. Pulling it out he expected it to be his wife to say she was having such a good time that he need not wait up for her. But it wasn't his wife, it was him again. "Still waiting for your answer, are you returning our money or delivering more product. I must know now, I do not play games." He felt his stomach tighten when he read those words. He didn't like this pressure of delivering on demand. He needed time, and he sure as hell didn't want to give the money back.

Steadying himself with a deep breath he typed into his Blackberry "I don't understand what happened. Not playing games. Can we meet to discuss." He hit send and sat staring at his phone. It felt like forever before the reply came back. "No meet, product expired, new product in 7 days or money. Don't disappoint." He felt his heart pounding against his chest as he read the message and realized he had been holding his breath and let it escape between his teeth. Seven days, he whispered to himself. That was a litter better he thought. Maybe he could deliver in seven days, if he planned his time correctly. He knew exactly where to get the product, he had his eyes on it for a couple of weeks now. All he had to do was formulate a plausible plan and scout the area. He already had her address and knew her schedule, he had been following the young girl for over 2 months now.

Made in the USA
Charleston, SC
18 December 2014